A Damnation MC Novel

SERENDIPITY

GRACE MCGINTY

Janet. Do not read this book.

I'm serious.

G x

Shout out to the most versatile
4-letter word in the English language.
Fuck Yeah.

ALSO BY GRACE MCGINTY

Hell's Redemption Series

The Redeemable: The Complete Novel

The Unrepentant: The Complete Novel

The Fallen: The Complete Novel

The Azar Nazemi Trilogy

Smoke and Smolder

Burn and Blaze

Rage and Ruin

Dark River Days Series

Newly Undead In Dark River

Happily Undead In Dark River

Black Mountain Mates

Hunting Isla

Stand Alone Novels and Novellas

Bright Lights From A Hurricane

The Last Note

Castle of Carnal Desires

SERENDIPITY

PROLOGUE

He sat on his knees in the dirt as they lowered the coffin into the ground and we all stood around him, protecting his back, shielding him from prying eyes. He was crying silently like his heart was being shredded, but I knew what he was feeling was far, far worse. We were all heart broken, but his life had just been lowered six feet into the ground and guilt was eating him alive. It was eating us all alive. We had failed her. We had failed them.

When the sky opened up and rain poured down, it seemed fitting. It should rain when all the light in our lives was being buried beneath the dirt. I let a tear fall, hidden by the rain. I had to be stoic; I had to present a strong front, despite the fact that I wanted to be in the dirt mourning her too.

People were drifting off, helped along by a few of

our members, so the Pres could have some privacy. Two men stood off to the side, waiting to shift dirt back into the hole, sealing them away forever. We had insisted at gunpoint that they be buried together; Laura and the baby. She'd want them together, the little one forever cradled in her arms. We didn't care what the laws had said, what the undertaker had said, what anyone said. We were all wild in our grief, and anyone who stood in our way would have died too.

It rained even harder, the water rolling off my leather cut but soaking everything else. The dirt was turning to slush around our feet and the other two guys standing beside me, behind our President, sent me a look. It was time to go.

I knelt in the dirt next to him, putting my hand on his back. "We should go," I said in a low voice, not sure he'd hear me over his grief. "We have to go." I wanted to hug him, but I knew he wouldn't appreciate the gesture right now. I picked up a rose that was lying on the ground, and handed it to him. It was muddy and dirty now, but that seemed right too. Nothing we ever touched remained pure, not a flower, and not her. We were a plague on those around us, and no one was exempt, not even the most innocent. Someone handed down one of the red roses as well. I tucked it in his hand beside the white one and tried not to think about how much it looked like blood.

I got to my feet, uncaring that the knees of my

black jeans were now caked in mud, and I pulled the Pres up with me. He stood on his feet, feeling insubstantial despite the fact he was two-hundred pounds of solid muscle. It was like all the life had leached out of him, leaving him just an empty shell.

His body shuddered, and he threw the two roses into the grave. One for his wife. One for his infant son who would never see his first birthday. A son who'd been killed by the sins of his father. Betrayed by his own blood.

I nodded to the grave diggers as they began to shovel dirt back into the grave. I grabbed his arm and pulled him away. Normally, I would have had a black eye for trying to drag him anywhere, and it worried me that he would never be the same President we had even a week ago.

However, if there was something that solidified the four of us, it was the need for revenge. We had all loved Laura. The need to avenge her death burned through my veins like acid.

When we turned, a man was standing behind us, and my gun was out and pointing at him in an instant. He didn't freak at having the barrel of my Desert Eagle in his face though. He didn't even look at me, he just stared at the Pres.

My Brothers had their guns out as well, searching the empty cemetery for an ambush. But there was no one else left. Just the grave diggers and this guy. He was dressed in black jeans and a t-shirt, completely out of place at a funeral. My heart was thumping like he had just pulled out an Uzi and my brain was screaming for me to run, but the man was just standing there, both hands in his pockets. He didn't have a gun, or any weapon that I could see.

"I know what it's like to have your love torn away from you," the man said in a smooth voice that sent chills down my spine. Who was this fucker?

The Pres just seemed numb. His hand hadn't even gone for his gun. It was like he was kind of hoping this dude was here to shoot him in the head.

I could understand the feeling.

"You wish for revenge? The most brutal kind of revenge. You want her pain and suffering to be avenged sevenfold?"

The Pres finally snapped out of it. He nodded slowly. We all wanted that, the entire Club. But especially the four of us.

The man in the t-shirt nodded. "I can give you that. I can give you the ability to exact revenge on all your enemies until they are buried so deep that no-one will find them. And I will promise you that death will provide no relief for those you mark. You will be strong enough that they will all fear you and none will ever come for what you consider yours again."

Fire lit in the President's eyes, the first sign of life in

them in days. Anger. I would take that over the god-awful blankness any day.

"In return, you become mine for eternity. All four of you."

"What?" One of my Brothers whispered behind me.

The man didn't take his eyes off the President, and I didn't take my eyes off him. "I will give you power, money, whatever else it is that you desire. But more importantly, I will give you what you want most; the strength to never fail anyone again. Any of you."

"And you get what?" I asked, wanting what he was offering despite my gut churning. I wanted to be able to protect my Brothers-In-Arms. I wanted to be able to protect the Club Family. That was my job and so far, I had failed.

The man shrugged. "I get your souls." A chill swept through the air at his words. "You'll ride for me when I need you, but I can't see that happening in the near future. I have a lot to do before then."

"Yes," the Pres whispered.

"Yes," both of my Brothers behind me murmured into the fading light of the worst day of our lives.

Finally, the man looked at me, the depths of his gaze chilling me to my bones. But still I nodded. "Yes."

The man smiled. "Good. From today, you will no longer be who you were. You will no longer be the

Punishers MC. You will no longer have your own names. You will be the beginning of the Damnation MC." I was mesmerized; I couldn't look away from him if I tried. My gun fell to the dirt as my hands went limp at my sides.

He reached past me so quickly I couldn't see his hands, placing his fingers on the chest of our Sergeant-In-Arms. "Goliath."

My Brother dropped to the ground like his bones were liquified, and I jumped away. My eyes whipped between them.

"Solomon." He did the same to the Captain, who went down in a heap. My eyes searched for signs of life and I let out the breath that had been caught in my throat when I saw their chests rise and fall.

He looked at me, and I stepped away. He didn't pursue me. I had a feeling I had to come into this willingly. "They aren't hurt. The swell of power just takes a while to settle into human bodies. Come forward, my Horseman." I stepped forward even though my feet tried to carry me away. He placed a hand on my chest. "Cain."

Something rolled through my body like a freight train, dropping me to my knees and then onto my back. I tried to stand, but it was like my body was paralyzed.

He stopped in front of the Pres, and I struggled to keep my eyes open. I needed to protect us.

"Judas. That is your name now. Own it. Revel in it.

You will never feel weak again." Then the Pres was on the ground beside us, but awake like me. "Your sacrifice needs to be greater, Judas. It is always hardest being the leader." He leaned forward and pressed his thumb into the President's eye socket, popping out his eyeball like a grape. The Pres screamed and I roared as I struggled on the ground like a dying fish. The man waved a hand, and the Pres passed out.

"It's always an eye for an eye in these stories, no?" he said softly to me.

As my limbs came back online, I struggled to my knees. "Who?" I croaked out, but I already knew. I just needed to hear it before my mind shattered into a million pieces.

The man smiled, and it wasn't a pleasant expression. There was a flash of huge black wings splaying either side of his shoulders, gone so quickly that I wondered if I'd seen it at all. But when I drew my eyes back to his smiling face, I knew I had.

"You can call me Luc," he said softly, and then he disappeared.

1

CAIN

I couldn't help but look at the girl in the passenger seat, my hands flexing around the steering wheel as I drove down the freeway too fast. Judas was going to murder me; just put a gun to my head and paint my brains all over the Clubhouse walls. Wouldn't do much, but fuck it would hurt.

The girl, woman, whatever, slid her eyes to me, catching my gaze with her own violet ones. I swallowed hard and tried to ignore the bump of her stomach. Nah, Judas would take one look at her round belly and let me off the hook. He might be pissed that I'd agreed without consulting him or the rest of the guys, but he was a sucker for a woman in distress. We all were, after what happened to...

I snapped down my mental walls on that thought. This wasn't the past. We weren't who we were any longer. We were better able to protect the more vulnerable. Better able to close ourselves off to that emotional bullshit. I took the turnoff, pulling up behind a bar and strip club. On the other side of the lot was the Clubhouse. It had its own bar, with a bunch of rooms out back. That's where I'd take the woman. I'd get one of the Prospects to clean it something fierce, because let's face it, it had seen more bodily fluids than a fucking spank bank, but she'd be safe here.

A former customer had dropped her off like an abused puppy at Pestilence Tattoos, my shop in town. The redhead, Hope was her name, had come in once before looking like she'd been beaten half to death, and I'd wanted to rip the head off the pretty-boy she'd come in with, despite the fact that he had a real fucked up vibe that made the hair on my neck stand on end. But Hope apparently remembered, so when this woman, Serendipity, needed a place to stay, why not send her to your friendly local tattooist with a bad attitude? I don't know why she decided I was the safe option, considering I had so much blood on my hands that I could have painted the town red, but she'd taken one look at me and decided I was the good guy. She was wrong; I wasn't a good guy. But I'd never turn away a woman in trouble.

I couldn't fathom how Hope knew that, but she'd picked the right person.

I'd always been a sucker for a battered woman.

Even before I'd joined the MC. Back when I was little and my father used to smack around Mom, it had broken something inside my head. Now, the idea of a man hitting a woman made me snap. I'd put my father in the ground, and joined my local chapter of the Punishers Outlaw MC. Then I'd loved a woman who'd had her life ripped away from her in the most brutal of ways, and my heart had died. Now, all that was left in my chest was the black lump that pumped with the near-demonic need for vengeance against those who would use women and children as pawns.

I wanted to punch myself in the head to chase away any thoughts of Laura. She was dead. A ghost. The only thing keeping her alive now was that guilt that infected my soul like the plague.

I got out, grabbing the woman's bag. *Serendipity. Not the woman*, I chastised myself. What kind of backwards, new age name was that anyway?

"Come on, we're gonna have to pass you staying here by the Pres, but I'm sure it'll be fine." I hope I sounded more self-assured than I felt.

Serendipity looked around, her eyes flicking between the stripclub and the Clubhouse, and all the motorcycles in between.

"You're a biker?"

I raised an eyebrow as I passed her the tote bag with her stuff. "Will that be a problem?"

I desperately wanted to get on my bike and ride

away from all the shit that seemed to be bubbling up inside me at the appearance of this chick, but I had to get her settled first.

"Cain, what the actual fuck, man?" Solomon appeared from nowhere, which was basically his superpower and his most annoying trait. I winced and turned, transforming my face into a menacing scowl.

It must have been a pretty good one because the woman backed up a step. "What the hell was I supposed to do? Some piece of ass came in, said this one was being stalked by some guy who knocked her up and what? I was just going to leave her there to be murdered by some psychotic asshole like–"

"I get it. Judas isn't going to be happy though."

Yeah, tell me something I didn't know. I nodded at Solomon, and he smiled at the woman. Serendipity. Shit, I had to start calling her by her name in my head. Solomon was a lady killer, and I was fairly sure he'd have her on her back with his face between her thighs before the night was through. He was tall, with golden hair like some kind of hair care model. Hell, he probably could have been a model if he wasn't such a cold blooded murderer. He had tattoos up and down his arms, most of them compliments of me, and I was a badass fucking artist. He had a few scars, most from before our time at Damnation MC. "Hey, Sweet. I'm Solomon. And you are?" He gave her that Hollywood smile, but she didn't smile back.

"Sera," the woman said quietly, her eyes taking his measure. Not as a man, but as a threat. Whoever was stalking her had really done a number on her. "And Hope isn't a piece of ass. She's an angel and you won't speak of her that way." She was frowning, her eyes blazing intensely and I swear to fucking Satan, I got harder than a rock.

I looked over at Solomon, who had a shit eating grin on his face and a growing bulge in his pants, but I wasn't surprised. I liked my women feisty. Solomon just liked them breathing.

"No last name, Sera?" Solomon basically cooed. Geez. Women actually fell for this shit?

She shook her head. "Not for you."

I grinned, the expression reaching my eyes. Fuck yeah. Apparently, the woman was immune to Solomon's ability to charm a nun out of her panties. Solomon just grinned, smug bastard. Of course he'd see it as a challenge.

I thumped him on the arm. "Don't get excited, Douche. Still gotta pass it by Judas."

Solomon waived me away and grabbed Sera's tote bag. "Let me take that for you," he murmured. "Come this way. Judas is in his office. I'm not missing this for anything."

I rolled my eyes and waved Sera forward, following up the rear. Despite the fact she had to be three or four months pregnant, the woman was too thin. She had a big round baby belly, but I could see she was nothing more than skin and bones underneath her clothes. Her body was all but wasted.

Solomon pushed through the doors of the Clubhouse, and all conversation ground to an awkward halt. There were dozens of people in that bar, patched members and their old ladies, some sweet butts that were on their knees beneath tables. I placed my hand on Serendipity's lower back, trying to ignore the heat coming from her skin and the way her spine was beginning to curve into an amazing ass. She flinched but didn't step away, so I kept my hand there as I directed her past the bar to a long hallway down the back. At the very end of the hallway was the large room where we held Church. Just up from it was a heavily fortified door where Judas' office sat.

Solomon banged on the heavy door, and the grunted response from the other side had him pushing it open. Solomon threw me an amused look. "Hey Pres, your VP brought you a present." I was going to put my fist through his face next time I got the opportunity, just for being such a jackass. Still, I straightened my shoulders and pushed the girl into the room gently.

She froze in the doorway, the first sign of hesitancy I'd seen in her yet. So far, she's taken the whole thing in her stride with sass or stupidity, I wasn't sure which, but standing in front of the Pres was enough to make her quiver beneath my hand. Maybe she wasn't so stupid after all.

Judas was a scary man. After he'd had his eye plucked out, it had healed roughly and now he wore an eyepatch like a fucking pirate. Combined with the five o'clock shadow and his shaved head, the guy looked like a demon. The irony was real.

Amusingly enough, Judas looked just as stunned. I didn't smile though. I liked my intestines where they were. Judas broke from his shock first, his stormy eye finding me and pinning me to the spot.

"What the hell is this? Get this bitch out of my office and back to wherever you picked her up from, Cain. We talked about this, no more strays."

He said that like I picked up women in desperate circumstances every day of the fucking week. I don't. Sometimes I offer the street kids a place to crash and get on their feet, but they work fucking hard for the Club. And never the girls. This was no place for a woman who wasn't an old lady or someone who wants to be passed around. But I made an exception for this woman. She needed us. I could feel it in my bones.

Apparently being called a bitch would knock the shock straight out of a person because Serendipity was no longer frozen. She was rigid with indignation. This was going to go south real quick. I put my hand around her forearm, shaking my head to deter her from what-ever tirade she was about to launch to verbally shred our President. It wouldn't endear him any more to the idea of her staying. "You don't even want to hear me out?" I say softly, not keeping any of the disappointment from my voice. I loved Judas like a brother. Hell, he was my brother. More than that even. We were bound by something greater than blood or love or any other such existential bullshit.

Judas sighed, dropping his pen and standing up. As he did so, I saw his whole body go rigid. He must have missed the rounded bulge of her stomach. I didn't blame him though, her face was pretty damn distracting. His one good eye shot to me, and there was a world of feeling in it for a moment before he shut it down. Yeah, bro. I'd been there. There had been a reason I couldn't say no despite the 'no more strays' mandate.

"Speak."

I rolled my eyes at his command, like I was a dog or something, but I let it slide. "Some piece–" Serendipity glared in my direction, "Uh, a customer from a few months ago brought her in. Real sweet kid. I told you about her and the blond guy who felt a little like someone from our past. Do you remember?" Judas nodded. "This customer, Hope, said that Serendipity needed our help."

The Pres switched his gaze to Serendipity. "So you decided to get in a car with a stranger who dragged you to a biker bar?" He raised his eyebrows. "Can't protect against stupid, Cain. Gotta have some self-preservation instincts to start with. Take her to a women's shelter somewhere."

Solomon's gaze was bouncing between the three of us like he was watching a trainwreck, which he probably was. Serendipity growled. "I trust Hope's judgement and somehow she knows the giant has a good heart. She wouldn't have sent me with him otherwise. I trust that he doesn't hang around with the kind of person who rapes women and kills children." She lifted her chin, daring him to prove her wrong.

Judas' body was so rigid I worried he was going to snap. I edged a little closer to the girl, and noticed Solomon doing the same. Judas' jaw flexed as he got himself under control.

"Tell me."

She frowned, her nose screwing up in a way that was fucking adorable. "Tell you what?"

Judas crossed his arms over his chest and gave her a look that had made grown men piss themselves.

"Everything."

2

JUDAS

I was holding myself so tight, I could feel my muscles twitch. My gaze kept drifting to this woman's midsection like it was magnetized. I gritted my teeth, willing them back up to her face, but her eyes were just as bad. They were like the Mediterranean Sea during a storm, and I was pretty sure I was drowning.

"I met a man," she said softly, her backbone rigid. I didn't need to know any more about this fucker. I already wanted to pound his face into a pulp. "He was beautiful. Like inhumanly beautiful. I don't normally..." She trailed off, a soft rose color lighting up her cheekbones. "I don't get close to people, but with him, I couldn't help myself. We had one night, and it fucking sucked. He was pretty but selfish." She looked over at Solomon. "You know the type, right?"

Cain laughed at the subtle burn, and Solomon opened his mouth to defend himself, but I waved a hand at him, stopping him before he could speak. I could see the laughter dancing in her eyes. "Anyway, the next morning he seemed disgusted with what he'd done. He called me all sorts of vile things. He punched me in the face, knocking me out, and when I woke up, I was in a place of darkness."

My eyebrows drew down at her odd phrasing. She was holding something back, but I let it go. "He kept me there for months, though he never came back. But his friend did." She swallowed hard and the first sign of true terror crossed her face and I wanted to fucking trash my office. I wanted to growl and howl and fucking kill any person who had ever hurt her. I fucking hated her for it. Instead, I waved for her to continue impatiently. "I was dying. I was covered in wounds, cuts and bites where I'd been tortured."

Cain let go of the same emotion that I was holding so tightly to my chest. He turned and put his fist through the drywall. Solomon was beside him almost instantly, but I didn't fail to notice that he placed his body between the woman and Cain. We both knew the big man would slit his own throat before he hurt her, but something about her put even the most easygoing of us on alert.

"Continue," I grunted, and annoyance flared in her eyes. Good. It was better than that dead expression.

"Anyway, Hope found me, rescued me. She dropped me off with... someone else. But when I began to show, I realized that that *fucker* had knocked me up. Despite the condoms. Despite the fact I'd been starved and beaten for months. When this other person realized I was pregnant, we decided it wasn't safe for me to be there anymore."

I growled. "What kind of spineless bastard kicks out a pregnant woman on the run?"

Her shoulders straightened and she looked me right in the eye. "One that wants what's best for his kids."

So it was a guy. I didn't like the fire in her expression when she thought about this other savior. I was going to fucking beat him until he couldn't lift a hand to touch her, kids or not. I clamped down on the thought.

I didn't give a damn who she fucked. I had no interest whatsoever in this woman. Not sexually or emotionally. She was Cain's fucking problem.

"And what, exactly, are you not safe from? What mess are you bringing to our door?"

She paled, and shook her head. "The bad kind. The worst kind you can think of. You don't stand a chance." She looked completely desolate in that moment, and I wanted to wrap my damn arms around her and tell her that I would keep her safe from the very hounds of Hell. She took a step toward me, her eyes desperate. "I just need a place to stay until the baby is born. Then I'll know."

Cain placed a reassuring hand on her arm, and I wanted to rip it off and beat him with it. "It's okay. You're safe here," my VP said softly. His eyes dared me to disagree.

I scowled at him then looked back at the girl. "Then you'll know what?"

"Whether the baby is a monster."

Solomon flinched back like she'd struck him. I wanted to flinch too, instead I felt my hands ball. Solomon stepped away from her like she'd tried to spit on him. "No baby is a monster," Solomon said on a soft growl.

For the first time, tears gathered in her eyes, but she didn't let them fall. "You don't understand and I can't tell you. But its father was a monster, and I'm not much better." But as she said it, she curled her hand around the swell of her stomach as if she would love the baby anyway.

It got too much for Cain, and he pulled the woman into his arms. She stood stiffly for a moment, but eventually all the strength that had been holding her upright ebbed away and she curled into him.

"You'd be surprised what we understand. We understand violence and monsters better than most," I informed her softly. I breathed deeply through my nose and flexed my hands. I detached my mind from the scene in front of me. "You can stay. Cain found you, so he can be your keeper. You fuck up, he gets punished, so don't fuck up. Stay until the baby is born or after, I don't give a shit. But you have to follow the Club rules. You got secrets, I don't give a shit about that either. Keep them. But you lie to us, you're out. It's honesty or the highway." I sat back down behind my desk, dismissing them all.

Cain ushered the woman out of the room, but Solomon stayed behind. He looked totally conflicted, and knowing what I knew about his past, I could see why.

I sighed and scrubbed my hand over my face. "Go on and say it."

"Goliath is going to shit."

I shook my head. I knew it. We all dealt with Laura's death differently. Cain became a fucking mother hen, nurturing the sweet butts and picking up strays like the pound. Solomon turned into a manwhore who refused to commit to anyone for anything more than a night, but he worshipped them in his own way. Goliath got his revenge, we all did, and then he went on to hate women with every ounce of his being. A woman had broken his heart into a million pieces, even if it wasn't her fault she died. The dude needed some serious therapy. Actually, we probably all did, but a shrink wouldn't be welcome in the

Clubhouse, and I probably couldn't pay one enough to step across the threshold anyway.

"Goliath can deal. I'm President. I say she stays. Just keep her out of his way if you can."

Solomon nodded. "She's still hiding something though. She feels..."

Yeah, I knew exactly what she felt like. She felt off. Wrong. Ever since Laura's funeral and a visit from, well, Lucifer I guess, we had changed. It had been thirty-five years, and we hadn't seen him again. It took us a decade to work out what he'd meant by us riding for him when we were needed. He didn't need an outlaw motorcycle club. He needed harbingers of doom. We were the fucking Four Horsemen of the Apocolypse. How'd I know?

Because the first time I'd shot a man after Laura's death, I'd seen his soul leave his body. I've seen Cain take two best friends and turn them against each other with only a few words. Solomon could ensure a man never got satisfaction from food or a buzz from alcohol ever again. I wasn't sure how he did it, but I'd seen men go mad from the results. And Goliath...

Goliath got a perverse pleasure out of stomping other Clubs, gangs, government agencies, anything that was a threat to Damnation, into a bloody wreckage beneath his boot.

Death. War. Famine. Conquest.

It took us two decades to figure out we were now

immortal. To realize we never aged. We couldn't be killed. Goliath had been riddled with more bullets than I could count on two hands, and yet he lived to see another day. Over and over again. We'd been damned alright.

As the same cycles of life repeated over and over again, I began to think of people as sheep; they had the same beige feeling about their souls. Like cardboard cutouts of one another. Even the patched Club members, most of them still riding with us since the beginning, and their sons. They knew we were different, but they were ride or die. They feared us as much as they loved us.

But this woman, Serendipity, she felt different. She felt like fireworks. Like a punch to the throat. I didn't know why, but I was sure of one thing. She wasn't an average Joe human, and I wanted to know what we'd invited into our Clubhouse.

Solomon was still in his own head, and I cleared my throat, bringing his focus back to me. "Find out what the hell she is, then let me know."

Solomon grinned, his eyes twinkling with mischief. "She's certainly hot though. Beautiful even. Pregnant women aren't really my kink, but you know, I'm willing to make an exception for her," he winked, giving me a shit eating grin that told me he knew I was attracted to her and wanted to pummel him in the face for his teasing words.

I didn't give him the satisfaction of biting though. "Do whatever you want, Sol. But if you see Goliath before I do, send him to me before he sees the woman. Someone should give him a heads up or he'll explode and then Cain will smash him into the concrete."

"I don't know, man. My money would be on Goliath."

A smirk curled the edges of my lips. "As epic as their showdown would be, I'd rather keep the peace. We are Brothers. We are Horsemen. No woman is going to come between us, got that?"

Solomon lifted his hands in the air, giving me that smug grin as he backed out of the door of my office. Sometimes I just wanted to punch him in the face.

I collapsed back down on my chair and rested my forehead against the cool wood of my desk. There was trouble on the horizon, I could all but smell it in the air. This woman was going to change everything, and as the President, I should have kicked her out. Sent her out of our lives before she burned everything we'd created to the ground.

I just couldn't do it.

3

SERENDIPITY

The room smelled like old sex. Cain bustled around, opening curtains and windows, even if there were bars on the outside. The bars should have freaked me out, but they didn't. I knew they weren't trying to keep me here. Cain's president would probably be over the moon with happiness if I left. His scowl made me feel three inches tall, but I'd battled beings bigger than some biker with an attitude problem.

Cain continued to fuss, dragging the table to the window and tucking the single chair underneath. "I'll get some of the Prospects and Old Ladies in to clean this shit up. I'll make them scrub the entire place." He screwed up his nose at what seemed to be a suspicious substance on the wall. "Just drop your bag there. It'll be safe, I promise."

How a mountain of a man, who looked like he could rip off a person's head and feed them their own ass, could be so sweet was beyond me. But damn, he was basically adorable. Huge, covered in scars and tattoos. I don't think I'd ever felt as safe as I did right then.

The baby kicked, and I unconsciously moved my hand up to press the spot. Cain's eyes followed the action, his eyes filled with an emotion that I struggled to pinpoint. I swallowed and moved my hand away. I didn't know what to do about the baby. Love it, I guess. Every day that passed, when it moved around, let me know that I wasn't alone and I got a little less detached.

But what if it was like him? What if it was cruel and barbaric? What if it was a sociopath who did terrible things just like its father? Could I still love it then?

It turned and kicked again, and I knew I would. I would still love it, I mean, him or her. I would protect it from everything and everyone. Even the Devil himself if need be.

I placed my tote bag on the table. It was laughable what my life had amounted to. One small bag of underwear and clothes. A toothbrush. A battered paperback. A rainbow hair clip from a small girl who had dealt with her own share of monsters. A small Hulk figurine from a young boy who had seen too much to ever really be a kid again.

That was it.

Thoughts of Marco and the kids made my heart hurt. What I'd told Judas was the truth; I'd had to leave my old hiding place because I was a threat to Marco's children, and he loved those kids above all else. But I thought, maybe for a moment, he'd might learn to love me like that too. I'd been wrong. He hadn't said a word about me leaving. Hadn't even waved goodbye.

I was exhausted. More exhausted than I'd ever been in my long life. I didn't know if it was the pregnancy, or the torture, or the emotional rollercoaster I'd gone through since I'd been out of Purgatory.

My heart stuttered at just the word. I felt the darkness claw its way into my chest, clutching at my lungs until it was hard to breathe. That was the secret that I was keeping from these humans, these bikers who were used to being the top of the food chain. I hadn't been kept in some dank basement. The person chasing me wasn't just some sociopathic stalker. I'd been seduced and abducted by an Archangel. I'd been kept in the darkness of Purgatory for months. I'd been tortured by another Angel. I'd been saved by the Angel of Death and an empathic woman who wasn't altogether human either. The baby in my womb was an anomaly, even more so than me. I was an immortal mistake. But this baby was a ticking time bomb that threatened to destroy everything we believed about what was right and wrong, about faith. My breathing got choppy and the darkness crept into my vision. No, not the darkness.

I was stronger than this. The darkness was in my mind. *You aren't there anymore. You aren't there anymore.* I repeated the mantra but it did nothing. PTSD didn't listen to reason. I whimpered, pressing my hands to my head as if I could chase it away.

Two big arms picked me up, banding me tightly to a warm body, walking me to the bed. Cain sat down, tucking me under his chin, my cheek pressed against his chest.

"It's okay. You are safe," he whispered over and over. I clung to the sound of his heart, to the whispered words, to the pressure of his arms that were crushing me tightly to his chest. His words and warmth chased away the darkness for now, but I wasn't stupid enough to think it would ever be gone for good. I'd suffered from night terrors every day since I'd been pulled from the nothingness, and there was no end in sight from the terror of my dreams. Sometimes, like today, those terrors crept into the daylight hours too, so there was never any relief.

I took a shaky breath and willed my heart rate to slow. I wiggled off Cain's lap, embarrassed. "Sorry."

Cain shook his head, standing to his full height. "You never have to be sorry for that. What was the trigger? Is there something I can remove from the room?"

I smiled, because how could I not? "Thank you, but

no. The triggers are all in here." I tapped the side of my head and then put a huge smile on my face. "But I'm seriously hungry. Must be the pregnancy thing."

Cain just gazed at me intently, his soft brown eyes full of sympathy that made my throat clog. "Sure thing. Do you have cravings? The, uh, other pregnant women we've known had cravings for hotdogs and crepes. Sometimes together."

I gagged a little. "Uh, no. But pancakes kinda sound good?" He held the door open and I gave him a small smile. "Do you collect many pregnant women here at your Club?"

His smile was tight. "Just one other." His tone told me that was the end of the conversation, even though I wanted to know more. But I wasn't ready to overstay my welcome just yet, so I let it go.

I followed him down the hall, through several security doors, and down the stairs. The stairs emptied out onto the bar, and there seemed to be two dozen people still there. Most of them were in leather or denim cuts, patches with a demonic horse head on the back and the words Damnation MC on the top rocker. There were men of every size, shape and level of hygiene in the room. Young guys with Prospect on their patches, grizzly old dudes with big beards and loads of tattoos. There were women too, of every shape and shade. Beautiful bottle blondes, latino women with curves for days, one short, round woman with huge boobs and an even bigger laugh.

Some of the women looked scrawny and strung out, some looked over the group with a predatory expression. One had her head thrown back in pleasure as she rode a man in a darkened corner. It was really a hedonistic free for all.

Cain whistled. "Trigger, take it back to one of the hot boxes," he shouted to the guy with the woman riding him like a pony. The guy stood up, zipped up his pants, and pushed a cowboy hat onto his head as he strolled past me like he hadn't just had his dick in some chick.

"Ma'am," he said, winking.

Cain huffed. "Trigger, this is Serendipity. You'll keep all your appendages away from her unless you want to lose them." He looked at me. "Trigger is our Secretary-Treasurer. He's good at it too, under all the fucking weird down-home getup." He pointed to the hat.

Trigger just grinned. "Sure thing, VP." He swaggered away, the girl in the short skirt chasing after him, her cheeks flushed and she was all but panting. I shook my head.

"Prospect!" he shouted, and two guys literally appeared from nowhere. "Go clean room seven. I want it so clean you could lick the walls. If I don't think it's clean enough when you're done, that's exactly what you'll fucking do. Got it?"

They nodded, and took off up the stairs. Cain

gripped my elbow and led me toward the bar. A man with a huge red beard and yellowing eyeballs lifted his chin at me. "Serendipity, this is Shots. Shots is the bartender and his Old Lady is the best cook around." A pole thin woman with rosey cheeks and twinkling eyes stuck her head around the door that was behind the bar. "Sweetie, this is Serendipity," Cain introduced again.

I smiled at the woman, the first friendly, not flirtatious face I'd seen. "Call me Sera, please. Serendipity is a mouth full."

"Nice to meet you, Sera. Hang on, my burgers are burning!" She ducked back inside the kitchen.

Solomon plopped down on the stool beside me. "You certainly are a mouthful," he said, grinning at me. Cain reached around my back and slapped him in the head. I smothered my grin as he rubbed all that spun gold hair. "Same goes for you as for Trigger. Keep it in your damn pants."

Solomon just smirked, and bit his full bottom lip. Damn. He was really super pretty. It was a shame that my weakness for pretty guys got me into my current situation. I was swearing off men for life, especially humans with guns and bad attitudes.

Cain rolled his eyes. "Shots, do you think Sweetie could make Sera some pancakes?"

Shots grinned at me, though all I could see was a

flash of white beneath the big ginger beard. Shit, how did he eat though that thing?

"Sure thing, VP." He turned, pushing through the swinging doors to the kitchen.

Someone turned up the music, and one of the girl's stood on a table, and danced around in her tiny skirt. I was pretty sure she wasn't wearing underwear, because the guys sitting around the table were looking up her skirt like it held a feast.

Solomon leaned closer. "Dancers from the strip-club up front." He wasn't apologizing, or rationalising. It was what it was, and he was just giving me more information. If he thought I was perturbed by a few strippers, he was sorely mistaken.

Shots returned to the bar, pouring me a coke. "Sorry we don't have any juice. I'll get some in. And some milk. That's what Sweetie wanted when she had our kids."

I gave him a smile and murmured my thanks. Cain took a huge gulp of beer. We sat in silence for a moment, like none of us knew what to say. Well, I certainly didn't. If I asked too many questions, they'd start asking questions. Questions I couldn't answer. I watched the room with ancient eyes, cataloguing the people, the feel of the humans in close proximity.

Sweetie bustled out of the kitchen, a huge stack of pancakes in her hands. She placed it in front of me and death-glared the guys on either side of me. "There you go. Keep your hands off," she said to Cain and Solomon. "When are you due, love?"

I swallowed hard. In all honesty, I had no idea. Time moved differently in Purgatory for everyone, though I'd been there at least five years earth time, but only three months Purgatory time. But after I came out, it felt like my body and my baby were trying to play catch up. Was it because it was a Nephilim baby? How quickly did they grow? From what I'd searched on the internet, the baby was moving enough to be in my third trimester. I could feel its kicks, it's movements. I had no reference here and I wanted to cry. Instead, I sucked in a deep breath. "In a couple of months." Non-specific enough.

She nodded sagely. "Taking your vitamins?"

I shook my head. I couldn't tell her that I'd been imprisoned in Purgatory for the previous five years, but needless to say that there weren't any prenatal vitamins there. When I'd been rescued, it had all been so crazy; realizing I was pregnant then calling Hope and getting shipped off with Cain. There'd been no time to think about things like prenatal vitamins. And now I wanted to cry.

Sweetie must have seen it coming, because she reached across the bar and squeezed my hand. "Don't worry about it, love. I'll pick you up some on my way here tomorrow. Some of the other Old Ladies have had their share of kids and probably have a bunch of baby stuff cluttering up their garages if you want some of it."

Solomon took a swig of his beer. "I'll buy her new stuff, if she wants it."

I was shaking my head before he'd even finished. "No, thank you," I said softly to Solomon. I didn't need to be indebted to these men more than I already was. I smiled at Sweetie. "If anyone has anything they are going to donate anyway, I'll happily take it. Nothing too... big."

No furniture that I couldn't take with me when I had to leave. If I had to run.

Sweetie nodded knowingly, her eyes sad. She nailed Cain with a stern look. "Fix this." Then she strutted back into the kitchen.

Cain shook his head. "You wouldn't know that this was a patriarchal club with the way she speaks to us."

Shots looked nervous. "Sorry, VP."

Cain waved him away. "Don't stress it, Shots. Sweetie has us by the balls and she knows it. She hooked us in with her food and now she may as well be Pres."

Solomon laughed, finishing his beer. "Do you dance, Serendipity?" he purred.

I loved to dance. Was I going to dance with this man? Every ounce of my self-preservational instincts screamed no. But when was the last time I'd done anything as simple as dance with a handsome man?

So ignoring my brain, I nodded and stood. I narrowed my eyes at Cain. "Don't eat my pancakes," I said, embarrassed by how much it sounded like a growl. Cain threw back his head and laughed, drawing the eyes of every person in the room.

"Go on. I'll protect your pancakes."

Solomon walked me onto the dance floor, pulling me into his body, though he kept enough space between us to keep it just this side of respectable. He placed a large warm hand on my waist and laced his fingers with mine, tucking our hands close to our bodies. The sound of some old bluesy country song came over the speakers, the beat slow and meandering, the singer crooning about how his lover was like a bottle of whiskey. Solomon rocked us from side to side in a two step that was surprisingly graceful. He moved my body as if he knew it intimately. He didn't speak, happy to just press my body to his chest and I rested my head on his shoulder. It felt nicer than anything I had had in a long, long time. Years. Decades.

Of course, the baby took that moment to intrude on the normalcy of my life, kicking where my stomach rested against Solomon.

He looked down at me. "Hungry?"

I couldn't help but smile. He thought the baby kick was my stomach rumbling. "No. It's the baby kicking."

The look on his face made me laugh out loud. It

was somewhere between shock, joy and horror. He settled on joy. "Can I?"

I swallowed hard. My first instinct was to say no. I was in denial. Like, if no one else felt the baby kick, then maybe I was just constipated or something. I took a deep breath and nodded. He placed a gentle hand on my stomach, still rocking us gently. The baby obligingly kicked his palm. His awe at the sensation was a little contagious, and I found myself grinning. Before I knew what was happening, Cain was there, grinning down at me with the same question in his eyes.

Solomon twirled me into the huge man's arms. "You should dance, Big Man. The baby likes it," he said over his shoulder as he walked back toward the bar.

I nodded, and Cain wrapped me in his arms. His hand spanned most of my lower back, and he moved in large, awkward steps, not nearly as graceful as Solomon. Still, he kept the beat and tucked me under his chin and it felt soothing. Safe.

I let him place his hand, which was even bigger than Solomon's, across my stomach. "I wanted to do this earlier, but I'm not that damn rude. I got the feeling that the whole baby thing wasn't sitting well with you," he murmured against my hair.

I bit my lip, working hard to keep my body loose. "It's been a surprise. I mean, I didn't know. I didn't realize until I couldn't ignore the signs anymore. I mean, I was starving, terrified," his hand flexed ever so gently in mine. "And then I was free of that place and him and that was supposed to be the end of it, you know? But then I realized there was this constant reminder growing inside of me and I resented the shit out of it. I felt terrified he'd find out and I'd end up back there again." I swallowed hard and snapped my jaw shut. I'd said too much. My nervousness had made the baby do acrobatics inside my womb, giving Cain the show of his life.

The man in question tightened his arms around me and petted my stomach. "We can keep you safe from everything, from a stalker to the damn Apocalypse. Trust me. Trust us."

The front door of the bar opened, and Cain stiffened in my arms. "Shit. He wasn't meant to be back until tomorrow."

He turned me so his back was to the door and I was completely hidden behind his broad body. He gave a low whistle, and Solomon turned from where he was talking to Shots. I saw him mouth the word fuck and jump to his feet.

"The Pres wants to talk to you," he said to whoever was on the other side of Cain's broad shoulders.

I leaned to the left to get a better look, and caught a glimpse of a tall, tattooed man. He was a similar height to Cain, which seemed impossible because Cain was huge and what were the chances of there being two ridiculously large dudes in one MC? Cain pulled me back into his body, which felt kind of nice even though I knew he was hiding me from the newcomer.

"I need a beer," a low voice growled. It was rough and deep, like he'd had one too many punches to the throat. He strode past Solomon, and Shots was glancing between the three of them like his eyeballs were made for pingpong.

Solomon stepped around him. "The Pres said now."

The man let out an irritated huff. "Fuck off, Sol. I'm back early and the Pres can just-" His voice snapped off as his gaze landed on Cain. "Who's that?"

Cain stiffened, but then his shoulders went loose. Like a fighter. Well, shit. Who was this guy?

My own body tensed, and I stood stock-still, like prey.

Cain stepped to the side, revealing me, and I met stunning grey eyes filled with shock, and then hate. The heat of his hate hit me like a wave. I'd never met this man before, how could he look at me with such open disgust?

His eyes fell to my cursed stomach, and the disgust turned to horror. What the hell? He stood up, pushing the beer that Shots had placed in front of him off the bar onto the floor.

"What the fuck is going on!" he roared.

I flinched and much to my embarrassment, I hid behind Cain like a chicken-shit. Semi-immortal I might be, but being beaten to the point of death wasn't something I was eager to repeat ever again. The guy was huge and angry, and I had no idea what I'd done. The whole room was quiet now, everyone watching the scene with wary eyes. Solomon stood between Cain and the big guy who looked like he wanted to chew me up and spit out my bones.

Now I could see him a bit better, he made my breath stick in my throat. He was heavily tattooed, even more so than Cain. I couldn't see an inch of his body that wasn't tattooed, except for his face. Even the back of his head, beneath the shaved sides of his scalp, was tattooed, right down the edges of the nail beds of his fingers. He had a huge, old scar that traveled down from his forehead, across the bridge of his nose, and over his cheek.

His face was red as I watched him, like my slow perusal of his tattoos was making him even angrier. He pointed a tattooed finger at me. "She needs to go," he growled, and I shrank back.

Judas was suddenly there, all up in the big man's face even though he was a couple of inches shorter.

"When I say I need to see you immediately, I mean it, Asshole."

The man grunted a low, primal sound, and I was kind of convinced that he was about to rip Judas' head clean off his body.

"She needs to leave," he said again, in a lower voice

that seemed more like an animalistic whine. He sounded in pain. What had I done?

I didn't realize I'd whispered the question out loud until all four men looked at me. Solomon looked over his shoulder, his smile sad.

"Nothing, Sweetheart. Just existed. Don't worry." He stepped toward the scarred man. Both he and Judas talked in a low voice, but the huge dude didn't take those penetrating eyes from mine. Eventually Solomon and Judas dragged him out back towards Judas' office.

Cain's hand felt heavy and comforting on my shoulder, like a security blanket. "And now you've met the last of my brothers. Goliath. Just avoid him if you can." Yeah, that wasn't going to be a problem. If I saw him coming, I'd be running the other way. "Come on, Sera. I'll take you back to your room. We can throw things at the Prospects until they're finished." He gave me a smile, and I swallowed hard as I nodded.

I looked back at the bar, but my pancakes were gone. For some stupid reason, probably goddamn hormones, I wanted to cry. As I felt the sting behind my eyelids, I realized I was crying. Fuck.

Shots looked panicked, and even Cain looked around for someone to pound into dust. They seemed to realize at the same time I was crying over goddamn pancakes.

Shots raised his hands. "Hey, it's okay, they just got

cold." He turned and rushed toward the kitchen doors, yelling Sweetie's name in a panicked voice.

Sweetie appeared once again like the goddess of baked goods, holding a plate covered in aluminium foil. "Ah, love. It's okay. I was just warming them for you." She handed the plate to Cain, and gave me a quick, tight hug. God, that hug from a complete stranger meant so much to me at that moment. "Go on up and have a lie down. I remember what my first baby was like. I kicked Shots out of the house for five months. Every time I looked at his big stupid face, I wanted to cry or throw something at him. Hormones are a bitch."

All I could do was nod as Sweetie loaded Cain up with a bunch of snacks so I wouldn't have to walk up and down the stairs to the bar unless I wanted to. She was an angel.

Cain smiled warmly down at me and gripped my hand. It was a bit of a liberty considering I had only just met him, but I felt like he was my only anchor at the moment, so I gripped it tightly.

If I was going to weather this storm, I was going to need a rock. I looked up at him as he walked with single-minded focus toward the stairs. Luckily for me, I'd managed to secure myself to a mountain instead.

4

GOLIATH

I put my hand through the drywall. I was surprised to find a hole already there, but it wasn't enough to shake me from the red haze of rage that had come over me at the sight of the woman in Cain's arms. Nothing shook me from my rage much anymore.

I felt the satisfying crunch of drywall cutting my knuckles, but I knew it'd be healed before I drew it back to my body.

"Are you done chucking a tantrum like a child?" Judas said flatly, and I snarled at him, more beast than man. He just waited there like a fucking king and I was a peasant. I wanted to slam my fist into his face instead. The crunch of bones was even more satisfying than drywall.

Instead, I sucked in a deep breath through my nose and gritted my teeth. "Who is she?"

Her face blurred over another one from my past, another blonde. Another baby.

"She's one of Cain's strays, that's all."

I curled my lip. She'd been dancing awful close to Cain for some stray. He might collect the damaged ones, but he never held them in his arms. Not since... the other one.

"Her name is Serendipity. I would have introduced you if you weren't such a psychopath," Solomon said.

I flipped him the bird. The way Solomon said her name, I thought perhaps she wasn't just Cain's stray. "She needs to go."

I sounded like a fucking broken record, but it was the truth. Women were poison. They'd poison the Club, poison my Brothers, leave us all broken in the dirt, and I wasn't sure I could get back up again.

"She stays. It's time you got over this. It's been thirty five years, man. You have to let it go. Serendipity isn't Laura," Solomon said softly and I whirled on him, grabbing him by the throat and slamming him into the wall. Judas made no move to stop me, but his eyes were full of disappointment and pity. Fuck him. I didn't need his pity and I no longer gave a damn about disappointing him. Still, I dropped Solomon and he landed on his feet like a cat.

Judas stepped closer, putting his hand on my shoulder. I flinched away and he sighed. "Sol is right. The girl is staying until after the baby is born. You just need to stay out of her way. If you so much as raise your voice at her, you'll answer to me. Do you understand?" I growled again and nodded. But Judas wasn't done. "It wasn't Laura's fault she died, G. We killed the bastards who took her life, but she never would have left if they didn't take the choice from her. It wasn't her fault, anymore than it is Serendipity's fault some fucker knocked her up and kept her locked in a basement for months."

I jerked at his words. Someone had kept her in a basement? "Who?" I kept my voice as impassive as I could so no one knew the emotions rolling around in my gut.

Judas shook his head, darkness clouding in his eyes. My own darkness rose to meet it. If misery loved company, then my darkness enjoyed bathing in blood with someone else.

I had no doubt about what I was. I was damaged. Broken. Tainted by evil.

Solomon growled. The pretty boy was dangerous when he wanted to be. Hell, we all were. "She wouldn't say, thinks we can't help. She doesn't know, but I'll be damned if I didn't want to tell her that there was nothing walking this earth that could take us on and survive."

Solomon was cocky. There were several things not

walking this earth that could crush us like bugs under their boot heels. First and foremost was the cause of this salvation and damnation. Luc. Lucifer. Even thinking about the Devil sent chills down my arms, and I looked around like he might appear because I thought about him too hard.

"Find out. I need to kill something."

I turned and strode out of the room, down the hall to the tiny storage room at the back where I slept. It was the size of a closet, but I prefered the close confines. The only decoration I had in there were guns taped to the undersides of different pieces of furniture. Judas said they were a security blanket. I said they were smart. Had to agree to disagree on that one.

I walked into my room, kicking the door shut with my foot. I slipped off my cut and hung it over the only chair in the room. I slipped off my holsters and put them there too, checking the safety was on first. The glorified janitors closet had an ensuite, basically a waterproof room because it was small and I was huge, so I didn't fit inside conventional shower stalls.

I peeled off my clothes which were stuck to my body after my long ride and then the sweat of my rage. The rage was still burning through my blood about the woman, and I grasped the feeling. I would take any feeling at all right now.

I turned on the hot water to max, and let the water heat up until it burned me. I let it sear my flesh, absolving me of my sins, but nothing would wash the blood from my hands. When the room got too steamy and I was worried I'd pass out, I switched the cold all the way on until it rained down on my skin in punishingly icy rivulets. Hopefully, it would cool the rage that was heating my blood.

I thought about the woman. She looked tiny in Cain's arms, but she really wasn't. She was average height, her body waif-like, like she'd been starved. It made the swell of her stomach even more conspicuous. Her wide, weird colored eyes popped into my head, her pretty pink lips parted in shock at my anger. The image of her on her knees in front of me, that look on her face, as I slid my cock between those pretty lips formed uninvited in my head. My dick responded immediately, hardening even though I wanted to twist the fucker off for its betrayal.

Instead, I wrapped my hand around its length, the only untattooed part of me, and squeezed hard. I imagined fucking her with all the brutality in my soul until she was a tangled, unrecognizable mess. I tugged at my cock angrily. This wasn't a release. It was a punishment.

Because women were the fucking downfall of man. Eve was the downfall of Adam. Laura was the downfall of me. I wouldn't let this woman, this Serendipity, be the downfall of my Brothers.

I pumped hard, the pain making my balls tight,

until I blew hot streams of cum on the shower wall. I stared at my dick like the traitor it was.

I climbed out of the shower, dressed again in clean jeans and a t-shirt. I pulled on my boots, and laid down on top of my blankets to stare at the ceiling. I willed my body to sleep, but I knew it was useless. I didn't sleep much anymore, and despite my exhaustion, I was still too riled up. I reached beneath the bed and pulled out a bottle of Jack. I tipped the bottle to my lips and gulped it down.

I couldn't will myself into unconsciousness, but I could drink until I passed out. I needed the release of sweet oblivion before I did something I'd regret.

I MUST HAVE BLACKED out a bit, because I woke to a blood curdling scream. I was up, with a gun in my hand before my eyes had even opened. I had the reflexes of someone constantly at war. I was out the door and up the stairs before my brain even caught up with my instincts.

My heart was pounding in my ears as I kicked down the door in front of me. My gun was raised, and I searched the room for intruders.

But there was just the woman, whimpering and crying like she was being tortured. She was twisted in her bedsheets, the fabric pinning her arms to her sides. I could see her struggling, tasted her animalistic fear in the air, but she was still asleep. I wanted to turn and leave.

No one in the Club was being attacked. This shit wasn't my problem. I watched her struggle, a pained whine leaving her pretty lips like someone was jabbing her with red hot pokers. I grunted a frustrated sound, and walked over to the bed. I pulled at the sheets, but she must have been tossing something ferocious because they were a hard rope. I slipped my knife from my boot and cut at the fabric.

Of course, that was the point those slow ass fuckers finally arrived. When I was standing over the bitch with a knife.

"What the fuck?" Cain roared, and was across the room, leveling an uppercut at my face. I took it.

Solomon and Judas weren't far behind him, and I noticed a few of the other members were behind them. Fuck. I let Cain get one more good hit in, but then I grabbed his wrist.

"She was having a night terror. Got herself caught up. Take better care of your Property, Brother," I spat at him, and shouldered past him. Judas stepped aside to let me through, his eye like a laser. As alway, Judas saw too much.

I growled at the members of Damnation MC, all in varying states of undress. This is why I slept clothed. I stomped down the stairs and into the bar. I walked around the back and pulled out another bottle of Jack and downed half of it in one go. I wouldn't die from alcohol poisoning, no matter how hard I tried. And fuck knows, I'd tried.

The burning liquor began to thrum through my veins, blurring my vision and setting off a ringing in my ears. Huh, that was new. Maybe I was actually killing brain cells. Good. Maybe I'd kill the fucking weak ass man who still wanted to save damsels in distress. I thought he was dead, but apparently I hadn't worked hard enough yet. I took another deep swig, hoping this would be the day where I tipped the balance of blood versus liquor in my veins toward the direction of death.

"She was tortured." A voice said from the darkness. I knew the voice, knew it as well as my own. Before he'd been my President, he'd been my friend. My best friend. More. We grew up in my Daddy's Club. Had the MC life shoved down our throats until we were old enough to patch in. When my father died, Judas fought for the Presidency. Then Laura happened.

I growled in Judas' direction and slugged down the booze. I was going to need it for this conversation.

Judas came around the bar, standing opposite me, the polished surface between us. "From what she was gasping about just now, he tied her up, cut her, and let the rats feast on her. Guess that's why she doesn't like being restrained."

I wanted to fucking vomit. Then I wanted to peel

the flesh from whoever this fucker was until I could piss on his corpse. I grunted and scowled. If he wanted a declaration of pity or empathy or some other fucking emotion, he was going to be waiting a long time. Apart from disgust, because rats were fucking gross, I had no soft emotions left in me.

"I can see you shutting down, G. But ask yourself this. If you care so little, if so much of your humanity is gone, why were you standing over her with a knife?"

I drank the dregs of the bottle, and I was swaying on my feet now. "To slit her pretty little throat, *Pres.*"

He huffed out a laugh, but it wasn't a joyful sound. "Sure thing, G. You are many things, but you aren't a fucking liar. Don't start now, and least of all to yourself."

With those fucking Yoda words of wisdom, he turned and left. I hated him right then, because he was forcing me to face something I didn't want to see.

Screw it. Two more bottles of Jack and I wouldn't see anything but the inside of a toilet bowl, and that was okay with me.

While Cain was trying to beat the back teeth out of Goliath, I was through the door and on my knees beside Serendipity's bed. She continued to thrash around, even though I didn't know how she could still be asleep. Sleeping through the heavy thuds of flesh hitting flesh, and Cain's goddamn roar, was nothing short of a miracle. Maybe she was sick?

I reached out and held my hand over her forehead like my mother used to do. She didn't feel any hotter than normal. I expected her to flinch away, but instead she pushed her head into my hand as if she was clinging to the last lifeboat left on the Titanic. Her screams turned into whimpers, then moans. Not gonna lie, her moans made my dick hard. I chastised myself.

She was moaning in fucking terror. That is not something to be hard about.

I kept my hand anchored to her forehead. "Serendipity. Sera," I said softly, and she twisted more in her blankets as if she was searching for me in her dreams. I could almost spot the moment where she felt trapped by her sheets again. She opened her mouth in a silent scream, and I was on my feet, ripping the twisted bedclothes from her body.

Guess that explains what G was doing. I didn't actually think he would hurt her. I have more faith in Goliath than he had in himself, despite the fact that he was a raging asshole. Hell, the same could be said for any man in this Club. You didn't join an MC if you were the soft, cuddling type.

Free of her bonds, she let out a shuddering sigh of relief but still didn't wake. I touched her head again, Cain watching me like a hawk.

"Serendipity." Fuck that was a mouthful. Sera didn't really suit her either. "Dippy. Wake up, Woman. You are stressing Cain the fuck out."

Cain sent me a half hearted fuck you, but his eyes were on the girl.

Judas growled for everyone to go back to bed. Her impossibly long eyelashes fluttered, and then she looked directly into my eyes and screamed bloody murder.

I fucking scrambled back on my ass, half from

surprise at the noise, and half to make myself as non-threatening as possible.

"Sorry, sorry! You were having a nightmare," I say quickly, my hands still raised. She shot up in bed, and her eyes took in the sheets, Judas in the doorway and Cain hovering near her ensuite. Thank fuck Goliath wasn't still here. There would have been no way to convince her that he wasn't a threat if she'd woken up with him standing over her with a knife like a psycho.

I could spot the moment everything came back to her, because although her shoulders didn't relax, the terror receded from her eyes. "Sorry. He, uh, he used to tie me up and let rats-" she let out a full body shudder, and I edged closer.

"Hey, it's okay. You don't have to apologize."

To contradict my words, Judas slammed his fist into the doorjamb with enough force to break bones, then left. Cain looked similarly pissed, but I gave him a look. The look said "It's the middle of the fucking night and we are two fucking bikers in her room, calm the fuck down before you spook the shit out of her." Or at least I hope it said that. It could have just said "Shut the fuck up" and that would have worked too. These guys had no idea how to act around women. Since Laura, they'd pulled into themselves, having little to do with women outside of fucking them. And in Cain's case, saving them from a shit life. But he never got attached. He fed them and then fucked them off. Rehabilitate and release.

I had a feeling he wanted to keep this beauty for his very own though.

I put my hand on the bed, leaving it there, not making a move to reach for her. She looked like she was still fighting off the effects of the dreams, somewhere between asleep and awake, the demons of her nightmares still lingering at the edges of the darkness. Her sleep shirt had slid up her body, gathering under her breasts, and in the soft light of the ensuite, I could see the round globe of her stomach. Also, a good stretch of her smooth long legs. I was a perv; at least I owned it.

I didn't stare though, looking back into those haunted purple eyes that seemed to shine even in the darkness. "Is there something we can get for you? A drink? A bath?"

She frowned toward her ensuite. "Is there a bath?"

I grinned at her. "Well, not in this room. Mine does. You are welcome to use it any time." I didn't even offer to wash her back for her. Seriously, I should get a gold star or something for good behaviour.

Cain snorted at me from where he stood, and I glared. She shook her head. "Not tonight. But maybe one day?" She took a deep, shuddering breath. "I'm okay now."

Because I was unable to stop myself, I reached over

and covered her hand with mine. "Okay. I'm just down the stairs, we all are. If you need anything, just knock on any of the doors and someone will help you. You're safe here, Dippy."

She snorted out a laugh, her eyebrows raised. It was so much better than the look of sheer terror. "Dippy?"

I nodded sagely. "I like it. It suits you. Besides, it brought you out of your nightmare so subconsciously, you must like it too." It was basically science.

She shook her head, grabbing the blankets and pulling them up her legs. "I don't mind being Dippy. It'll be nice not to be Sera for awhile."

She plumped her pillow and I took it as my cue to leave, even though I kind of wanted to crawl beneath the blanket with her.

And sleep. Me. Just sleep in bed with a woman? Where the fuck had that urge came from? I kept my shock locked down tight, and strode toward the door.

"Solomon?" I paused, a small part of me hoping she was about to call me back, ask me to stay with her. "Can you leave the light on? I... I don't like the dark."

I smiled softly at her, and switched on the overhead light. "No worries."

Guess that explained why the light to her ensuite was on. I strolled down the now quiet hallways with Cain.

"She's..." he started, but seemed to lose the words. Didn't matter. I had enough words for both of us.

"Fucked up? Beautiful?"

He nodded, and cocked his head toward the sound of Judas and Goliath in the bar. We turned, heading back toward our apartments at the rear of the Clubhouse. "I screwed up with Goliath though. I just saw him there with a knife and I fucking reacted, you know?"

I didn't say anything. He had fucked up, and he'd have to make it right. But I wasn't so sure I wouldn't have thought the very same thing if I'd been the first through the door. Goliath was unpredictable, and although I trusted him with the safety of the Club, I wasn't sure I trusted him with Dippy.

But there was still a little bit of the man I used to know, the man who lived before Laura, deep down in there. That man I trusted above all else. That man was still hard and brutal, but he had a heart so big that when it broke, it shattered like crystal. Now nothing was left of it but dust that threatened to shred the hands of all those who reached for it.

It didn't help that he was Conquest. Violence was his duty now, and he reveled in the darkness of it all.

Cain stilled his feet outside his own door. I doubted any of us were going to be sleeping, but we all needed space. "Maybe G is right. Maybe she does need to go."

I stepped back in surprise as I tried to read his face.

"What the fuck? You were the one who brought her here, remember?"

Cain glared. "Yeah, I remember. But she's different, I can feel it in my bones. I feel like she could, fuck I don't know, she could destroy us. Destroy me."

Ah, Cain felt it too. The pull. I noticed as soon as I walked up to her. I couldn't resist. She was like the sun. We were getting so close that we were going to burn, but I hadn't felt more alive in thirty years. I was loath to give that up because these assholes couldn't tell the past from the present. Maybe that was dangerous in its own way.

"She stays, Cain. We aren't throwing her out on the streets because you guys can't fucking control yourselves for five minutes."

His eyes narrowed and I could tell he wanted to hit me. I'd probably welcome the sensation at this point. "I never suggest we throw her on the streets," he growled. "Just that she shouldn't be here. We could assign some of the boys to watch her. Maybe Shots and Sweetie, because Sweetie knows this baby shit."

"And you don't trust any of the other single members not to climb between her pretty white thighs, right?"

Cain turned and had his hand around my throat in an instant, shoving me into the wall with a thud. "Watch your mouth," he growled again.

I just grinned back, a big shit-eating smirk spread

across my lips because I knew it would rile him more. "You know, if you're gonna keep choking me out like this, you should at least let me have my cock in my hand first."

Cain narrowed his eyes, but I saw his lips twitch. He let go and I dropped softly to my feet. "Sorry man. She just makes me feel things."

I slapped him hard on the back. "There's nothing wrong with feeling shit, Cain. It's what separates man and beast. But protect your heart too."

I just hoped I could take my own damn advice.

6

SERENDIPITY

I rolled out of bed the following morning, although the light told me it was late. I felt like a zombie, my sleep broken and fragmented. Waking to find half of Damnation MC in my bedroom hadn't helped. Not because I felt threatened, despite the fact they were huge, scary bikers. That would have been way too sane for me. Instead, I kept imagining the way Solomon sat back on his haunches, his eyes soft, his hands curling gently into my sheets, and it made me... horny. Yeah, that was the word. Horny as hell.

I huffed out a laugh as I stepped into the shower and set it to as hot as I could stand it. If I could punch my libido in the face, I probably would. It got me in this situation. It could calm the fuck down.

Under the cleansing rush of hot water, I could

think about what happened in Purgatory. Uriel stealing me from my bed the morning after I got shit faced and had really uninspired sex with the giant, beautiful douche. He was an ugly kind of beautiful. Perfection on the outside, with fire-red hair and a physique like he'd been moulded by God himself, which I guess he had. Cruelty had danced behind his eyes, but when you've lived as long as I have, even cruelty is better than feeling nothing. But he ended up being a two pump chump, then zapped me to fucking Purgatory to hide his sins. Then his friend visited.

I twisted the tap on the hot water higher as the chill in my bones made me shudder. Dalius. He'd been an Angel too. He believed in punishing the wicked with the fervor of a zealot. It made him very creative in his punishments. But the rats were the worst. The beatings I could take. The deprivation of light, heat, food, everything necessary for life, I could deal with. But the scrabbling of tiny nails over the stone floors, the feel of them scratching across my skin, biting at my flesh, that is what broke me.

Bile rose up in my throat and I vomited all over the shower floor. Another reason why I only thought about my time in Purgatory while in the shower. I could wash my weakness right down the drain.

I stepped out and pulled on some clothes. My t-shirt was so tight it rolled up. I was going to need some maternity clothes or something soon. I pulled on my jeans, and sucked in a deep breath to button them up. When it didn't happen, I pulled the tie from my hair, letting my blonde locks cascade around my shoulders in a golden wave. I hooked my hair tie through the buttonhole then secured over the button. It would have to do. I wondered if any of the thrift shops around here had maternity clothes. My shirt rolled up my stomach again and I huffed.

I tiptoed out of my room, looking up and down the hallways like a thief. I padded softly down the stairs in search of Cain's room. He might loan me a giant shirt until I could get my own. I didn't want to walk around with my shirt looking like a crop top for the rest of the day.

I wracked my brain as to whether it was the third or fourth door that was his bedroom, but I couldn't remember, so I tried the one at the very end. I knocked softly. I could hear the heavy thump of boots behind the door, then it was wrenched open.

Behind it wasn't Cain. It was the guy from last night. He didn't look any less scary in the daylight, his eyes filled with rage and his face contorting into contempt as he realized who was on the other side of his door.

I backed up until my shoulders hit the wall on the other side of the hall. "I'm sorry. I was looking for Cain. I need a shirt, I mean, sorry. I'll just go. Shit. Sorry. Go back to sleep. If you want." I slapped a hand over my mouth. I wanted to run, but he pinned me to the spot with his gaze. I felt like an ant caught beneath a magnifying glass, just waiting for the sun to move. "I'll just-"

"Don't move," he growled. Then he slammed the door. I told myself to move. But it was like my muscles were frozen. The door wrenched back open, and a ball of fabric was thrown at me.

"Cain is there." He pointed at the door three feet from my head. Then he slammed the door again. I looked at the fabric in my hand, shaking it out until I realized it was a t-shirt. It was fucking huge and smelled like motor oil and man.

I didn't actually mind the smell. I slipped the shirt over my head and it fell to my knees. He was huge. I heard a soft noise from down the hall, and I turned to see Solomon standing in the doorway of what I assumed was his room.

"I think Goliath's softening. It helped that he found you last night. He's not as heartless as he likes to pretend to be."

I stared back at the giant's door. Goliath. It suited him. "He was there?" I whispered as I walked toward Solomon. He gave me one of those panty-dropping smiles, and nodded.

He shut his door and met me halfway. "Yep. Worked out it was your sheets freaking you out. Then Cain punched him in the face. It was all really exciting. Pity you weren't awake for it," he laughed.

I didn't know what to say to that. Heat warmed my cheeks at the idea they'd all seen my night terrors. I wasn't embarrassed exactly, although I hated appearing weak in front of them. "Sorry. I sleep heavily during the nightmares. It's like I'm trapped until it all plays out again."

I hated sleeping. But the baby was sapping my energy at an alarming rate, so all I wanted to do was sleep. It was an exhausting tug of war between my body and my mind.

Emotion raced through Solomon's eyes; pity, rage, empathy, determination. It was an interesting mix. He grabbed my elbow, leading me back down the hall. "It's late, Cain will be in the garage. How about we get some food in you and then you can see him? Sweetie won't be in the kitchen, but I can make you whatever you want. Or I can take you to the diner down the road. They have a great all-day breakfast."

I didn't want to tell him I had no money. Well, that was a lie. I had about two hundred dollars in the bank. I needed a job. I definitely challenged the stereotype that immortals were all rich and eccentric. I nailed the eccentric bit, but I was poor as fuck.

A little of it was my lifestyle. I'd never stayed in one place for long. I picked up money and jobs haphazardly. I didn't need money really. I had homes littered around the world, humble shacks that were all unfortunately traceable back to me. I needed to get rid of some, but couldn't do that without revealing I was alive and back on earth. So for now, I was poor.

I would take this safe haven for as long as I could, then I would take the baby and run. Live like a human. I thought about the redheaded woman who had rescued me from the depths of my own personal hell. Hope. Such an apt name. She might know someone who could hook me up with some fake identification. I looked at Solomon who seemed to be waiting for my response.

"Uh, I'll just have toast, if I could. I'm having trouble accessing my money right now."

Solomon actually rolled his eyes at me. "Stop. If you need money, we can give it to you. You need clothes?" His eyes took in Goliath's huge shirt. "Though I kinda like the way you look in a Damnation shirt."

I looked down at the shirt, the horse head motif from the patches screen printed on the front. It was pretty cool. I didn't say that though. Instead, I frowned at him. "I can buy my own clothes and breakfast. I don't want your money."

Solomon laughed, and held up his hands. "Sure, Dippy. But I'm starving so we are going to the diner. Let's ask Cain if he wants to go too."

We walked across the parking lot, the doors to the strip joint chained and padlocked shut this early in the morning. There were a few cars and bikes in the carpark even now.

We found Cain in a workshop tucked beside the strip club. He was standing in front of a dismantled bike on some kind of platform, his big hands working in the tight spaces with ease. There seemed to be a half a dozen bikes around the room in various states of dismantlement. Old school metal music played over the speakers and Cain sung softly as he worked.

Solomon put his fingers to his lips and whistled. Cain's head shot up and he smiled our way. Holy shit, what a smile.

He pulled a remote out of his pocket and turned off the music.

"Sera. How did you sleep?" Then he seemed to realize what he was saying and grimaced. "You know, after we left?"

Solomon laughed and slapped him on the back. "Good work, asshole."

I gave Cain a soft smile. "I slept fine, thank you."

He looked at my shirt and frowned. "Why are you wearing Goliath's shirt?"

I flushed, and pulled it out, looking for his name somewhere. How the hell did he know that it was Goliath's shirt?

Solomon wrapped an arm around my shoulder and squeezed me tight. I tried not to stiffen at his touch. "We all have colors associated with us. Goliath's is white, hence why his horsehead is white." He looked at Cain. "She was looking for you, so she could borrow a shirt, but found Goliath's room instead."

Cain's face went from surprise to worry and back again. "Was he... civil?"

Laughter bubbled up from Solomon's chest until he was bent over, sucking in air like he was about to die. "Civil. Fucking civil. Goliath," he hissed out between gasping breaths. It was the kind of laugh that you couldn't help but giggle along with, even if you didn't get the joke.

I shook my head at Solomon. "He was perfectly polite, if scary as hell."

Solomon was still wheezing, and Cain punched him in the kidney. "It wasn't that funny dickhead." He looked back at me, his eyes soft. "Do you have everything you need?"

Solomon finally straightened. "I'm taking Dippy to breakfast and then to buy some clothes so she doesn't have to keep taking her life in her hands by borrowing G's. If you would like to come and chaperone, you're more than welcome."

Cain threw down his wrench and picked up his cut, slipping it over his inked arms. "I could eat. Let's go."

We stopped outside the workshop in front of a couple of bikes. Not going to lie, it took me an embarrassingly long time to work out that we were going to ride to the diner. On a bike. Because they were bikers.

"Uh, I thought you said it was just down the road. Maybe we should walk? You know, exercise is good for pregnant women." Yeah, I was playing the pregnancy card right now.

"Aww Dippy. Don't you trust us?" Normally, I would have taken the challenge head on. I mean, I couldn't really die from a little bike accident. I was like one of those everlasting lightbulbs. I'd just glow and glow for all time, unless someone got a baseball bat and smashed me to pieces.

But the baby? I didn't know, and I found myself not wanting to take the risk.

Cain looked over at me, and he must have seen the worry, the indecision on my face.

"It's a couple of miles down the road, we can drive if you want. But I promise, you'll be as safe on the back of my bike as you would be in a car. I won't let anything happen to you or the baby."

His words sounded like so much more than a promise not to ride like a lunatic and kill us both. No, his words sounded like a vow, and they poked tiny holes in the armor around my mummified heart. I swallowed hard, blinked back emotional tears that threatened to gather in the corners of my eyes and make us all uncomfortable, and nodded.

Solomon gave me a reassuring smile and handed me a helmet. I placed it on my head, and Solomon's deft fingers tightened the chin strap. He looked me in the eyes, like he was mining them for my secrets as his fingers brushed the sensitive skin of my neck. I swallowed hard, and he must have felt it because the corner of his mouth twitched. His thumb came up and brushed lightly along my jaw. It was the whisper of a caress, and then he was turning away, throwing a leg over his own bike and I wondered if it had even happened.

One look at the way Cain narrowed his eyes on the other man told me that it had. He hopped on his own bike, huge booted feet resting on either side, holding it steady.

I walked over and glared at the bike. "Are you sure there's going to be enough room on there for all of me?" I waved a hand at my belly. He nodded, turning around to slap his hand on a little square of leather that I assume was supposed to be a seat for anyone crazy enough to hop on.

Apparently, I was that anyone. I slid onto the back of the bike, and wrapped my arms around Cain's waist. It wasn't my first time on a bike, I'd lived a heck of a long time, but it was definitely different.

The bike roared to life, and I involuntarily squeezed Cain harder as the rumble of the engine vibrated through my body. Solomon looked over at me and grinned, his eyes covered with sunglasses and he pulled up a face mask with a smiling skull to cover most of his face. Cain looked over his shoulder. "We're going just down the road, so you should be fine, but don't talk or bugs will fly in your mouth," he yelled over the bike and then he revved the engine and pulled out of the lot beside Solomon.

We rode for a couple of miles, and the wind picked up my hair and streamed it behind me. I held my face to the wind and enjoyed the way it bit my cheeks, even if it was making them a little pink from the cold. I was never going to take fresh air and the sun on my face for granted ever again.

Too soon, we were pulling into a diner, the parking lot full of potholes, cracked pavement and breeder buses. It was a small, box-like beige building, the kind of diners that popped up in the seventies and still had all the original ripped vinyl booths.

When we walked through the squeaky front door, all conversation muffled and every eye swung in our direction. The weight of judgement fell heavily onto my shoulders, though not from the waitress of the little diner. She smiled at Cain and Solomon like they were there to raise the sun in the sky.

She waved them to a spare booth at the back near the kitchen doors, with a clear view of all entries and exits. A criminal's table. There were hushed whispers as we walked over, Cain leading the way, tattooed and menacing with a swagger that promised violence, and Solomon too close to my back, his hand hovering over my spine.

I could feel the silent judgement, some of the looks people were casting in our direction bordered on disgust, but more than one woman looked at both Solomon and Cain with raw lust.

The waitress fell into the latter category, as she placed two cups of coffee in front of them and smiled from beneath her lashes.

"Hi Cain. Hi Sol. The usual?" Her eyes passed right over me like I didn't exist, like she couldn't see me right there beside Solomon.

Cain nodded. "Thanks Becky. And a menu for Sera here. Want milk or juice or something?" he asked, completely oblivious to the sharp looks Becky was throwing my way. I wondered if Becky would spit in it.

"Uh, just bottled water please." I smiled at the girl pleasantly. Given the way she was smiling at Cain, it was obvious she had a huge crush on the man, something Solomon confirmed when he leaned close to my ear.

"One of Cain's old rescues. Found her turning tricks on the corner near the shop. Got her a job here, and she got herself a job over at Apocalypse. The strip joint," he clarified. "Anyway, now she's more than a little in love with the big guy. They always end up in love with him, the broken dolls. Never given any kindness, then Cain comes in, swoops them up from shitty situations and boom, he's their saviour and sexual conquest all in one."

I frowned. "He sleeps with them?" That seemed wrong. But Solomon was shaking his head. "Never. He never gets attached. He just doesn't like to see women in danger. It's a trigger or some shit for him. He finds them somewhere safe, and sends them on their way. Some of the guys he'll let patch in, and they tend to hang around the Clubhouse as prospects or apprentice mechanics or whatever. But never the girls. The Clubhouse is no place for a single woman."

I frowned. Why was I different? "What about me?"

Solomon grinned, a full, wide smile that made Becky stop and stare during her conversation with Cain.

"Dippy, you are shaping up to be the exception to every fucking rule we've ever had over at Damnation," he laughed. Cain quirked an eyebrow in my direction, but Solomon ordered before he could ask what we'd been talking about.

"I'll have eggs and bacon, and Dippy here will probably have a giant stack of pancakes. What do you say?"

I wanted to say that I wanted scrambled eggs or something, just to make a point, but the fact was I really did want fucking pancakes. Even the idea of eggs made me want to vomit right across the table.

I narrowed my eyes at Solomon. "Pancakes would be great."

Becky bustled away, though I was fairly sure if she

could take her break and wrap herself around Cain like a cat in heat, she would have. She'd probably hiss in my direction too.

Cain pulled a small spiral bound notebook from his pocket, flicking past numbers and rough sketches of bikes and tattoos to a blank page.

"What are you going to need for the baby, Sera? I know Sweetie offered you some of her stuff, but honestly, Shot's kids are like thirty now and I'm not convinced it isn't all coated in lead paint and BPA."

"What even is BPA?" Solomon asked, making a little gaspy noise after sipping his coffee. Sweet caffeine. God I missed it.

Cain shrugged. "Fucked if I know, but everything seems to be free of it these days, so better safe than sorry."

Honestly, I had no idea what babies needed. In all my long, long years wandering the face of the Earth, I'd never been able to conceive. Closest I'd ever come to rearing anything more complex than a kitten was in the thirteenth century when I adopted an orphan just after the fall of Constantinople. It was so long ago now, I barely remembered his face, or his name. My mind protected itself by forgetting, allowing me to adjust, renew myself for each Age of Man. But I remembered the happiness I felt in caring for someone else. I hoped that was how this would feel now, when this tiny, helpless thing burst forth from my body like an alien.

I was saved from admitting my ignorance by loud voices at the other end of the diner. Cain shifted his eyes over my shoulder, and I turned to see who was yelling.

Two boys, well they were probably in their early twenties, so not quite boys but not quite men yet either, were harassing their waitress. Not Becky, but a middle aged woman whose uniform strained across her love handles and her hair stuck up in a frizzy halo around her head. The waitress was trying to appease the situation, but apparently failing miserably.

One guy pushed his coffee cup off the formica table and it shattered on the floor, splashing up onto the waitress' legs and leaving an angry red mark.

I was standing before I realized I was doing it, only noticing that Cain and Solomon had stood too when Solomon placed a hand on my shoulder.

"Sit. We've got this."

Cain's face was folded into a mask of rage. Yeah, they had this alright. I raised an eyebrow in his direction. He flashed me a quick smile before he was sliding out of the booth and strolling over to the group like he didn't have a care in the world. Solomon swaggered behind him, stopping to whisper something to Becky, who was watching the situation with wary delight.

Cain cleared his throat. "You should tip your waitress," he said quietly.

The guy who'd pushed his coffee on the ground

swung around to look at Cain. For a split second, he looked ready to shit himself, but it was quickly covered with bravado when his eyes switched back to his buddies.

"You tip the fat bitch. That coffee was the worst thing I've ever put in my mouth."

His buddies all laughed, and Solomon laughed along with them. "Well I'm sure that's not true. Bet you had that fuckheads diseased dick in your mouth last night. That's infinitely worse than Gloria's coffee."

Their eyes swung between Cain and Solomon, finally taking in their tattoos and cuts. The coffee douche started to look a little panicked. But apparently he was a douche with commitment because he doubled down on his dumbassery. "Why don't you go fuck yourself and Gloria's huge ass while you're there."

I didn't even see Cain's fist move. But in the blink of an eye, the guy was on the floor, blood pouring from his nose. He was yelling and his voice sounded wobbly as if he was going to cry. "What the fuck, man? What is wrong with you?"

Solomon grinned. "Ah shit. Looks like you got a real bad nosebleed there, kid. You should go get cleaned up. But first, tip your waitress." He lifted his shirt in a real subtle movement, flashing the gun that I knew sat there. I hoped no one else saw it though.

Coffee-Douche's friends all blanched a pasty color, throwing down fifties and moving out of the diner like their asses were one fire, one of them dragging a still ranting douche with them.

Gloria smiled between Cain and Sol. "Thanks guys. You didn't need to step in though. I had it under control." She didn't, but I could respect her need to think she was a badass in that moment. She gave them a shy smile. "I know how the cops hound you down here. I don't want you to get into trouble over me."

Cain waved a hand and smiled. "Don't worry about shit like that, Gloria. This diner is in Damnation territory, and I'll be fucked if I am going to let entitled little shits mouth off. You are a waitress, not a punching bag for trust fund kids."

Sol wrapped an arm around Gloria's shoulders and whispered something in her ear that made the middle-aged woman blush right down to her ankles. I'd only known Solomon a day or so, but I instinctively knew that he was a ladies man, so whatever he was whispering was probably dirty as hell and going in Gloria's spank bank for the rest of eternity.

They strode back towards me, their shoulders tense despite the casual nature of their violence. I shook my head. I'd fallen into the trap of stereotyping them all; Cain was the kind one, Solomon the lady killer, Judas the alpha enigma, and Goliath was the crazy one. But in all honesty, they were all crazy killers. They weren't the Spice Girls. They didn't conform to a trope. They were all dangerous. They were all so fucking alpha my brain didn't know if I should run away or throw my panties on the floor like a fucked up orgy gauntlet. They were all lady killers, though in Goliath's case, I think he literally killed ladies.

Cain sat down, his gaze brushing over me warily, as if trying to judge my response to the random act of violence. Flight or fight. I could almost taste his indecision on whether he'd stop me or not.

But I'd lived a long time. Sure, every couple of centuries, my memories got fuzzy, like it had too much stored in my brain and needed to archive some shit. But violence was the one constant through the ages. Unless you'd seen a warrior king cut off his enemies head and drink his arterial blood like a fine shiraz, you hadn't really experienced real violence. That wasn't to say these guys weren't as dangerous as that king of old, they definitely were, but I wasn't one to be scared off by a little deserved retribution.

I reached over and grabbed Cain's notebook, letting my fingers brush over his barely reddened knuckles. They were rough and hardened by years of throwing hits. I ignored his quick inhale and the weight of Solomon's eyes.

"I think I need one of those portable cribs. Just for when the baby is little. Then when we move on, I can take it with me. I don't need more stuff than I can carry. This isn't my life. I'm not nesting or whatever pregnant women are supposed to do. I can't, while he's out there." I swallowed hard. Nope. Not thinking about Uriel.

I watched Cain's fingers curl gently around the edge of the table, and heard the ancient formica groan ominously.

"Gotcha, Pretty Girl. Travel gear only. Cain, write this shit down, then we are hitting up one of those big box baby stores." He pushed the spiral notebook back to Cain, as if he was distracting the tattooed monster. "If you need to drag shit around, you need it to be quality. And you need one of those holsters where you carry your kid around like a rich girl with a toy dog."

Cain looked at him like he was insane, but wrote down "Baby Holster".

A small, hysterical laugh filled up my chest, before it bubbled over my lips like laundry liquid in a fountain. I was still giggling at the idea of carrying my baby on my hip like a six-shooter in a western film, when Becky returned with the guy's food.

She placed it down reverently in front of them, making sure to put her boobs right in Cain's face. "What you guys did for Gloria was amazing, just so you know. Not enough real men left in the world." If she wasn't basically eating the two men in front of her with her eyes, I would have lifted my hand for a high five.

Solomon stuffed a piece of toast in his mouth. "Didn't do it for Gloria. They crossed into the wrong territory to start shit." He leaned back in his chair as he chewed his toast, exposing a little slice of golden skin just above the low waist of his jeans. I wanted to worship at the alter of those abs.

Cain cleared his throat, and I realized both me and Becky had been staring. Becky's cheeks went red, but she cleared her throat and continued. "Locals respect the rules. If only we didn't have to let outsiders in." She eyed me none too casually that time. Yeah, message received bitch. No need to beat me over the head with it.

Unlike Sol, who was hoovering his food like a starving man, Cain looked pointedly at the empty table in front of me.

Becky pressed her hand to her chest. "So sorry, in all the excitement, the kitchen forgot your food. It will probably be another twenty minutes or so." Wow. Give the girl an Oscar. If she faked an orgasm the way she faked sincerity, she'd be out of here in no time.

Solomon waved her away. "Don't worry about it, Becky. She can share ours. We'll get those pancakes to go."

He then stabbed a piece of bacon and held it out to me. My eyes shot to Cain, who was putting bits of his breakfast onto his side plate, no eggs though. How he knew eggs made me gag was a mystery. Becky was looking at them like they'd sprouted another head each, and I swear to God, I was going to cry again.

Instead, I took Solomon's fork, shoved the bacon in my mouth, and focused on chewing. "Thank you," I said around a mouth full of food, one so they wouldn't know I was getting choked up, and two, so they wouldn't know that I wasn't just thanking them for sharing their food. It was for willingly sharing everything with me. An outsider, like Becky said. I wish I knew why they'd taken to me so strongly, but I wasn't going to search this safe harbor for cracks just yet. I would take a couple of days to bask in the fact that I was safe-ish for now. Let myself feel free for the last time.

They chatted about things a baby might need, putting pieces of their breakfast on my plate again as soon as it was empty. I only opened my mouth to veto big ticket items like fancy strollers and bassinets.

When we'd finished eating, they'd bundled me up, threw some cash on the table before I could think about protesting, and walked me outside sandwiched between their bodies again. Sol wrapped an arm around my shoulders again, and I was surprised when my muscles didn't automatically bunch. If I read too much into the soft smile on Solomon's face, I thought he might have been pleased by my reaction too. "Wanna ride with me this time, Dippy? I'm way safer than Cain, and my bike is a sweeter rider too."

I grinned when Cain flipped him the bird and called him a name that wasn't really fit for repeating.

After my initial fear of riding, I found I was eager to taste that freedom again. "Okay."

Cain grunted. "Fine, but she rides with me back to the Clubhouse." If I didn't know better, I'd think he was pouting. If Solomon's shit eating grin was anything to go by, he was definitely pouting.

I slid onto the bike behind Solomon, placing my feet where he pointed and wrapping my arms around his waist. His trim, muscled waist. Gah. Drool.

W e pulled up outside a store aptly named *Baby, Baby*, a baby boutique in one of the swanky areas of town, out of Damnation territory but not in anyone else's either. The main business district was neutral territory. Too hard to patrol, too hard to control. Better to let it be.

Solomon had his hand on the hollow at the base of Serendipity's spine, and I wanted to rip it off and throw it in the dumpster near where we parked our bikes. I loved Sol, he was my Brother, but he had this disarming thing that allowed him to touch Serendipity where she froze like a deer any time anyone else got within three feet of her. I'd noticed she even avoided people on the street, and looked uncomfortable in crowds.

But not with Solomon, that smooth fucker.

I consoled myself that she allowed me to dance with her last night, and she came to find me for a shirt this morning. Then I mentally punched myself in the vagina. I didn't care who she let touch her. I didn't want to get involved with her. After Solomon's talk last night, the hypocritical fucker, I decided that I would ignore the pull between us. Because she was nothing but heartache wrapped in a pretty package. End of story.

I held open the door, giving Sol a squinty-eyed glare that didn't scare him in the least. But he did remove his hand, which was damn lucky.

The shop assistant looked up, and I watched the fake, happy expression melt from her face when she took in my tattoos and our cuts. In the 2.4 seconds it took her to look us over, she had us judged and found wanting.

I didn't mind it. I'd lived with it my entire life. But sometimes in the bubble of Damnation Territory, where we were just part of the scenery, granted like a fucking barb wire fence in that scenic picture, I forget that the rest of the world reacted like this.

She looked at Serendipity, who's waif-like frame made her belly seem huge and drew even more attention to Goliath's Damnation shirt, and her nose screwed up. Ah, she'd judged Sera too, but where she feared us, she was disgusted by Sera. Double standards at its finest.

I decided to ignore the shop assistant, who was yet to do any assisting.

I pulled the list from my pocket, and rattled off the first few things. I watched Solomon reach down and pluck a onesie off a display, watched the light dim in his eyes. I knew what, or should I say who, he was thinking about. My heart thudded painfully in my chest as I struggled to keep the memories in their box. I knew this was going to happen. It was time.

I chanted that over and over to myself. I could save them this time.

Sera looked between us, her brow creasing adorably. Then she reached out, ran her hand over the onesie that Solomon wasn't really seeing, before twining her fingers in his. I swallowed hard. Fuck. She looked over at me, her eyes appraising me with gentle empathy. "Let's look at baby holsters first?" Her voice was soft, and I knew that wasn't really the question she was asking.

I wanted to kiss her. Just wrap her in my arms and kiss her until her cheeks were flushed and she was gasping for air. The urge hit me like a freight train, but it wasn't like it had come from nowhere. I'd been staring at that freight train for a long while now, as the light got closer and closer, and the danger became so intense I wanted to run the fuck away. But I was also drawn like a moth.

I was so screwed.

We found the right section, staring at the insane amount of baby *carriers,* not holsters, they weren't fucking weapons. I slapped Solomon up the back of the head for making us look like idiots.

I didn't miss Sera looking at the price tags of everything and wincing. I noted the ones she stared the most longingly at, and made a note of the brands and colors.

We made it to the portable cribs when Solomon swore softly under his breath. I glanced over his shoulder and swore a little louder.

The fucking attendant had called the fucking cops. I curled my lip at the woman behind the counter, and felt some satisfaction that her prejudicial ass cowered. Probably didn't help my standing with the cops though.

There were two of them, one who looked pissed to be here doing a nuisance call. And the other guy. The other guy set my teeth on edge. He was a cowboy, I could tell that in an instant. It was in the way his hand was already resting on his gun despite the fact he hadn't even spoken to us yet or the fact that we hadn't done anything more threatening than look their way. He puffed out his chest and swaggered over to us, and I just knew he was going to be trouble.

"Easy," Solomon said softly as the power flooded my veins. I tried hard to reel it in. We didn't need this to go further south than it was already threatening to go.

Solomon gave the cops an easy smile. "Can we help you, Officers?"

The Cowboy Cop smirked. I wanted to punch it off his face. "You all need to leave this establishment. The shop assistant is evoking her right to eject you from the premises."

Solomon raised his hand, and the Cowboy Cop pulled his gun and trained it on my Brother. Rage was now flooding my veins. There was no stopping it. Solomon showed the cops his palms. "Woah, let's calm down. We are happy to leave. We were just looking for some baby shit for our girl."

The man sneered. "Our girl, huh?" He looked at Serendipity like she was scum and the edges of my vision began to turn the most beautiful shade of crimson. "How about you take your criminal asses down the road to Walmart, then?"

This guy was going to die. His partner looked at the Cowboy Cop like he was tempted to put a bullet in the back of his head too, but he had his gun out and pointed at my chest. Sera reached out and placed her hand on my arm. At her movement, the Cowboy Cop moved his gun in her direction and that was it.

"Get your fucking gun off her," I growled, the sound low and primal.

Both guns swung to me, and the Cowboy Cop

grinned. Fuck. "Get the fuck on your knees," he yelled, and I wanted to rip out his throat and dance on his corpse. "On your fucking knees," he shouted, and I knew this is what the little badged cocksucker had wanted all along. He wanted me on my knees, wanted the world to know that he held all the power.

"No."

"On your knees now! Hands on your head!" The guy screamed in my face, waving his gun haphazardly.

I looked at Sera, her eyes wide as her gaze flicked between me and the cop. I swallowed hard.

I wanted to kill this arrogant asshole. But I didn't want Sera to be scared ever again. So I did something I didn't think I'd do for anyone but the fucking Lord of Hell. I knelt.

The victorious smirk on the pig's face made bile rise up in my throat. He looked at Solomon. "You too, Pretty Boy!" he said, waving his gun at Solomon. His gaze landed on Sera. "Actually, you too. Though, I bet being on your knees is not such a big issue for you as it is for these guys, am I right?" His eyes were lecherous as they landed on her pregnant stomach. I growled low, ready to stand and smash this fucker into his next life.

Apparently, that was a line for his partner. "Fuller! That's enough."

The cowboy cop, Fuller I guess, rolled his eyes. "Fucking relax, Weston. These guys aren't going to go to internal affairs. They don't want people poking around in their shit, do you boys?"

I bared my teeth. I wanted to rip his throat out with my hand and then bathe in his blood for disrespecting Sera. For disrespecting us, and the Club.

Then Solomon looked at me, his face as serious as I'd seen it in years, the faint glow of power drifting through his eyes. "Doughnuts," he whispered on the air. "Doughnuts."

Then I started laughing and couldn't stop. I didn't stop when the cop screamed at me, or when he slammed his baton against my skull, making my ears ring.

Solomon. The fucking Horseman of Famine, had just basically cursed a cop to forever be physically ill at even the sight of motherfucking doughnuts.

Who knew that Solomon still had a sense of humor?

Somehow, laughing had been worse than ripping out Fuller's throat, because we were all in cuffs and in the back of separate squad cars, being hauled downtown within minutes.

Worth it.

8

JUDAS

I f the universe had a sense of irony, it would be embodied in Damnation's lawyer, Thomas McCool. There was nothing even remotely McCool about Thomas. He was old as dirt, his eyes had started to yellow from too many business lunches rolling into business dinners and damaging his liver, and he wore ugly brown suits all the time. He's snorted more coke than a music exec and has three ex-wives who all hated his guts. But he was a damn fine lawyer. The best, in fact, you could get that would willingly damage their reputation by representing an unruly pack of bikers.

"You guys can't do a damn thing without being arrested. I was taking some goddamn German future clients to the strip club and now that stupid ass-licker Reginald is going to bust a stiffy in his fucking tan chinos and embarrass the whole lot of us, just because I have to come down and bust you and your latest piece of ass out of the fucking lock-up because you were trying to play house in the wrong damn part of town," he ranted without pausing for breath.

He was the only one I let speak to me like this. If he'd been a prospect, I would have had him on the ground and be kicking his teeth in before he'd finished the first sentence. But I kind of liked McCool, and I knew how much he liked the girls in Apocalypse. Besides, he had a way with words that was pretty much unrivaled.

"Just fix it, Thomas. I didn't ask for your opinion. And she is not a piece of ass. If you don't want your dick to be detachable, you better keep that shit to yourself from now on."

McCool wasn't intimidated by my calmly delivered threat, probably because I'd been giving him the same threats for thirty years. He harrumphed and spun on his polished Oxfords, marching up the stairs.

I leaned against my bike as he stormed into the police precinct, Goliath in the truck beside us. He'd take the guys back to get their bikes from where they still sat in some shitty alleyway beside the boutique they'd been detained in. Not arrested, detained for doing nothing more than looking at baby crap and looking scary.

I watched as the doors opened and out came

Serendipity. She was dressed in Goliath's shirt, looking like a damn goddess and I shifted my eyes across to my Brother to gauge his reaction. In anyone else, I'd say he was completely unphased by the beauty in front of us, her hair flashing gold in the late afternoon sunshine. But I saw the gentle tick of his jaw, heard the squeak of the suspension as he shifted his considerable bulk in the driver's seat of the truck. Goliath did not fidget.

She did look damn beautiful. I could admit that. But she was also trouble, and that I couldn't have in my Club. She'd been here a day and already she'd caused two of my Brothers to be arrested.

She stopped at the top of the stairs, gazing at me warily like she knew my thoughts about her at the moment ranged from horny to disgruntled and back again. Slowly, because she was either brave or stupid, she walked down the steps, her eyes shuttered and cautious. Brave it is then.

"Where's Cain and Sol?" she asked softly, her voice low and smokey, seductive even though she didn't mean it to be.

I shrugged. "Probably still locked up. It is easier to free a pregnant woman who was falsely detained than two bikers. They are probably looking for long lost warrants to keep them there and make it seem like they weren't beaten under the guise of being arrested for nothing." They wouldn't find any. We changed our legal names every twenty years or so, and we paid a lot of money in clean-up over the years to ensure that nothing ever came back to us. Still, they'd hold them for as long as they could.

I looked over at Goliath, who was staring straight ahead but kept sliding looks at Serendipity, and nodded. "Wait for them. Pay McCool. Head straight back to the Clubhouse. We need to hold Church and we've had enough fucking excitement for one day."

Goliath didn't nod, didn't acknowledge the order in any way, but I knew he would do as I asked. He was an ornery bastard, but he was loyal.

I passed Serendipity a helmet, and pointed to the back of my bike, my eyes daring her to say no. I hopped onto my bike, waiting. Her jaw tensed but she took the helmet and slammed it on her head. She climbed onto my bike like she'd been doing it her whole life, and held my waist with a firm but impersonal touch.

Good. I didn't want her to get any ideas. Her warm body wrapped around mine meant nothing.

I kicked over my bike and it rumbled to life, the low hum reverberating through my blood like always. I flicked my sunglasses down, and eased into traffic. I let myself get lost in my thoughts, my bike like a trusty steed, moving me toward where it thought I needed to be. Of course, my bike wasn't actually alive, it was my subconscious directing that lump of metal. Either way, we didn't hit the highway, the fastest way back to the Clubhouse, but I didn't second guess myself. I just let the bike hug the road as the woman behind me hugged my back. She seemed unfearful. Content even.

But I needed answers.

Even when we pulled into an abandoned rest stop, a boarded up gas station in the background, she didn't seem worried. That told me more than any words she could utter.

I kicked the stand on my bike, and she slid off the back without me asking. She walked a few feet away, her gaze wary but not fearful. I could see her hand subconsciously cupping her stomach, which told me that she was more worried for the baby than for herself.

This woman was an enigma that I intended to solve. Right fucking now.

I slid my sunglasses off and stared at her, like really looked. I looked past her beauty and her pregnant stomach. I looked past the standoffish stance and her fight ready fists. I looked into her soul, and saw her soul looking back at me.

"What are you?"

Her eyebrows rose high. "Excuse me?"

I tilted my head to the side, letting it crack as I sucked in a deep breath through my nose, a breath that inhaled her scent on the wind. "I said, what are you?"

She narrowed her gaze, like she was trying to figure out if I said *what* are you instead of *who* are you on purpose.

"I am what I am. Unemployed. Knocked up."

"Not human."

She stared at me stonily, neither confirming or denying. No outrage. No quick lies. Just slow, deliberate appraisal.

Then she shrugged. "Not human." She took a step closer, which told me that whatever she was, she was used to being either the top predator in the pyramid, or she was invincible. "What about you? Throwing accusations like that around tells me that you aren't exactly 100% dyed in the wool sheep either."

I quirked an eyebrow. This wasn't how it worked. I was asking questions and she was answering them.

She let out a long breath. She ran her long fingers through her hair and huffed out a sigh. "There's no real name for me. Well there is, but it would be inaccurate. I was the only one, until now." She ran her palm across her stomach. "Or maybe this one is a different beast altogether. I don't know. So much I don't know."

My heart was thudding in my ears at her words, but I kept my features blank. Stoic. Show nothing. Feel nothing.

"Make me understand." I'd let a wolf into my Clubhouse. I was the only wolf allowed.

She paced back and forth, her hair streaming out behind her. So fucking beautiful. How anyone could think she was human was beyond me. She was more.

So much more. My phone buzzed in my pocket, and I slipped it out to look at the message from Goliath.

THEY ARE OUT. Heading back to the Clubhouse now.

I HAD lots of faith in McCool, that wrinkly old fuck. I slid my phone back into my cut, and glared at the pacing woman. I watched her eye the road, as if wondering if she could outrun me, pregnant and alone. Whether I'd chase her at all. Would I chase her?

Yes.

I wanted to rationalize that it was for Cain, who would be heartbroken if she disappeared, despite his protests to the contrary. Maybe the fact that Cain was so attached was enough reason to get rid of her. She wouldn't be the first woman I'd buried.

She stilled her feet, turning to me and squaring her shoulders. She swallowed hard and stared me directly in the eye. "Nephilim."

I held my breath, even though my heart was pounding and the baby was doing somersaults at my turmoil.

"Nephilim?" he said softly, the edge of disbelief tainting his words.

I nodded. He gazed at me, his eye travelling down along my body. "Aren't Nephilim meant to be giants or deformed or some shit? You look pretty good to me?"

I rolled my eyes. "You haven't seen all of me. Maybe I have three vaginas and they all have teeth."

His gaze stilled on the open zip of my jeans. Great work, Sera. "Is that an offer?"

I scoffed out a laugh, because this was getting damn ridiculous. "To see my piranha cooch? Sure thing."

He chuckled, a soft low sound that sounded like his

bike. "Okay. You're a Nephilim. Just to make sure we are on the same page, that's half angel half human, right?" I nodded warily. "Who's your angelic parent?"

Now it was my turn to shut down. No one needed to know that. I stared at Judas, refusing to look away, until he rolled a single eye. "Fine. Keep your secrets. I couldn't care less if you're a fucking flying purple people eater. Are you going to be trouble for the Club?"

I swallowed hard. There was no hedging this one. "Yes." I briefly wondered if he'd kill me then, which seemed like an overreaction, but you try being a Nephilim in the Dark Ages. You got burned if you were too ugly. You were burned if you were too beautiful. You got burned if you survived the plague, which seemed a little redundant to me. Anyway, it made me cautious of people's responses.

Judas raked his hand over his face, and even though he looked in his late thirties, he *felt* a lot older at that moment. "Tell me."

I winced. I had no way to sugar-coat this. "You won't believe me."

He gave a humorless laugh, easing back to rest his ass on his bike. "You'd be surprised what I would believe."

I shook my head. "It doesn't matter. There is no way you can protect me. I'm Nephilim, my enemies are bigger than petty stalkers. The monsters under my bed are the real thing." He stared at me, unblinking, waiting for me to crack. And crack I did. "Fine. I warned you." I sucked in a deep breath. "The baby belongs to an Archangel. Uriel to be exact." I took in his blinking face, the silence heavy in the air between us. "Well, originally I thought it was Lucifer's, but I got that story set straight pretty damn quickly."

At the mention of Lucifer, Judas' face went slack with terror, but he quickly got it back under control quickly. Huh. I guess the Devil inspired that kind of reaction in the vast majority of beings.

He stood and looked around, as if he expected Lucifer to appear. "But it isn't Lucifer's right? You're sure?"

I nodded, confused by his panicked response when literally nothing I'd said so far had rattled him at all. "Really sure. The baby belongs to Uriel. His isn't a face I'm likely to forget."

I shuddered at the memory of his face twisted in rage and disgust, and I felt the blood drain from my face. Judas stepped forward, his hands cupping my arms. "Hey, it's okay. Damnation has you. We said we would protect you, and we will."

I actually laughed in his face, a dark, bitter thing that bubbled up from the hopelessness that had made its home in my chest. There was no protecting me against God's fucking chosen angels. There was no defending me against a being so powerful that he was literally unstoppable.

I choked on the powerlessness of the whole thing. Or maybe it was the tears streaming down my cheeks. Judas pulled me closer, wrapping his arms around my shoulders. "It's going to be okay, Dippy. Trust me. Trust us." I smiled at his use of Solomon's nickname. I let myself be weak for a moment longer, then pulled away.

I wiped my eyes on the sleeve of Goliath's shirt. "Sorry. Hormones." Yeah right. "So, now we all know what I am, what are you? Because you aren't human." He had too much presence. A few humans had that kind of presence, and they either ended up humanitarians or cult leaders. But for all four of them to have it, Judas and Cain, Solomon and even Goliath, they had to be a different race of being. The question, as always, was what flavor of supernatural were they?

Judas gave me an enigmatic look and turned, sliding back onto his bike, giving me a great view of the way his denim jeans hugged his thighs. "Get on the bike, Serendipity." The way he said it made goosebumps rise across my skin, not in fear, but in pure, unadulterated lust.

Still, I wasn't that easily sidetracked. "Seriously. I showed you mine. You totally need to show me yours now. Fair's fair."

He just gave me a bemused look and, his eyes

sliding at the seat behind him, before he pushed on his sunglasses and pulled up his skeleton face mask.

I huffed and slid onto the back of his bike. I had to let myself trust. It wasn't just me anymore, and without help, both me and the baby were as good as dead.

WHEN WE PULLED into the parking lot of the Clubhouse, it was filled to the brim with stripjoint customers. Huge tattooed guys in black stood sentry on either side of the door to Apocalypse, the red neon sign giving them an otherworldly glow.

My heart leapt at the sight of Cain and Solomon's bikes parked at the front of the garage, as well as the truck. Thankfully, Goliath wasn't in it.

Thinking about Goliath made me realize I wasn't going to be able to give him his shirt back anytime soon. Instead of hitting up a thrift store, we'd been arrested, so my wardrobe was still significantly lacking. Hopefully he wouldn't mind me hanging onto it for a little longer.

When the bike stopped, my legs were dead and the baby was sitting on my bladder, making the threat of peeing my only pair of jeans a very real possibility.

I groaned in frustration, jiggling my legs, trying to get blood flow back. Judas slid off his bike, reaching over to grab me by the waist and haul me off the back.

His huge hands spanned my waist, holding me upright until my legs felt steady enough to support my weight.

As soon as my muscles were back online though, I gripped my stomach with two hands and ran towards the Clubhouse doors. "I gotta pee," I yelled over my shoulder, and Judas' low chuckles chased me on the wind. I burst through the door, and every set of eyes turned to look at me. I looked desperately at Shots. "Bathroom?"

He pointed at a short dark hall off the main room, and I sprinted toward it. I almost peed myself at the sight of the toilet sign, like my bladder thought *welp, close enough!* But I prayed to the gods of pelvic floor muscles and burst through the door. The first sign I was in the wrong bathroom was Trigger taking a piss in a urinal, before spinning in a magnificent golden arch of piss when the door slammed against the tiles.

"Fuck!" I yelled, hustling to the only toilet, although the size of his giant dick was enough to almost still my feet in amazement. But it wasn't quite that impressive. "I'm so sorry! I have to go!" I said as I slammed the cubicle door, not even worrying about locking it as I struggled with the hair-tie holding together my jeans, that I couldn't even see over the bulge of my damn belly. "Shit, shit, shit why won't you come undone?"

Trigger had the gall to chuckle, before clearing his voice. "Do you, uh, need a hand or something?"

Pride made me want to say no. The fact I was barely hanging on had me yelling, "Yes!"

Trigger pushed gently through the door, quickly surveying the issue, his hands deftly flicking open my jeans.

I pushed him unceremoniously out of the cubicle. "Thank you!"

Few things in life are better than good sex in my opinion. Taking a too tight bra off after a long day. The miracle combination of perfectly flakey pastry, gooey rich chocolate and perfectly ripe strawberries, and the relief that comes after peeing when you've had to hold it for a long time. I let out an audible sigh of pleasure.

Trigger laughed, and it sounded like he was cleaning up. "You know, normally when I have women in the men's bathroom making that noise, I'm in the stall too."

I grinned to myself. "From what I just saw, I can believe it. But I gotta say Trigger, flirting is not overly sexy when you are cleaning up piss and I'm too pregnant to get my pants down when I need to."

His laughter echoed off the wall, and I chuckled along. "I better get out of here before Cain realizes this bathroom was occupied and removes my appendages." I heard the squeak of the door opening, and I wondered if it made that noise before I'd burst in. "Hey, Serendipity?"

"Yeah?"

"You pee like a racehorse," he laughed, and left.

I screwed up my nose. "Well you're hung like a racehorse," I yelled back, realizing too late that that probably wasn't an insult.

Finishing my business, I buckled myself back into my pants which was way easier when I wasn't desperate, and washed my hands. There was only a tiny mirror in the bathroom, no bigger than a dinner plate, and I looked at myself.

I looked... alive.

Sure, I had a serious case of helmet hair, and my cheeks were just a bit too red. I picked a bug out of my teeth and gagged.

All in all though, I looked kind of content. It wasn't a feeling I thought I would experience again so soon.

I wiped my hands on my ass because there was no paper towel, and did the waddle of shame back to the bar. Well, not that I was waddling just yet. My stomach was growing at an exponential rate though. I wasn't an expert by any means, but I didn't think I should be this huge this quickly.

The somber thought burst through my good mood like a pin to a soap bubble. I entered the bar, and I felt more than a few eyes on my back. I got some sympathetic looks from the Old Ladies. Probably ones who'd had kids. The sweetbutts, easily recognizable by the fact they were either dry humping members - in the case of one couple in the corner wet humping - or dancing on tables in too short skirts with beer bottles in their hands.

I sat down at the bar in front of Shots who slid me a glass of milk and a cookie like I was five. But I happily munched my chocolate chip cookie. Because I wasn't turning down chocolate.

I couldn't see any of the guys in the room. Not even Trigger was present. "Where is everyone?"

Shots wiped down a glass. "Been holed up in the Pres' office since they were released. Pres went straight there. Trigger walked back that way a moment ago. Pretty sure they are having a meeting."

Three guesses what that could be about. I searched the room, trying to pick if everyone in the Club was supernatural, or just Judas. I reached out with that sixth sense that tugged in the back of my brain, the one that said this was something else, something bigger than the natural order of things. But everyone in this room felt normal. Sheep with a fleeting lifespan and an allegiance to a man so compelling that he had to be something more.

Were they going to be a threat now that he knew what I was? He said no, but I didn't live this long being trusting.

Tiredness consumed my body down to my very bones. I drank my milk like it was tequila, stuffing my cookie into my bra. "I need a nap. I'll be upstairs," I told Shots who just nodded and looked confused. I didn't know why I was telling him either. He wasn't my keeper.

I staggered down the hall, pausing outside Judas' office for a moment. Someone once told me that prying ears rarely ever heard good things about themselves, but I couldn't help it. It was muffled, as if they were keeping their voices down. I heard the odd word like danger. Help. A distinct Goliath growl that had no words but was threatening all the same.

They were going to kick me out on my ass and I couldn't blame them. I would too. But first I needed a motherfucking nap.

I growled low, wanting to beat the sense into every single one of them. We'd gone through all the club business in thirty minutes, but we'd been at this for nearly an hour, going over and over the same fucking shit. Does she stay or does she go? Even Trigger seemed smitten with her, and he hadn't even said three words to her. Kid just loved pussy.

"Kick her ass out. We don't need her problems. We've got enough of our own."

That might be a bit of an exaggeration. There was a Cartel that was trying to set up territory on the edge of ours, and who kept killing off our pushers, but I'd take care of them soon enough. I would bathe in their blood and they would realize why Damnation MC had held this territory for so long. We squashed incursions like fat kids squished fucking ants. But death didn't stop the pulsing bloodlust in my veins anymore. Killing, killing and more killing. Just a lot of the fucking same. Every fucking day. I was so damn tired but I didn't deserve a day of fucking rest. I would do this shit until Lucifer ripped my heart from my chest.

"Fuck off, G. She's been walking around wearing your shirt all damn day. What do you think that means, Big Guy? Wanna take a guess? I'll give your dumb ass three," Solomon poked. I briefly wondered if Lucifer really needed Famine. If I ripped his head off now, would the apocalypse still go ahead, or would we all just turn to dust?

Judas flicked his eye to Trigger. "Go get the girl and bring her down. Wake her gently. Keep your dick to yourself."

Trigger grinned and saluted. "It's all good. I already got her out of her pants in the men's bathroom anyway." Then he slid out of the room and slammed the door before Cain could reach him to wrap his hands around the young guy's neck and squeeze. Kid had balls, I'd give him that. He was a legacy, and slid easily into the position held by his father before he died. I figured that Smoke, Trigger's Daddy, suspected we weren't all human and passed the knowledge onto his son, but they never let it slip in words or actions. They were fucking fearlessly loyal, and I respected the shit out of that. We'd never tell him unless we had to, but it was nice to know he had our backs like that. He wasn't a snitch.

When Trigger was gone, Judas gave us a look that made my heart sink. It was a stark look, completely devoid of emotion like he'd put his shit on lockdown. "I had a good chat with our little housemate. She isn't human."

"Fucking duh. She feels like a fucking predator to me."

Cain raised his eyebrows in my direction. "Did you just say duh? Like a fucking schoolgirl?"

I flipped him the finger, which was better than pounding his face like I wanted to do, and continued. "What is she?" It must be bad. I knew there were other unexplainable things in the world. I wasn't delusional enough to think that we were in any way special.

"Nephilim."

Solomon screwed up his nose. He didn't have Judas' poker face. "That's like an angel right? Kinda explains her tits."

Cain slapped him so hard on the back of the head, he almost sprawled on the floor. "No, pregnancy explains her tits, Jackass. And it's only half angel." Solomon just grinned and seemed completely unrepentant. Dude could take a hit, that was for sure.

I let out a disgusted noise. "As much as I wanna do her family tree for her, I assume she's been kicking around a lot longer than us. What's the fucking drama now?"

Judas gave me one of his disapproving looks that was meant to make me piss my pants but no longer had any affect on me whatsoever. "The fucking drama is that the her stalker, abducter, baby daddy is the goddamn Archangel Uriel. Is that dramatic enough for you, Goliath?"

Holy fucking shit. Not much stunned me anymore, but getting knocked up by an Archangel would do it. Her story of being tortured, which I knew in my soul was true because you can't fake those kinds of mental scars, seemed a whole lot more ominous. How much punishment could a Nephilim body take? I found myself wanting to find out personally.

Cain paced around, the room too small to hold his energy. "Do we tell her? What we are, I mean?"

I slammed my fist back on the filing cabinet, denting the door a little. "Fuck no. We tell no one. Just because she's a similar type of freak to us, doesn't mean she needs to know. What if Uriel gets her again? Pretty sure he'd pet her little head for giving up Lucifer's fucking Horsemen, don't you?"

Solomon opened his mouth, probably to give me a serve, or suck Cain's dick, but Judas lifted his hand. "I agree with G," I grinned smugly at my Brothers, but my smile fell at his next words. "I don't think we tell her yet. We'll see how it plays out. Maybe she'll have the kid and run off, no harm, no foul. If shit goes fucking sideways, then we can tell her. But she knows we aren't human, so she'll be watching. Keep your damn shit together." He eyed me then and I scowled at him.

Cain stepped forward. "So she stays?" He looked like a damn little kid asking Daddy if they could keep the stray cat he found in a junkyard. Judas nodded and I punched the filing cabinet again.

I could hear Trigger coming down the stairs, cooing shit to the woman. She walked through the door, and looking at her was like a punch in the balls. She looked all sleepy, her eyes hooded, her hair mussed and poking up at odd angles. Her belly looked even bigger than it had this morning, which was impossible. Fuck, maybe it wasn't impossible for a Nephilim fucking Archangel bastard. Maybe they came in litters. Who the hell knew?

"Thanks, Trig. Shit is starting to get rowdy out there, go tell them the beer is on the house. But if they smash up the place again, I'm taking it out on their fucking flesh, got it?"

Trigger was young enough to still be scared shitless by Judas. He just nodded and fucked off out of the room faster than I could see. Probably off to get his dick wet with one of the dancers. They all loved him and that stupid cowboy hat.

When the door closed again, the woman looked

more alert, like she realized that she was surrounded by fucking killers.

Her face turned down, and she swallowed hard. "You're kicking me out, right? It's okay, I don't blame you. I don't want to put you in a position to have to fight a battle you can't win."

My inner Horseman growled at the idea we would lose any battle we started. I was fucking Conquest. If Damnation wanted the girl, we would fucking take her no matter who else wanted her. Judas gave me a pointed look that said "Control your fucking self" and turned back to the woman.

"No. We aren't kicking you out. We think we can still protect you if we have to and we aren't going to send someone to their fucking death because we are too chickenshit to try. You stay until you want to leave."

I stubbornly ignored the flash of relief in her eyes and focused on Judas' words. "But there's rules. One, we aren't going to tell you what we are. Deal with it. Two, if you sense trouble, you tell us immediately." She nodded warily. "Three. No using your powers on anyone in the Club."

She laughed flatly. "I spent fucking years being tortured in Purgatory. Other than my near immortality making me the perfect fucking canvas for sick angels, I have no damn powers." The bitterness in her voice, the darkness dripping from her tongue, made my own stir. I wanted to carve up the people who hurt her, which had less to do with her and more to do with the fact I wanted to make someone bleed. I made a low humming noise in my throat, pleasure at the thought, and the woman gave me the side-eye. "Is that it?"

Judas nodded. "For now." He seemed to hesitate. "Let the guys help you. It would help assuage some of our past sins."

My eyes snapped to the Pres. I'd atoned for our sins. I'd bathed in the blood of that atonement. I didn't need some bitch soothing my hurt feelings. I curled my lip menacingly, and was happy at the fear that made her shoulders tense. Good. She might be part-angel, but we were the damn harbingers of the End of Days. She should be scared.

She nodded and turned toward the door, but hesitated. "What will you tell everyone else?"

Cain stepped toward her, his hand alighting softly on her spine. "We'll hold Church. Put it to the members. But it's in our code that we offer sanctuary to women. We'll tell them we expect trouble, and if they want to send away any of their Old Ladies, they can. We'll put a ban on the sweetbutts for a while too, though they can still go to the strip club. Then we'll vote. It'll be fine. The four of us, and Trigger will vote for letting you stay. No one will go against all five of us like that."

He grinned at her, an expression I hadn't seen in

decades. Maybe the Pres was right, maybe she was helping them overcome their past sins.

Not me though. I was steeped in sin. Blackness flooded from my pores and spewed past my lips. I was beyond saving, and I wallowed in my filth happily.

Judas clapped his hands together, the sound overly loud in the tiny room. "Good. Let's fucking party."

Solomon hefted the woman in his arms and whooped, and her stunned squeak made my lips twitch. "Let's go. I'll drink your share, Dippy."

He skipped out of the room, Cain's snarl to watch her head trailing them and the woman's light laughs bouncing off the walls.

Judas turned toward me, his face not showing any of the lightness that the other two had. I understood. His grief was an endless well that he filled with anger and tyranny. He seemed fair, but underneath that reasonable exterior hid a monster that could bring nothing but death and destruction. There was no relief from the horrors of the things we had seen and done, and some woman would not absolve him of any of it. "You sure about this?" I asked one last time now that Sol and Cain weren't in the room. Something good remained in them. Something that wanted saving. I wanted death and so did Judas. If not my own, then someone else's.

Judas sighed. "I am sure, G. I can't explain it, but my gut says she needs to be here."

I nodded. More than any touchy-feely bullshit, or whatever bleeding heart crusade that Cain was on this week. I trusted my Pres' gut. Judas slapped me on the back. "Let's go drink with our family and forget the past for a little while, hey?"

Now that plan I could get down with.

It made so much damn sense now. She was an angel. The more I stared, and seriously I was only a trench coat and a chubby away from being a fucking creeper as it was, the more I could see she wasn't normal. Even with the beauties from the strip club dancing around, drinking and flashing more skin than they did at Apocalypse, so many eyes kept wandering in her direction. She was something fucking else. Magnetic.

I wanted to pluck the eyeballs from every man who even looked her way. I wasn't the violent one in the Club, that dubious honor went to Goliath. I wasn't even the most deadly, that one was Judas all over. Hell, I wasn't even as silently menacing as Cain. But when anyone cast even a single heated look in her direction, I wanted to jump the fucking table and pummel them to death. These were my Brothers. My Club. I shook my head to chase away the thoughts.

My eyes drifted away from where she sat with Cain, listening to him talk shit about god knows what, and over to where Judas and G sat at the end of the bar, watching the room but not really a part of it. But their eyes were focused in the same place as mine, as much as they wanted to fight it. I didn't mind them looking. With them, I'd share. We'd always been a set, a band of brothers, even before that day over Laura's grave when Lucifer had made us so much more.

Laura had bound us all. She'd been our world and I wasn't sure we could do it again. But I wasn't sure they'd just let me have Dippy either, despite their protests.

And fuck knows I wanted her. I downed my beer, excusing myself from the table where Trigger had his hands up some girls skirt, a different one from last night though, but she didn't seem to mind. Timo and Stag just grunted and went on talking about who had the better bike.

I walked toward her like a moth to a fucking fireball. I'd ask her to dance. I could tell she loved dancing. When I had her in my arms last night it was like our bodies had been made to move together. She was light on her feet despite the bulge of her stomach throwing her off.

I contorted my face into something casual and less

desperate, sitting down beside her in the booth oppo-site Cain. Shots and Sweetie were on the other side, as well as Taylor, Timo's Old Lady. She was short, round, and had the biggest laugh of anyone I'd ever met. She was infectiously happy, and how she ended up with that grumpy old fuck Timo was beyond me. But she loved him with all the ferocity of a hurricane. She was petting Dippy's hand enthusiastically.

"Don't even worry about it, Doll! My youngest just had her sixth kid and made her husband get fixed or she was going to chop his dick off herself," she said, roaring with laughter. I caught Timo's fond look as if he was drawn to the sound of her laugh. I'd met Timo and Taylor's youngest. She wouldn't hesitate to cut off a man's dick. "You can have whatever baby stuff you need. I'll bring it over next weekend, and anything you don't want can go to charity. She won't be needing it, and her older brothers are all done too. You'd be doing her a favor really."

Ah, Taylor was a smart woman. Dippy wouldn't take charity, but she would help lighten another's load. I could sense that about her.

I leaned toward her, ignoring the pointed look Cain was giving me. "Want to dance again, Dippy? This time Cain can wait his turn and Goliath has already had his temper tantrum. We can dance until the sun comes up," I promised softly.

She looked at me from under her lashes and then

gave a soft nod. I slid out of the booth and held out a hand. When she took it, I felt that spark of attraction again. I'd felt it when I'd seen her slide out of Cain's truck in the car park yesterday. I felt it last night when she danced in my arms. I felt it now, and I needed to tell myself to go slow. She wasn't a sweet butt or a stripper. She was damaged, even if she did hide it well.

I struggled with slow. I wanted to live, because I knew how quickly it could all be taken away. One minute, Laura was there. We were fucking happy too. Sure, one woman and four men was unconventional, but we were fucking one-percenters. We didn't do conventional things. And when the baby had been born, I'd been fucking ecstatic.

Then it had all gone in a moment.

Unlike my Brothers who'd closed themselves off, I took the opportunity to feel whenever I could. Like I could build a callous on my heart so if it ever happened again, it wouldn't hurt so bad.

I pulled Dippy into an empty bit of floor and tucked her close, closer than I'd held her last night. And she let me. She stood stiff for a moment, but eventually the heat of our bodies and the thrum of the music had her melting against me. "Been a hell of a day, hey?" I said softly.

She sighed, and I felt the fight leave her body. If I let her go now, she'd slide to the floor boneless. "I've had worse."

I bet. I didn't miss the part about Purgatory. About her torture. It made me want to tear down the world, and that wasn't a feeling I was used to when it came to someone I'd just met. I'd practiced the art of no-strings. Now I felt like a marinette. "You sure you don't have some kind of enchantment power, Dippy?"

Again her laugh was all bitterness on her tongue. "I've been alone forever, Solomon. If you knew just how old I was, you wouldn't ask me that."

"I'm a lot older than I look too, you know." Judas would kick my ass for hinting like this, but there was no harm. She knew we weren't human.

"Oh Solomon. I'm, like, 5000 years old. Old enough to know your namesake. Old enough to have seen terrible and wondrous things."

My arms dropped and I felt my mouth fall open. Holy fucking shit. "Fucking hell," I growled, blinking rapidly. She gave another sad laugh, standing there with her arms wrapped around herself, looking vulnerable. How? How could a woman who had lived so long have any vulnerability left, any soul at all?

I shook my head and grabbed her back in my arms. Shit. Shit, shit, shit. I was going to have to tell Judas.

"You can't die at all?"

She shrugged, her body stiff again in my arms. "Not that I can tell. I have a theory that if you cut off my head and carved out my heart and then burned my body I'd be pretty damn dead. Thankfully, no one has tried to do that yet. You aren't going to be the first, right?"

I shook my head vehemently. "No fucking way. You're safe here. We live by our oaths."

I wanted to mine her brain for secrets, I wanted to know everything about her and the things she'd seen. I wasn't much of an academic, but even I knew that her brain would be filled with answers to things that had plagued the world for generations.

Cain would call me a fucking nerd.

"Why alone?" That was the real question. She was so fucking beautiful. Men would have razed civilisations for her if she'd asked. She could have been a queen. A goddess.

She swayed, her stomach pressed firmly into my abdomen. The baby was kicking furiously. She enjoyed dancing like her mama too. "It was just easier that way. You can only watch so many people you love wither and die before it takes a mental toll. People notice you don't age like others. Superstition kept people alive back then. There was a science to things, but it was easier to believe that I was causing crops to fail, or women to be barren, or cows to die of some weird disease. So I moved around constantly. Never staying in one place. Always alone."

I flexed my hand where it rested on her spine. "Not anymore. Never again."

She rubbed her belly, thinking I was talking about

the baby. I didn't correct her. I convinced myself that I meant the baby too. "I guess not. Unless Uriel finds out and gets rid of us both."

I couldn't suppress the swell of power in my body, the spirit of the Horseman flooding my body. I breathed deeply through my nose before everyone died of emaciation. I'd learned that one the hard way. I had to have complete control of my power or people died.

Dippy moved away, her eyebrows drawn together as if she could feel the swell of my power. Hell maybe she could. "What are you?" she whispered.

I struggled to wrestle the Horseman back down. He normally sat dormant, a kernel of power just glowing next to my soul waiting to be called out. He was hard to get back into his box though. Unlike my Brothers powers, Famine had been locked away for decades. Today, I let him out against the cop, and he'd tasted freedom. Now he wanted more.

Judas was suddenly beside me, his hand curling around my arm. "Take a walk, Sol. Get your shit together." He looked over his shoulder at G, who was staring daggers at Dippy like it was all her fault. "Goliath, go with him." He lowered his voice so Serendipity couldn't hear. "Knock him out if he can't get it under control."

Both G and I nodded. It would hurt like a bitch

tomorrow, but I didn't want to inadvertently hurt my Club.

I let G drag me through the front doors of the Clubhouse and down into the back corner of the lot behind the building. I could hear the hoots and bad R'n'B music of Apocalypse, taste the coming of winter in the air. I breathed that shit in through my nose and out through my mouth and tried to cajole the Horseman back into his box.

G was muttering about how this was all Serendipity's fault, and he was the kind of asshole who didn't say much but would rub an "I told you so" in your face whenever he could. I mean, it was her fault to a degree. If she hadn't been here, I wouldn't be this wild. This close to the edge. But I couldn't find it in me to wish we'd never met. Something had changed when she'd slid from Cain's truck, and I don't think I could go back. If that made me a pussy, so be it.

I looked at the murderous giant in front of me. Looked him dead in his flint grey eyes. "I'm going to have her, G. Whether you guys want her or not is up to you. But she's meant to be with us, man. I feel it here." I banged the left side of my chest, my power still pulsing in my body. "You would too if you just let yourself."

G bared his teeth. "There's nothing there anymore, Solomon. Nothing but hate."

Then he punched me in the face and it was lights out. Motherfucker.

12

J udas ordered Cain to take me to bed like I was a naughty child, like he'd caught me and Solomon doing something forbidden. I'd desperately wanted to dig my heels in, to tell him to go fuck himself, he wasn't my President. But I didn't want to bite the hand that fed me just yet. And in all honesty, I was still fucking exhausted. Trigger had woken me from my nap, but lethargy still made my movements sluggish. So I'd let the domineering dick-head have his way and obediently followed Cain upstairs.

I couldn't stop thinking about the swell of power that had suddenly emanated from Solomon. One minute, he felt like a normal human. The next minute, I was being suffocated under a power so indescribable, so malevolent, I was suffocating on it. What the hell were these guys? Demons? Warlocks dabbling in things they didn't understand? I mean, I'd seen that kind of power over the years. But Solomon's power didn't really feel like that.

I turned it over and over in my head, but I couldn't pinpoint what they could be. There'd been other "supernaturals" in the world, beings that had died out over the years as humans populated to near plague-like proportions. Things that would have been considered magic, but were just different evolutions of the same general mould, had been abundant in my first thousand years. Then natural disasters, the rise of the human population, and disease had wiped them out one by one. But I couldn't remember anything that fit these guys.

Cain was silent as he walked me to my door, his brows drawn together. I looked up, up, up into his face. He looked worried. I hated that I'd put that look on his face.

"I'm sorry about this. I know that this wasn't what you expected when Hope dropped me off at your shop."

One side of his mouth tugged up in a sad smile. "None of this is your fault. Though, that reminds me of something. Hope rescued you, you said. From Purgatory?"

I just nodded warily. Hope's secrets weren't mine to tell.

"How'd she get there?"

I leaned against the doorjamb with a sigh. "Uriel."

"And how'd she get out?"

This time I smiled. "She killed an angel, summoning the Angel of Death, who gave us a ride out of Purgatory."

Cain blinked at me. Then he blinked again. He shook his head. "You keep some fucking weird company, Serendipity. Makes me wonder if your name is less of a monikker and more of a warning, you know?"

I laughed, and the sound echoed down the empty hallway. "I know. I gave it to myself a couple of thousand years ago. I don't even remember the name I was born with."

More blinking. Then he bent down, kissed my cheek softly. "Should have changed it to Trouble. Goodnight, Sera."

Heat flooded to my face, and I wanted to pull him into my room and fuck him senseless. Up until twenty minutes ago, I'd been all but ready to go to bed with Solomon as he moved my body like it belonged only to him. Apparently my traitorous libido was hopped up on pregnancy hormones and any stick would do the trick. I pointedly ignored the fact that no matter how pretty Trigger was, he did nothing for me. I also ignored the niggling attraction I had to Goliath, the absolute psycho who looked like he wanted to carve out my heart and fuck the cavity it left behind.

Apparently, hormones also made me stupid.

I kicked the door shut and bolted it after last night's little impromptu nightmare party. I could deal with the dreams like I had for the last few months, with cold sweats and terror. I didn't need my new guardian angels to fucking watch me sleep every night. I hated being this pathetic.

Water started leaking from my eyes again at the thought and I laid back on my bed, put the pillow over my face and screamed in frustration.

Eventually I must have dozed off, because I startled awake in the middle of the night. I looked around groggily, the thickness of the darkness telling me that it was the early hours of the morning and the clock on the bedside table confirming that it was three a.m. I struggled to drag myself from sleep, my rest not disturbed by nightmares for once.

A subtle thudding noise fought with the muted sound of the strip club, and at first I thought it was my heart until I realized it was a discordant rhythm. Slipping from bed, I walked over the window, looking through the bars to the parking lot.

Two shirtless bodies fought beneath the moonlight, the heavy crack of flesh against flesh echoing even up here. Whoever these two were, one of them was going to end up dead because they weren't pulling their punches. They danced around each other, one with a distinct height advantage to the other. When one shifted to the left and the weak streetlight hit his face, I gasped. Goliath.

I realized the bars on the windows unbolted from the inside, and outside it was a fire escape. I couldn't imagine that the building would be up to code if you could die in a literal barred room. Before I could think about it, I opened the window softly, and it swung back on silent hinges. I climbed through the window and onto the fire escape, the night chill lifting goosebumps on my legs and making me regret not grabbing my jeans first. I was still in Goliath's shirt and my boyleg underwear which seemed respectable enough.

Someone grunted and my eyes drew back to the two fighters below me. Goliath fighting was a thing of beauty. He fought like his body was a weapon that he knew how to expertly wield, but whoever he was fighting could hold his own. I was climbing down the ladder before I registered my movements, drawn to the mesmerising brutality of the whole thing. I got to the last rung before I remembered that I wasn't a lithe immortal right now. I was a heavily pregnant woman and that eight foot drop to the pavement suddenly seemed a lot more ominous.

Apparently I'd lost all my courage in Purgatory.

I began climbing back up, chastising myself for being such a dumbass when the rung creaked loudly, protesting my weight. The fighters stopped mid-punch, and when the second fighter turned around, I recognized Judas. He didn't have an eyepatch on, the sewn up socket looking hollow and empty in the darkness.

He ran across the parking lot inhumanly fast and was standing beneath me in the space of a blink. "What the fuck are you doing?" he growled, and honestly, even though he was yelling at me, that growl was hot as hell.

"I saw you two out here fighting..."

"So you decided to climb down a forty year old fire escape that hasn't been maintained since Richard Nixon was in office? Are you completely damn stupid?"

Looking down at him was giving me a touch of vertigo, but there was no way I was going to look away first. "What kind of President doesn't maintain the fire escapes of his goddamn Clubhouse anyway? All it would take is one molitov cocktail or whatever it is gangbangers use and your whole MC would be wiped out." If all else fails, deflect your stupidity onto someone else. That had to be in a handbook somewhere.

Judas huffed. Goliath had wandered over to stare daggers at me. "I hate women that always need saving."

The knife of his words hit their target. I hated that I needed saving at all. Letting out a strangled sound, I climbed back up the ladder. Stupid, stupid, stupid. The ladder groaned again, and jerked downward. My foot slipped and then I was falling. Fuck!

I wrapped my body protectively around my middle, but it was literally in a single breath before I was landing on the hard ground.

Actually, it wasn't all that hard. Then I opened my eyes and looked into furious grey ones. Goliath had caught me?

He looked disgusted with himself, and I struggled to breathe as I registered his strong arm banded around my chest, my face pressed to his bare chest. Fear and adrenaline and lust made my skin tingle, my breathing choppy. He slid me slowly to my feet, not letting go until I had my feet planted firmly on the ground. Like he cared if I fell.

His next words dispelled the idea that the giant was warming to me.

"I should've let you hit the pavement. I would have enjoyed the sound of your bones shattering."

Then he shoved me gently back, Judas' hand shooting out to steady me, and strode out of the parking lot without picking up his shirt. Judas watched him go with lowered brows. He looked pensive, trying to solve the riddle of Goliath's actions too.

His eye flicked to me, and he looked angry all over again. "What were you thinking? Why are you here, endangering my Club, all the people who are my responsibility if you aren't going to take any care of yourself?"

I didn't have any excuse. I couldn't tell him that their fighting was mesmerizing, that their combined power drew me closer and closer like I under some kind of compulsion. I swallowed hard, trying to choke down my pride. "I'm sorry."

He sighed heavily and walked away from me to where he had his stuff in a haphazard pile beside the building. He pulled his shirt on, picked up Goliath's and threw it at me. I caught it, bundling it in my hands in time to see him pull back on his eyepatch. He picked up a bottle of Jack and took a long swig.

"Come on, I'll walk you back to your room."

I followed along behind him, watching his back muscles move beneath his shirt. He had a body made for sin. Long, with huge broad shoulders and a lean waist that led into the perfect slope of his ass. He opened the door and turned back to me, his eye widening when I wasn't fast enough to drop a mask over my obvious 'fuck me' face.

He growled low in his throat again, reached out and grabbed my wrist. He pulled my body to his, despite the awkwardness of the bulge of my stomach between us, and covered my mouth with his. His kiss was hard and punishing. He devoured me with his lips, his tongue, his teeth. It was a kiss that was meant to possess, and when my back hit the wall beside the heavy door of Clubhouse, I kissed him back. I kissed him with all the pent up anger, turmoil and lust that was raging through my bloodstream.

Then the heavy metal door slammed shut, making me jump and breaking the kiss.

"Fuck!" Judas yelled, slamming his fist against the wall beside my head. I flinched, and his eye moved back to my face. Something soft and vulnerable flashed in it. Then he ruined it by wiping his mouth with the back of his arm.

He stormed back into the darkness of the Clubhouse, leaving me weak kneed and confused by the door.

What just happened?

A banging on my door had me up and alert before my mind caught up with my body. I pulled open the door, and flinched away from the feral look Judas was giving me on the other side.

"Get control of your fucking property, Cain, or so help me fucking god."

Then he stormed down the hall and slammed his own door shut with enough force to rattle the windows.

Panic seized my body as I pulled on my jeans, tearing out of my room barefoot. I started with Sera's room, but it was empty, the window open and the curtains fluttering softly in the night breeze.

I ran down the stairs, taking the hall that emptied out into the back lot. As I tore around the corner, I saw her. She was sitting beside the door, her body curled in on itself. She looked up with big wet eyes, looking more lost and broken than she had at any time in the last two days. What the fuck had Judas done?

"Sera?" I said softly. "Are you okay?"

She inclined her head, but buried her face back in her knees. We sat in silence for a moment more, and then I bent down and picked her up, tucking her body against my chest. She didn't protest. It was like all the fight went right out of her. I hated it.

I bypassed her room and took her to mine, who gave a fuck what propriety said. I'd felt the power coursing through Judas when he banged on my door. I trusted and loved him. He was my friend. My Brother. But we all made mistakes, and Sera made us all a little wild. She could stay with me for the night and I'd watch over her.

She didn't even let out a peep when I placed her on my bed. I tucked her in, pushed her hair off her face. The whole thing felt too intimate. Too much. But I couldn't help myself. What was it about this woman that fucking had me cut off at the knees so quickly?

She'd closed her eyes, and I breathed out through my teeth. "Want to tell me what happened?"

She shook her head. I had to know though.

"Did Judas hurt you?" I'd hurt him right back if he had. I would return that shit sevenfold.

Her eyelashes fluttered open. "He kissed me."

I would have been less shocked if she'd slapped me. "Did he force himself on you?" I couldn't believe it.

"No!" she said quickly, some of her spirit coming back. "No, I kissed him back. I wanted it. Wanted him."

I let out a long, relieved breath. "Thank God." I tilted my head at her, trying to see past her sadness. "Then why are you crying?"

Apparently, pointing out she was crying was the wrong fucking thing to do because she just cried harder. Fuck, fuck, fuck!

I stroked her hair, mumbling dumb, reassuring shit and making promises I probably couldn't keep. Anything to stop her from crying. Finally, I hummed the lullaby my mother sang to me. It was in Russian, so I couldn't sing the words, but it soothed something dark and terrible in my soul. I could still imagine my Mother as she did this to me as a boy, stroking my hair and singing in her lilting accent. Her favorite colour was bottle green and she always wore too many bracelets. She was fiery and strong, but my father made her weak. He'd taught her how to break, and she did it with such ease that eventually she'd laid down one day and let his fist put her down like an unwanted dog.

She hadn't fought for me, but damn I missed her still.

Sera had exhausted herself, and I didn't want to move. She might wake up and start again. I needed to

talk to Sweetie. Was she supposed to be this heartbroken? Was she supposed to cry like that? It couldn't be
good for her or the baby.

The urge to lie down beside her, to curl her body
into mine, was like a physical punch to the chest. The
smudge of her eyelashes against her high cheekbones,
the way her bottom lip jutted out slightly in her sleep,
it was like she was made to tempt me. Instead of giving
in, I slowly slid from the bed and moved across to the
closet.

I pulled the extra blanket down from the top shelf
and threw it down on the ground by the door. If Judas
came in, I'd be in the perfect position to punch him in
the balls. I let my eyes close, let the memory of my
mother's voice in my head and the soft hush of Sera's
breathing lull me to sleep like my new favorite lullaby.

THE GENTLE BRUSH of a boot to my chest woke me with
a start. My hand struck up and wrapped around the
ankle, making someone fall against the door with a
huff. By the time I had enough brain cells to tell me
that the ankle I was holding was small and delicate,
and that there was no boot just a soft, bare foot, Sera
was looking down at me wide eyed.

"What, not even going to say goodbye?" I teased
softly, and a small smile curled her lips. Her eyes were
still puffy and red, but she wasn't crying anymore and I

sent up a small thank you to whoever the patron saint of hormones was.

She waved a hand. "Oh, you know my type. Hit it and quit it," she joked back. I was desperately trying not to look at her long, bare legs which seemed neverending from my position on the floor. I was really, really trying to be a gentleman and not stare up her shirt at the tiny little booty shorts that were the only thing separating me and my dream of pulling her down on my face right now and feasting on her pussy.

My dick though, he never pretended to be a gentleman. I was getting harder than rebar and soon she was going to notice. I sat up, but I kept my fingers wrapped around her ankle, keeping her still.

Fuck, now I was the perfect height to sling one of those perfect long legs over my shoulder and bury my face in the middle of her thighs. Shit.

I sucked in a deep breath, letting it out in one long, hot breath. It fanned over the front of her thighs, and I felt her body go rigid through her damn ankle. It was like every muscle in her body locked.

"Cain?" she whispered.

I struggled to keep my body loose and easy. "Yeah?"

She let out a whispy breath. "I'm a fucking disaster."

My eyes shot from her thighs to her face. "What?" Did I misread this whole damn thing? Solomon was right, my seduction skills were getting rusty.

"I'm a mistake. Cursed even. From the day I was born, I've been a screw up of literally biblical proportions. I was meant to die, and sometimes I wonder if the universe is fucking with me to right the balance. Any man I've ever loved has died. Any friend I've ever had has turned against me eventually. But I could always depend on myself, depend on my mind, and now I feel like I'm losing that too, and I'm so fucking scared."

I wanted to protest. I wanted to drag her into my arms, wrap my body around hers and promise we would never turn against her. But she stilled me with a wave.

"I'm also fucking selfish. Out of control. I need an anchor and an outlet for this rage that seems to be burning me up inside. For the lust that seems to crawl over my skin whenever I see-" she stumbles over her words and I hold my breath. "Whenever I see you. Or Solomon. Or Judas. Even when I see Goliath. That's how I know I'm really fucking losing it because that man would rather break me then befriend me. I basically threw myself at Judas last night and now he hates me. I want nothing more than to sit down on your lap right now and fuck you until I can't see straight." Shit, the blood was rushing in my ears, and my brain had shortcircuited on the way her lips formed the word fuck, but those lips were still moving. "But it's wrong. I won't use you guys like that. You've given me a haven and I'm not going to fuck it up because I'm a disaster that can't get her hormones under control."

I gaped like a fucking fish as she stepped over me, opened the door and walked out. I felt like I was always a step behind with Sera. Always knocked on my ass, wondering what the fuck just happened.

I scrambled to my feet, uncaring that I was only in my boxers with a boner so hard I'm pretty sure it would snap if I ran into the wall. I caught up to her quickly as she padded down the hall quietly, trying not to wake the slumbering beasts. I had my suspicions that a couple of those beasts were fucking wide awake, pulling their cocks and imagining fucking this angel in the flesh. But not me, I was going to go one better.

I reached her, tangling my fingers in hers, yanking her gently backwards until she was in my arms. Then I kissed her. I don't want to be a pussy and say the earth shifted or there were fireworks or whatever. But when her lips moved against mine, the knowledge that shit was never going to be the same settled in my soul.

My hands moved of their own volition, travelling down her back to cup her ass, pulling her tighter against me. I wanted to touch her everywhere she'd let me. I wanted to bury my face between her thighs, I wanted to taste her skin, I wanted to bury my cock deep in her delicious body. I wanted all those fucking things right now.

Instead, I forced myself to pull away from the kiss

so we could both breathe. "Use me. Please. For whatever you need. I'll be your rock. I'll fuck that delicious body until you can't think terrible things about yourself. I'll take care of you for however long you'll let me. Just let me in."

I dropped to my knees. I'd never begged for anything in my life, but right now I would happily beg for a taste of her. She was breathing heavily as I moved my hands up the outside of his legs, wrapping my hands around her thighs, letting my fingers brush along her wet underwear. Fuck. Her heat, her scent, it was intoxicating. I forced my hands to keep moving, even though I wanted to just shift the crotch of her panties to the side and eat her like a savage. I moved them up to the waistband of those little boyshorts that cupped her ass and killed my IQ by 100 points. I hooked my fingers in the elastic and began to gently pull them down, watching her face for any sign of hesitation. She wasn't giving anything away, but she didn't say stop either.

Worry began to niggle in the back of my mind. "You don't have to do this, if you don't want to. We gave you our word. I'll be here for you, I don't want you to think that I-"

"Cain?" My heart stuttered. Then it stopped beating. Shit I had read this all wrong. I forced myself to grunt out something that sounded like, "Yeah?"

Her eyes were wide and frantic. "Please."

I needed to hear it. "Please what, Sweetheart?"

She swallowed. "Please make me feel better."

I frowned at the wording, but I knew I could do more than make her feel better. I could make her feel golden. I pulled her underwear the rest of the way off and let it fall near her feet. Then I was gazing at heaven and I couldn't breathe again. I was surrounded by the scent of her, and could feel the heat of her pussy against my face. I grabbed her calf and lifted one leg, sliding it over my shoulder, bearing her to me even more. Fuck.

Fuck.

She was so fucking perfect. I braced my hands on the wall beside her hips and turned my head, nipping the thigh that was hugging my cheek. She sucked in a breath and I kissed the small hurt. I wanted to tease her, to push her to such desperation that when she came she shattered into a billion pieces.

But Sera wasn't the only one who was desperate. I leaned forward and ran the flat of my tongue along her soaked slit. I knew I'd never forget that first moan. It was like fucking music to my ears. When I swirled the tip of my tongue around her clit, her knee shook and she grabbed my wrists in a grip that threatened to shatter my wrist. Worth it.

I feasted on her like a starving man until she was whining, no longer worried about being quiet. Good. I wanted the whole Clubhouse to hear me pleasuring her. She was fucking mine now. Mine.

"God Cain, I'm going to come" she gasped out. Her fingers gripped at my hair like they were a lifeline. I growled against her, pulling her closer and sucking her clit into my mouth.

"Fuck! Cain!" She flooded my mouth and I couldn't help the smug grin on my lips. I was basically holding her up now as her legs shook with the force of her orgasm. Giving her one long stroke with my tongue, I slid her other leg down and slipped my hands to her waist.

Her head was resting on the wall behind her and her chest was heaving as she panted. I stood, wrapping her back in my arms. I kissed her, spreading the taste of her satisfaction between us.

Her eyes were searching my face, and when I broke the kiss and pulled away, her lips parted like she wanted to say something. She shook her head softly, and I grinned.

"I know, Sweetheart. Let's get you tucked up into bed. It's been a long night." I leaned down and lifted her into my arms. I knew she could walk, but there was something about holding her in my arms that appeased my beast.

Sera burrowed into my chest, her body already relaxing into sleep. I walked her back to my bedroom, the door still hanging open. Before I stepped over the threshold, I looked down the hall.

I knew he was there. Knew the sound of her pleasure would draw him out, because how could it not? It was fucking beautiful.

Judas stood in the doorway of his room, his eyes burning bright in the darkness, the raw envy on his face contorting his features. I lifted an eyebrow at him, and then stepped into my room with the woman he wanted in my arms, kicking the door closed.

I knew we'd talk about this tomorrow, and I had a few choice words for my President. But until then, I had a woman to cover with my body and savour until the sun came up.

14

JUDAS

I 'd called Church for today, but all I wanted to do was put my fist through Cain's face. He kept giving me this stupid, smug, knowing look, and I was one dumb comment away from fucking shooting the bastard.

My mood wasn't helped by the fact that I'd gotten absolutely no sleep. After watching Cain eat out Sera in the motherfucking hallway last night, I'd had an aching case of blue balls to compete with the dark cloud of guilt that seemed to surround me after I'd kissed Serendipity.

Stupid dumb fuck.

"Are we ready or what? I have shit to do today that doesn't involve waiting for the fucking quilting circle to assemble," I snapped at the men piling into the room.

Everyone hustled their asses into their seats, and I

ignored Solomon's questioning look. I banged a gavel and everyone went silent. Gotta respect the sanctity of Church.

"I'm sure you guys haven't missed the pregnant chick roaming the halls. We've offered Serendipity the protection of Damnation MC, but she comes with some pretty bad shit tailing her. If you want to send your Old Ladies to visit their mothers for awhile, now would be the time."

Herb leaned forward, resting his elbows on the long mahogany conference table that was our round table. "If she comes with so much fucking drama, why don't we just send her on her way instead?"

There were a few murmurs around the room, and I noticed Cain mentally noting every single one of them. But this was the point of Church. They could voice their opinions here, but they knew that my word was law.

End of fucking discussion.

I leaned back in my chair. "When this Club was founded, it was on the premise that women were to be treated with respect. We might be fucking animals, but women would be safe here." We'd been raw from the death of Laura. Some of the old timers had remembered my wife. Remembered her infectious laugh and her bright eyes. Those same old timers remembered her battered body on the metal table in the morgue, almost completely unrecognizable. When we'd put it in our Charter that we were a safe haven for women and children, it had been unanimously agreed.

But some of the members around us don't remember those times. Had never met Laura.

I didn't care. They knew the rules when they'd signed on. "Do you have a problem with the Charter you signed up to, Herb? Because the door is fucking there. You knew what we were about when you patched in."

Herb sneered, and he just rocketed to the top of my 'punch in the fucking face' list. Herb was a legacy member, but he didn't have his daddy's integrity. He was a cowardly little shitstain, but he was still a member. A good President knew that they wouldn't be best buddies with every member, hell they really couldn't be best buddies with any of the members. Your members had to fear and respect you in equal measure.

Herb needed that fear beaten back into him, apparently. I looked over at Goliath, who had narrowed his eyes in Herb's direction too.

Herb crossed his arms over his chest but kept his mouth shut.

"If no one else wants to protest, let's get down to business already. We have a shipment of green to go out to the low level dealers this week..."

For the next hour, we went over the workings of the Club. It ran a lot more like a business than a civvy would know. We didn't just sit around, drinking, fucking and destroying shit all day long, though sometimes that happened too.

While we only dealt in weed and stolen electronics, we were trying to go legit. The time for illegal activities was almost over. We could make a shit heap of money in property and business now. We were slowly going legit, and while that still meant strip joints and tattoo parlors, at least they were legit.

I listened as Trigger explained how the economic downturn had been good for Apocalypse, bringing in crowds even during the week. Nothing like forgetting your problems by sticking a crumpled dollar bill in a stripper's g-string and drinking bottom-shelf bourbon.

By the time Trigger was done, so was I. I needed fucking coffee and a nap. I needed to get my dick wet in a woman who didn't look like sunshine. Who didn't make my heart feel like it would beat out of my chest. Who didn't make my skin crawl with guilt every time I thought about kissing her then remembered my dead wife and kid.

I slammed the gavel down. "Church is out. You all know what to do. Get the fuck out of here."

I waited until they all left, and the only people remaining were my four. I rubbed my eyes to ease the pounding headache taking root behind my forehead.

"Long night, Pres?" Cain asked, and I growled low

in my throat. He squared up to me, and I felt my nose flare as my anger flared.

Trigger, who was easily the smartest man I'd ever met, took a big step toward the door. See. Smart.

Solomon cocked his head. "Did I miss something?"

"Your *boy* here just kept me up all night face-fucking his property in the hallway."

I saw the flash of jealousy on Solomon's face before he shut it down.

Trigger slapped Cain on the back. "Way to go man. Does she taste as good as she looks?"

Every set of eyes in the room drilled into his skull, each look promising pain, even mine. Hell, even Goliath's. I took back what I said about him being smart. If he said something stupid like that again, I'd rip his tongue out.

Trigger held up his hands. "Woah, woah. Kidding. I have no interest in your girl, I promise. I also have no interest in whatever thing you guys have going on with her. I might just go out and see what Shots needs for inventory right now."

He fucking hightailed it out of the room like he was one second away from getting Goliath's boot up his ass.

Cain slammed his hands down on the table, his shoulders rippling with tension. "We need to talk about this shit. Yes, I went down on Sera. Yes, I fully intend on fucking her whenever and wherever she wants it." I watched the anger flow out of him. "She's not just a fuck. She's something more. I can't explain it." He narrowed his eyes at me. "I want to know what happened last night. I found her crying next to the back fucking door."

Every single eye turned toward me, and I knew how Trigger felt a moment ago. "I didn't hurt her!" Cain and Solomon looked like they wanted to draw and quarter my ass on their Harleys. Goliath let out a scary ass grunt that could have been anything from outrage to a lament that I didn't actually hurt her. Could never know with that fucker. He did save her last night though. He hadn't asked for his shirt back. Goliath's fucked up feelings were a problem for another day. "I kissed her. Then I felt guilty because I enjoyed it. Laura and Max are dead in the ground, and I was dying to kiss another woman."

Solomon's face softened in a way that made me want to slit his fucking throat, but Cain still looked hard and unforgiving. "Why would that make her cry?"

I shrugged, but I knew why. I wiped her kiss off my mouth like she disgusted me. But it wasn't her kiss that repulsed me. I disgusted myself. Then I stormed off like a fucking teenager. Sighing, I slumped down in the chair.

"We need to talk about this," Sol repeated softly. He was right, but I was scared. Fucking terrified. I couldn't tell him that though.

"Not fucking now, Sol."

Cain slammed his fist down on the table, making it creak in protest. "Yes, fucking now. Laura is dead, Judas. The men who loved her are all dead too. We aren't those men anymore. We are the fucking Horsemen." He swallowed hard. "I loved Laura so much that when she died, I didn't think I could possibly love another woman again. I felt like my heart had broken into a billion damn pieces and I'd never find them all to put it back together. Hell, I never even looked. I was happy to bury it down there with her." He took a deep breath. "But Sera, man. It's like she was made for us. It's fucking kismet. A half-blood angel wanders the earth for thousands of years and then magically ends up in the hands of the Four Horsemen of the goddamn Apocalypse?" He scoffs. "If she had any idea what the hell we are, I'd be suspicious. But she is just sad and scared and she needs us. All of us."

I shook my head, and Sol frowned. "Do you think we loved Laura any less than you? Any less than Goliath? Laura was my fucking universe. My best friend. The best thing that had ever happened to me in my shit fucking life. She would absolutely hate the way you two have closed yourself off. She would abhor that you made Dippy cry. She would have kicked your ass repeatedly for how you treat women, G. You need to give yourselves a chance. If not with Serendipity, then with someone else. Because you don't get to be fucking assholes while Cain and I do what Laura would have wanted and find love again!"

Cain raised an eyebrow at Sol. "Love?"

A slight red tinge lit Solomon's cheeks. He was fucking blushing. "You know what I mean. Don't be an asshole." He straightened his shoulders. "I love you guys. You are my Brothers. My best friends. I have your back 'til the literal End Of Days. But I want Dippy, if she will have me. I want to see where that goes. Eternity is a long time to be alone."

With that, Solomon turned and left, closing the door softly behind him.

We all stared at the door for a heartbeat. Then Goliath marched over to it, wrenched it open so hard the doorknob came off in his hands, and stormed away.

Cain sat down heavily opposite me, the table between us. I leaned back and pulled a bottle of Hennesy from the wet bar in the corner of the room. I poured us both a generous splash of booze and slid him the eightball glass.

"As soon as you brought her into my office for the first time, I knew she was going to be trouble for us. That she was going to fucking change everything."

Cain took a sip of his cognac. "Maybe things needed to be changed."

I nodded, downing my drink and repouring another. "Maybe you're right. But I'm fucking scared,

Cain. So fucking terrified we won't be enough to protect her and she'll die and it'll be that pain all over again. I can't do that a second time."

He nodded, but he was silent. He wasn't going to lie to me. There was a chance we wouldn't be enough again. We were better now. More equipped to protect what was ours. But the enemy that wanted to take her was far worse than anything we had ever faced.

I looked at Cain, trying to decipher why he was so damn calm. As if he could read my thoughts, he clinked his glass to mine. "I'm scared too. But she's worth the risk."

He downed his drink, and walked out of the room, leaving me alone with my what-ifs and guilt.

I need to beat something. I needed to feel bones crack and flesh give way beneath my fists. I'd jumped on my bike and rode away from the Clubhouse like the actual Hounds of Hell were on my ass.

I rode around the borders of our territory, hoping for some of those Cartel fucks to be edging their way across the line. Then I could pulverize them into the ground again. But everyone seemed to have learned their lesson, or were at fucking Church or who knew fucking what. Not even the freedom of being on my bike, riding too fast was calming the turmoil inside my body.

Cain and Sol and the woman. Disrespecting Laura's memory like that. Sol was wrong though. I didn't love Laura. I fucking hated her. I hated her with every dead spot in my soul. Hated the thought of her, the sound of her name, the memories of her that used to haunt my dreams. But more than I hated Laura, I hated myself. Hated this monster that rode shotgun in my body. Hated that I hated everything and everyone.

What I really abhorred though, was that I actually *liked* how the woman had felt in my arms last night when I'd caught her. That I'd liked her softness against my chest. Thoughts of Laura had been so far from my mind, that I realized I hadn't thought about the woman who was meant to be my everything in years other than as a catalyst for my darkness.

I roared into the wind, revving my bike, pushing it harder and faster, weaving through traffic and splitting lanes down the freeway.

Cain should have left the woman where he found her. Told the other bitch no. So, I hadn't been happy before she'd arrived, but I hadn't been this fucking confused either. I didn't have that ache in my chest before she arrived.

I drove past a strip mall, and a sign caught my eye. I flung my bike into the entrance of the car park, pulling into a bike spot. I left the keys in the bike. We were still in Damnation territory, and no thieves were stupid enough to steal bikes here. You couldn't scrap them down fast enough before I'd find them, and then flay you alive for dishonoring my machine like that.

I pulled off my sunglasses and tucked them onto

the collar of my shirt. The automatic doors in front of me slid open with a whoosh and I stepped into enemy territory.

The teenager by the door looked at me like she was about to shit herself. "Uh, hi. Welcome to Babyland Kingdom. Uh, do you, uh, need help or somethin'?"

I stared down hard at the girl. "I need maternity clothes."

"Oh, yeah sure. This way. Um, follow me?" She looked like she was really hoping I'd leave. I wondered if she'd call the cops like the boutique lady had done on Solomon and Cain. Hopefully I could get in and out before that happened.

"So, do you know what size you are after?" The girl squeaked out, and I huffed. I had no fucking idea.

"I don't know," I growled, making her jump. I clenched my fists and forced myself to be calm. "Sorry," I said softly. "I should have checked before I came. This is a waste of time."

I spun, but the girl made a soft noise. "Wait! We can work it out. It's okay," she said gently, and walked to the racks. "Wrap dresses are good. When you get to the later stages, bending down to put your feet in pants is exhausting to even think about," she winked. "Or so they tell me. Plus you can adjust wrap dresses to whatever you need, and it's a nice soft jersey, see?" She held out a black dress to me, and I obligingly felt the fabric between my fingers.

"I'll take it. And like ten more things." The woman needed more shit if I was ever going to get my shirt back.

The girl looked toward the counter. I narrowed my eyes at her. "Are you trying to signal someone to call the cops?" I growled.

The attendant, her name badge said Stephanie, whipped around to me, dropping the dress in her shock. "What? No? Why would I call the cops? Are you thinking about robbing the place? Coz, I gotta tell you, we've got like a hundred bucks in the till. Everyone uses card for transactions now."

My lips curled up. "Nah, I don't need your money. Sometimes people only see what they wanna see though." I waved a hand at my tattoos, my cut, my general killer demeanor.

Now Stephanie was over her initial fear of my warm and fuzzy persona, she decided I was no threat. "Pshh. I have six older brothers. Takes more than a nasty scowl to scare me. Okay, well I think you should get one of these knit dresses too. Take a guess at what size your, uh, wife is?" She asked, her question lilting at the end, asking a question within a question. I didn't bother correcting her. I didn't think about the reasons for that too hard either.

"I don't know. She's about your size, maybe a little bonier. She's got hips though, and tits." I made a weird gesture with my hands to indicate the size, and

Stephanie raised a brow. "I said I didn't know. This is dumb."

Stephanie rolled her eyes. "Don't be such a whiner. I'm a twelve, so she's probably a ten," she said to herself, and then she fucked off into the racks and apparently I didn't need to have anymore input. She was gone for fifteen fucking minutes before she came back, an armload of clothes.

"Okay, Mr Scary. I've got two pairs of maternity jeans, two pairs of leggings, four dresses and four t-shirts. I also put a pretty dress in there in case you wanna take your wife out for a nice dinner. Just because she's massive doesn't mean she wants to be stuck at home forever, you know?" She handed them to me to add to the dress I was already holding. "Anything else?"

I just shook my head, feeling a bit overwhelmed, not that I would ever admit it. I could torture a man for hours and not even blink, but a teenage girl and a fucking baby store made me a fucking pussy.

Stephanie led me to the checkout and I ignored the worried looks of the grey haired lady behind the other checkout. Her name badge said Karen. I knew without a doubt Karen would definitely have called the cops. But not this kid. "How old are you, kid?"

Stephanie had the fucking gall to roll her eyes at me. I'd beaten the shit out of a prospect for that level of disrespect. "Nineteen. Baby face. Two hundred and thirty six dollars, Mr Scary."

I handed the cheeky brat three Benjamins. "Keep the change." On impulse, I pulled out my business card. It just had my name and phone number on it. I handed it to Stephanie.

"No offense, Mr Scary, you're hot and all, but you're old as shit. I'm not going out with you."

Now, I rolled my eyes. "Get real. You're a fucking baby. No, keep the card. If you need a favor from Damnation, call the number. I owe you one."

She looked at the card, reading my name, her eyes widening. "I've heard of you. I don't think I'll be needing your type of help any time soon."

I nodded. I hoped she was right. I grabbed the bags and left the store. My bike was exactly where I left it, and I stuffed the plastic shopping bags into my saddle-bags. Then I hopped on my bike and roared out of the parking lot.

I rode around for a little longer, grabbing a hot dog from a street vendor who refused to take my money. When I took the back roads, I knew I was subconsciously avoiding going home.

Because then I'd have to give the woman the stuff I'd bought. What had I been thinking anyway? This was a fucking stupid idea, even though I hadn't planned it. Now she was going to start fucking thinking I wanted her to stay around. I didn't. I wanted her to have everything she needed so she'd fucking leave and let me get back to my damn life.

By the time I'd pulled into the parking lot of the Clubhouse, I was fucking furious. Rage coursed through my veins. I wrenched the bags from my saddlebags and stormed through the front doors, every single eye turning to me. I was used to it.

I moved through the room, not stopping to talk to the few people loitering around at the bar in the middle of the day. I climbed the stairs two of the time, my angry stride eating the distance to the woman's door. I thumped on it heavily. To prove she was an idiot, she opened the door.

She was still in my damn shirt. She looked like she was napping, which she probably was considering Cain was up most of the night eating her fucking pussy like it was his damn last meal.

I thrust the bags at her chest, and she clutched them instinctively. "I want my shirt back."

It popped out of mouth before I meant it to. Sure, that's why I bought her the stuff. I wanted my damn property back. That was it.

I was a fucking liar.

"Now? Don't you want me to wash it first?"

I curled my lip. "No. I want it now."

She gave me an angry look. Finally, she was showing some fucking spine. She dropped the bags at her feet, grabbed the bottom of my shirt and pulled it over her head.

Except, she wasn't wearing anything beneath it. My eyes shot to her full, heavy breasts, her dusky pink nipples hardening in the coolish air. Then I looked down at the swell of her stomach, then back up to her tits. I couldn't drag my eyes away. Well, at least until she threw the shirt at my head and slammed the door in my face.

I held the shirt in my fist. It smelled like her. Like jasmine and sunshine. She smelled like the light. I stood there for what could have been seconds or an hour, just staring at her door in shock. Not even a damn thank you. Did she even know what was in the bags? Fuck, I was such a fucking pussy right now.

When I turned, I saw Solomon at the end of the hallway, leaning against the wall like he was propping the damn thing up. I wondered if he'd see the whole thing. I snarled at him, pointing at his fucking smirking face. "Not a fucking word, asshat. I don't want to hear it."

Solomon mimed zipping his lips, but his eyes laughed loud enough that I could basically hear it bouncing off the walls. Fuck this shit. The girl needed to go.

I could hear Solomon's laughter as I reached my own door, and I slammed it so hard after me that it rattled the windows. I gripped the shirt, throwing it on my bed next to my pillow. I would throw it in the washing pile tonight. Get one of the Old Ladies to do my laundry, and then she would be erased from my life. I could go back to pretending she didn't exist. I'd given her a peace offering, what more did those fuckers want from me?

But when I fell into bed that night, I forgot to put it in the laundry pile. And the next night. And the night after that.

16
―――――
SERENDIPITY

When your life has been one big shit show for so long, two peaceful days of nothingness is like a holiday. Both Judas and Goliath avoided me, which hurt a little but I needed the breathing space anyway.

But Cain and Solomon seemed to be going out of their way to be in my company. Solomon had taken me out to see the ruins of Van Slyke Castle, then around the lake. I'd spent hours in the workshop with Cain as he worked on bikes, sitting on his office chair reading the baby books Sweetie had given me. Normal human babies were a lot of work apparently. What would a three-quarter angel baby be?

The whole thing had been nice. I should have known better than to get comfortable. Because it's when you are comfortable that life likes to karate-chop you in the damn face.

Solomon sat on my bed, looking around at all the crap that littered my floor. Even though Taylor had left with the other Old Ladies, she'd come back today, bringing her daughter and an entire truck load of baby crap for me to pick over.

I had strollers and bouncy chairs, a bassinet, a change table, so many tiny little onesies that there was a literal small mountain of them.

"I thought you were going to keep it light?" Solomon teased and I groaned. What the hell was I going to do with all this stuff?

I sagged onto the bed beside him, and when he wrapped his arm around my shoulders, I relaxed into his side. "I was. But they are so damn persuasive, and they made everything sound like it was 100% necessary or the baby would grow up to be a hooker giving hand-jobs in a back alley for crack."

Solomon laughed, the sound rumbling through his chest. "It's not that bad. You heard them, anything you don't want you can just donate."

I needed a nap. I looked up into Solomon's pretty blue eyes. I was pretty sure if I asked, he'd lie down with me. Maybe I could convince him to spoon me. Maybe I could convince him to do more than spoon me.

Cain had joined me in bed every night since the first time, though he never let it go further than giving me mind blowing oral sex every night, no matter how much I begged. I wasn't sure what he was waiting for, or if it was the whole pregnant belly that was giving him the heebie-jeebies. I frowned. I wouldn't want to fuck me either. I was about as sexy as a sea cow right now.

"Hey, what's wrong? You aren't really worried about this right? If you don't want to worry about putting everything away, I can send up a couple of the Prospects to do it for you? They pretend to bitch and moan, but I heard them wondering if the baby was going to be a boy or girl. I think they are excited about a baby in the Clubhouse. Very unscary of them. Might have to beat them a bit more so they aren't such fucking pussies."

I smiled, and I shook my head. "No, it's fine. I'm almost excited to put this stuff away. I think I'm nesting or some shit."

He ran his fingers through my hair and I all but purred. It felt so good. "Then what's wrong?"

My cheeks flushed, and I regretted not agreeing to the freakin' Prospects putting all this shit away.

"It's nothing." He raised a brow, and I sighed. He wasn't going to drop it. Solomon was perceptive and stubborn as hell. "Fine. But you asked. Cain won't have sex with me, and I'm pretty sure its because I look like a beluga whale." I indicated my belly.

Solomon blinked at me. "Uhh..."

I stood up, and walked to the pile of onesies, and angry folded them. I folded each one twice and banged them down on top of the small table in the room.

I heard his soft steps behind me, and I kept my shoulders tense. "Dippy, that's not it at all." He gently spun me so I was forced to look up into the empathetic look on his face. "I'm almost positive that Cain has the biggest case of blue balls, because pregnant or not, you are hot as fuck."

I snorted a laugh. "Eloquent."

Solomon gave a frustrated huff, then he leaned forward and kissed me. And holy shit, he could kiss. If Judas wanted to possess and Cain wanted to devour, then Solomon's kiss was pure pleasure. His lips pulled and sucked at mine as his tongue made love to mine like it was a different part of my body.

When he pulled back, he was grinning and I felt dizzy. "Uh..." I mumbled. "Again?"

"Now who's eloquent, hmm?" Solomon whispered against my lips. He kissed me again, his hands roaming up and down my spine, one reaching down to palm my ass. He groaned low in his throat, and I finally pulled away.

Cain. I'd started something with Cain. This wasn't

right. "I can't," I gasped out while I had enough working brain cells remaining. "Cain and I..." I trailed off, because Cain and I hadn't actually said anything about where this was going. Basically I cried and he'd made me feel better, then done it again the next night, and the night after and I couldn't tell if he wanted it or just thought he was doing me a favor. Ugh. Men were fucking hard. Now I remembered why I'd been alone for the last two thousand years.

Solomon refused to let me go, and I remained pressed against his body because it was nice. The firm plane of his chest, his broad shoulders, the way his hands spanned the width off my back. "Don't worry about Cain, Dippy. We've done this before."

I pulled away so I could see his face properly. "Done what exactly?"

"Shared a woman."

I felt my brows almost hit my hairline. "You've had threesomes?" Not going to lie, I wasn't opposed to the idea right now.

"No, I mean yes, we've had threesomes but that's not what I meant. I mean we've had a relationship with one woman. Actually, not just me and Cain. Judas as well, he was her husband. And Goliath."

"Goliath?" I couldn't keep the disbelief from my voice. I just assumed that he hated women in general, but maybe it was just me.

Sadness clouded Sol's eyes, but in the next second it was gone. "It was a long time ago, and a long story."

I stepped back. "I've got ti-"

A low siren interrupted my words. Solomon's body went on high alert. He went over to my window and let out a stream of profanities.

"We're under attack. Come on," he grabbed my hands and dragged me out of my room. We met Cain on the stairs, already holding a gun in his hand.

"Get her into the room at the back now. It's not just Uriel. He's brought friends."

He leaned forward and kissed me quickly on the lips. "We've got this, Sweetheart. Go with Sol," then he was back down the stairs. Solomon continued to pull me along as we pushed against the flow of men rushing around like ants. Solomon stopped in front of what looked like a storage closet, but instead he punched in a number into a number pad, and the door popped open. Inside was a huge cache of weapons. Everything from semi-autos which I'm pretty sure were military grade and illegal as fuck, to damn C4.

Solomon tucked me into the closet then threw guns at every man who went past. Eventually the gun safe was empty of everything but a bunch of bricks of C4 and some goddamn grenades.

Solomon herded me back into the hall, pulling the armory door closed behind me. "What about me? I need a gun too."

"Do you know how to use one? We will be in a

room filled with our own people. Are you sure you can hit your mark?"

I huffed as I followed along behind him. I was an excellent marksman with a bow. Guns were a reasonably new weapon, and I hadn't needed one. I was just a woman in this age. They didn't need me to fight wars. And I didn't need a gun to hunt for food when a bow was just as useful and cleaner. So no, I wasn't a good marksman with a gun, fuck it.

Taking my silence as an answer, he opened the door to a room with no windows and the door seemed heavier. A huge wooden table sat in the center of the room. "This is where we hold Church," Solomon explained, slamming the door shut. I noticed two prospects were here with me. Solomon stared at them, lifting his gun in their direction. "A single hair on her head gets hurt, I swear I'll fucking torture you until you scream for mercy. I'm starting with your balls."

They nodded nervously. Poor little guys. Couldn't be more than twenty or so. They should be in college or at home with their Momma's, not caught up in my fucking supernatural war.

Solomon leaned forward and kissed me softly. "It's going to be fine. It'll be all over soon."

Then he walked out the door, slamming it shut behind him.

I slumped down in a chair, holding my head in my hands. Fuck, fuck, fuck.

They needed help. They didn't understand what they were up against. I pulled my phone from my jeans pocket, and texted Hope. Then I called Marco.

I hadn't told the guys about Marco, I wasn't sure why. He seemed seperate to them, somehow a part of this shitshow but he'd gotten out. Dodged a literal bullet. I didn't want to bring him back into it. But if Uriel got me today, he needed to run. Because if Uriel traced me here, he was going to want to eliminate anyone who knew that I was pregnant. Anyone who knew the whole story. Hope was on her own, she had her own beef with the Archangel. But Marco and his kids, they were just innocent bystanders.

He'd laugh so hard if he knew I just called him innocent. He was muscle for hire. He was a crazy bastard who'd spilled more blood than the two kids who were meant to be protecting me right now. Hope, the woman who had rescued me from Purgatory, had met the guy while trying to bring down a dirty organization called Tenebrae. They were created by Uriel, but Tenebrae was little more than a venus fly trap for your soul. You were lured in by the power, the sex and the drugs, the sin, and you lived well. But when you died, you were marked for Hell. Tenebrae did some fucking heinous things, but I'd met a few of Hope's boyfriends, and they scared the shit out of me too. Maybe they were evenly matched, or maybe we'd all get our asses handed to us.

Either way, Marco needed to know. My heart hurt a little thinking about him. Leaving him behind had been the right thing to do; he had kids to protect. But it still stung how easily he'd let me go.

I pressed call on his number, and I waited for it to answer. There was silence at the other end of the line, but I expected it. Marco was mute.

"Marco, they found me. You gotta take the kids and run for a little while. If this shit all went bad, he'll come for you guys. I need you to run."

I could hear the hard thump at the other end of the phone, like someone slamming their fist on a table.

"Hey, listen. I wanted to say thank you. I never said it before, but you guys gave me a safe haven even for a little while, and I appreciate it more than you'll know. You gave me normalcy in a time that I didn't think I would ever be okay again. I owe you for that. Tell the kids that they are amazing. They are going to be wonderful human beings, and that's down to you, Marco." I took a shaky breath. "I gotta go. I hope I see you soon." I heard a strangled yell from the other end of the phone. I didn't know what happened to Marco that stopped him from speaking, but I think it was physical. That it hurt him to speak.

I hung up before anything got more touchy-feely. I looked at the prospects, but they had their eyes trained on the door. That's when I heard the first gunshots. I sucked in a shuddering breath.

I tried to call Hope but her number just rang out. Something rammed the building and the whole place shuddered. "I need a gun," I said to the Prospect closest to me. Stevie? Or Paulie? I couldn't remember. He looked back at me, and then looked at the other Prospect.

"Uh, I'm not sure, Ma'am. I've only got one."

I sighed, he probably needed it. The other Prospect didn't even make eye contact with me. I stood and paced, the baby kicking the shit out of my bladder, sensing my distress. I had to pee. Fuck this. I should go out there. These men didn't need to die needlessly.

I walked toward the door, but Stevie was there before me. "You can't go out there, Ma'am."

I pointed a finger at him. "Stop calling me ma'am." I sighed. "I can stop this. No one needs to get hurt for me."

Stevie was still shaking his head. "No, uh, Dippy." Most of the Club had adopted Solomon's nickname for me. "I can't let you go out there. And this is something we voted on. We want to protect you and the baby. When we signed onto Damnation, it was part of the oath. The Club Charter says that we protect women and children who come to us for help. It's part of the reason I wanted to be in this MC to start with." I narrowed my eyes at him, and he nervously continued. "My sister was murdered by her husband in her living room. I was only thirteen at the time, and she was eight years older than me, but I loved her so much. And he took her life like it meant nothing, just because he didn't like how she vacuumed the carpet." Stevie stepped forward and ushered me gently back to the chair. I went willingly. "She told her friends that he used to beat her, and she wanted to leave him, but he was a cop and she was scared. If she'd known that she could have run to this place, to Damnation MC and Cain, would she still be alive today? That's why I want to pledge. To help women like my sister. Like you. Let us help. It's why some of us are even here. Not Paulie though; he is just here because he thinks the cut makes him less of an ugly fuck, and will attract girls," he joked.

The other Prospect flipped him the bird, but his face was serious too.

I swallowed hard. I didn't know that about Damnation. Had Hope known that they protected women when she'd dropped me off at Cain's tattoo parlor? Or had she just known that Cain was good the way she knew so many things?

One day I'd ask. If I survived the next twenty-four hours. More rapid gunfire sounded and it rattled along my nerves. Were they down there, dead or in pain? Cain would be on the front lines. He was VP after all. Solomon too. Judas would definitely be there. He definitely wasn't a man who would lead from the back.

Goliath I wasn't worried about. He was the type of

man who lived for this mayhem. For the bloodshed and the war. He'd be in his element.

I could hear shouting now, getting closer and closer. I tilted my head, straining to catch the words. It was Cain yelling to pull back to the Clubhouse, and I could hear the heavy thump of boots on the stairs. Why was Cain giving orders? Where was Judas?

Finally, the doors snapped open, and both Prospects had their guns trained on the door. "It's us," Cain yelled through the gap in the door, and the Prospects lowered their weapons. I stood and rushed toward the door. I wrapped my body around Cain, kissing his cheeks. "Thank God you're okay. Everyone else?"

"Tito got a bullet in the thigh, but he'll be fine. We locked down the front, but they seem to be swarming. Where the fuck are all these mob guys coming from?"

"Tenebrae, I think. Human traffickers and fucking powerful men with their own private armies. I didn't think Uriel would bring them in. I didn't think he'd want that many witnesses. I'm so sorry, Cain."

Cain wrapped his arms around me and pulled me tight to his chest. I let out a gasping breath as I counted his heartbeats against my cheek. "It's fine, Sera. We aren't beaten yet. We have a few tricks up our sleeve, okay?" He kissed my forehead, then my cheeks. "Grab a seat, Sweetheart."

There was a call from downstairs. "Let them

through, they're with us!" It was Trigger's voice. The heavy wooden doors opened for the second time in as many minutes, and in walked Hope and the fucking Angel of Death.

There was an audible gasp in the room at the sight of Azriel's wings. Apparently, no one was even playing at being human today.

"How's it going, Sera?"

Cain growled. "We are being attacked by the fucking mob."

I shot him a look. "These guys seem to think that being pregnant has turned me into fine china that can't hold a gun. I need a gun." I needed for this to be over. I needed to be snuggled in bed with Cain, or Solomon. Hell, after this maybe I could sleep for a week between both Solomon and Cain. We just all needed to survive my mistakes.

Hope, bless her heart, whipped out a gun and handed it to me. Cain frowned, and Hope shrugged unapologetically. "What? She's about to cry? Do you want her to cry?" Cain stared at me in horror, and I blinked rapidly. I wasn't going to cry about not having a gun, but I felt like I was an inch away from a nervous breakdown. Hope knew too. She always knew.

Hope told me about attacking Uriel, showing their hand too early, and I could hear the regret in her voice. It didn't matter to me. It was bound to come down to this, and it was nice to be able to see the guillotine coming.

"Did you bring an army?" I asked, looking at the Angel of Death, though his wings had changed since I saw him last.

A voice from behind me sent chills down my spine.

"No, she brought the Devil."

I grinned, blood and gore running down my face and dripping in my mouth. I spat, but I didn't care. I lived for this shit. I had my gun in one hand, and a hunting knife in the other. I walked through their group, barely dodging their bullets as I dropped them like annoying little flies. Raw power flowed through my veins, and I let my beast out to play. A guy came up from beside me, and I whirled fast, using my blade to sever his head from his body. Fuck, I loved this shit. Another one came from behind me, and I spun quickly, putting my fist in his face, and then shooting him between the eyes.

It was like a dance really, a macabre ballet. I killed three more, and then this big golden fucker with wings appeared. I aimed my gun but he threw up his hands.

"Woah, easy there, Killer. I'm on your side. Cain called us in as reinforcements. Need a hand?"

"No," I growled, but spun away, shooting a guy trying to kick down the side door.

The Golden dude with wings pulled out a mother-fucking huge sword. "Bad luck, Killer. I got your back."

He whirled it, and then he was spinning through a swarm of armed guys in suits. Honestly, who comes to a fight in a goddamn suit? I threw my knife at a guy who was trying to sneak up on the blond angel. He grinned over his shoulder and I realized he was enjoying this shit too.

Fine. Killing was more fun with company. It was a pity he was so damn chatty though. "So, you're one of Luc's Horsemen, then?"

He said it like we were discussing interest rates, instead of him decapitating a dude, and talking about the fucking Horsemen of the Apocalypse. "Yeah."

"Not a big talker? That's okay. I bet you're Conquest. You seem way too happy to be covered in pieces of brain and skull."

There was a sharp whistle, and Judas yelled for us to pull back. I huffed, not ready to retreat yet, but in this situation, Judas was General. I fired my gun randomly, covering us as we moved back towards the door. Though the angel didn't seem all that worried, just strolling along behind me. "I'm Gus by the way."

"Goliath," I grunted, opening the door and firing the last of my clip around it. Gus walked into the back of the club, taking in the bullet holes in the walls and the destruction of the bar. "Nice place you have here," he laughed, and strode over to another angel. This one was huge and black, and he seemed to suck the light out of the room. He made my skin crawl with fear and it wasn't a feeling I was used to. "This is Mephistopheles. He hates small talk to. You guys would get along great." The big, black angel nodded to me, and then turned back to Gus. That was fine. I didn't want to chit-chat anyway.

I kept low, running toward where Judas and Shots were behind the bar. A bullet wouldn't kill me, but they hurt like a bitch.

When I crouched down beside them, and tilted my head toward the Angels, who seemed to be cutting the Tenebrae members down like they were picking mushrooms in a field. "Who the fuck brought the Angels?"

"The woman who delivered Serendipity to Cain. Apparently, Dippy keeps interesting company."

We were fighting angels. Had angels on our side. How do we know which was which? "How do I know which angels to kill, and which are on our side?"

Judas shrugged.

Trigger leaned around the door jamb. "They are about to break through," he yelled over the noise. As if summoned by Judas' words, a woman skipped down the stairs, followed by an Angel with wings the color of a sunset.

The next face down those stairs had black dots dancing around the edges of my vision. Lucifer was here. In the Clubhouse. We hadn't seen him in decades, and here he was, standing beside the woman and a bunch of other Angels.

The woman with the red hair smiled. "I brought a posse," she said happily to Trigger.

Lucifer's eyes focused on us, and his gaze could flay the skin from your bones.

"Judas," he said softly.

"Lucifer," the Pres returned. Lucifer's eyes switched to me, and he winked. He fucking winked. Blood rushed in my ears, blocking out the sound of the gunshots and shouts in the room. It was like all my focus was on the man, er Devil, in front of us. He'd changed my life irrevocably, and I had equally cursed him and thanked him for that every day since.

Judas looked between the Angels and the Devil. We were out of our league right now. "Damnation, fall back. Hold the stairs. No one gets to Dippy," he shouted. Gus looked over at us. "They are about to ram the doors," he said to Judas, who seemed less fucking freaked by the appearance of Satan than I was.

I ran toward the stairs, but Judas grabbed my hand.

"I need you up there guarding Serendipity. I don't trust anyone with her life more than I trust you. You and Cain are the last line of defense okay? She has to live, for their sake."

I nodded, and clapped him on the back. He was an idiot if he thought he was immune to the woman's charms.

I bust through the door, and almost got punched full of holes for my impulsiveness. It was only that Cain had good reflexes that I wasn't bleeding on the floor right now. I looked at the people packed into the room. "Get out into the hall. Shoot anyone who comes up those stairs that isn't one of us or the redhead."

"Hope," the woman said softly. "Anything with white wings is fair game too. They are on the other side."

"Of course her name is fucking Hope," I muttered, glaring at the rest of my Brothers in this room who were taking too long to move. Finally, the only people left in the room were the woman, Cain and me.

Cain was pacing, his body tense. This was war. His bread and butter, and he was caging the Horseman who was desperate to make someone bleed to be with the girl. Maybe he did love her. My Horseman had no problem being up here, but not because I wanted to protect the woman. Nah, I was Conquest. Someone wanted to take what was mine? No fucking way. I'd guard her until they were all dead at my feet. I would take what was theirs, because she was fucking mine now.

"Go, Cain. Spill some blood. I'll watch the woman," I said softly at Cain. He shook his head, but he was torn. His blood was up, and he'd tear this whole room apart soon. Or have an accident. You didn't want the power of the Horsemen slipping out without control. That's how good guys died by friendly fire.

I don't know what the woman saw, but she grabbed his arm as he paced past her. "Go. Help Judas and Sol," she urged softly.

Cain growled, pointing his gun at my face. "She lives or you die. I love you, man, but..."

I waved a hand at him. Yeah, I got it. Something about the woman had sent him mushy in the head. "I've got it. Go."

I all but pushed him out the door, but I saw a flash of the Horseman behind his eyes. I could hear him barking orders at the Club as the door shut. I walked away from the doors to melt into the darkness in the corner of the room where I had a clear shot. I noted the gun on the table in front of her, and I wondered if she knew how to use it.

"What's going on down there?"

Great, she wanted to make fucking small talk. "The angels rocked up. They seem to have shit under control."

She made a frustrated noise, and I briefly

wondered if she would pick up that gun and shoot me with it. I found the idea oddly fucking hot. I kinda liked her more now she'd brought some bloodshed to the party, rather than all the emotional angst.

I went back to ignoring her, though the building shook. Guess they'd finally rammed the doors. "What the fuck was that?" the woman asked, and I rolled my eyes.

"They rammed the doors with a truck, I guess." Now I was kind of envious of my Brothers. I was stuck in here with the fucking knitting circle when I could be painting the walls red. At least I got a little time to spread some gore with the big golden angel. If I hadn't seen Lucifer and the one that was all onyx colored, I'd think that all angels are this golden color. After all, the woman was half angel and she was cast from the same golden hues, even if it wasn't quite as potent. And no damn wings.

"Why do you hate me so much?" she asked, and I instantly regretted letting Cain leave. Now was not the time for touchy-feely conversations.

"I feel nothing for you," I answered, not even turning to look at her.

She scoffed. "That's a fucking lie. Even if it isn't hate, you definitely feel something for me. Disgust, dislike, apathy. Something." Oh, now she decided to grow some balls. Fucking fantastic.

I turned my head, looking over my shoulder at her. "I don't feel. Don't take it personally."

She stared back, her eyes holding mine, despite how dead they felt. Her eyes called me a liar.

"You make them weak. Women make us weak. I'll never be weak again."

She gave a little nod. "Someone broke your heart. The woman you shared with Cain and Solomon? And Judas?"

I narrowed my eyes at her. "Who told you about Laura?"

She shook her head. "No one. Not really. But I feel the ghost of her clinging to you all," she said sadly.

I turned back and stared at the door. I didn't want to talk about Laura. About women. I didn't want to talk to one woman in particular. I wanted to break bones and spill organs. Hell, I'd rather spill my own organs then continue with this conversation one second longer.

A soft brush of magic and the sound of feminine gasp had me spinning, raising my weapon toward the corner of the room.

A huge angel stood in the corner, blond, but not quite the same golden as the other guy, Gus. And his wings were all white. The kind of white that is unattainable in the real world because the world is inherently grey and dirty.

He gave me a smile that I guessed was supposed to be beatific, but was just fucking creepy. "I am Livinius, an Angel of Heaven's Legion. The girl is ours. She must come with me. She belongs to Uriel," he said, his voice so evenly modulated he sounded almost like a robot. I moved towards Serendipity, who was sitting still, trembling so hard I thought she was going to fall out of her chair. Terror. She was shaking with fucking terror. I moved around the chair, standing in front of her, blocking her view of the angel with the huge white wings.

"She belongs to us," I growled, lifting my gun. Then I shot him in the chest.

Serendipity gasped, but the angel just looked down at his chest. It didn't even leak any blood. "Your stupid mortal weapons won't hurt me. I will repeat. Give me the woman. She belongs to Uriel."

I dropped my gun onto Serendipity's lap and pulled out my long bowie knife. "You fucking hard of hearing? She'll never belong to him. She. Is. Mine." I launched myself at the angel, and for the first time in a very long time, let the Horseman take over me completely. It was a weird sensation, like a pale mist coating my body, filling me with power.

The angel took a surprised step backwards, fear on his face for the first time. Yeah, that's right fucker. Not so immortal faced with a fucking Horseman of the Apocolypse, are you?

"This can't be possible! We did not know Lucifer

had chosen." He tried to pull his fancy ornamental sword from his hip, but I was fast and made for bringing down angels. I was on him quickly, my knife slashing at his throat. He moved backwards, well trained as one of Heaven's legions should be, but not fast enough. I whet my blade with angel blood. His sword came down, but I danced away, aiming low and scoring another shot to his side. The angel hissed, becoming more enraged. I grinned, the blood crusted to my face cracking.

"You seem to be leaking, your Eminence." Fuck, this was better than fucking. This was everything. This made the bitter, dark life I lived totally worth it. This is the moment I was reborn for.

I spun again, feinting low, but slashing him across the face. When it came down to it, nothing I did would kill the angel. Only one thing could kill an Angel. The Sword of St Michael. But I could make him hurt. I could make him regret coming into my house and trying to take what was mine.

My hand moved faster than my eyes could follow, though the angel had his sword up now and was swinging just as wildly to block my hits. But my knife was a close range weapon and he couldn't get his sword high enough to get a good hit in. I'd be down if he did. I was starting to bleed ribbons of bright red blood from the various slashes, but none of them big enough to be mortal.

Finally, I got a good shot into his stomach, dragging my knife upwards until the barbs got caught on some ribs.

The angel gasped and stepped away. "The child is an abomination. The Father won't let this rest."

"Oh, I think you would be surprised what the Father would allow, Livinius," a new voice said, and I spun again, stepping back towards where Serendipity stood at my back.

"Archangel Michael," Livinius said breathlessly.

The new Angel, the motherfucking Archangel Michael, was equally as big as the one with my knife lodged in his gut. But he felt so, so much bigger. His power made my skin crawl, made the Horseman run and hide back in my body like a scared kitten. Shit. Fuck. Shit fuck shit fuck shit! I bared my teeth and stood over the woman. If I let her die, then Cain and Sol would die with her. They wouldn't be able to take that again. They'd only known her a couple of days, but they'd tied her fate to theirs.

I grabbed both my gun and the one Serendipity had. I held them out, but the Archangel just laughed.

"Relax, Horseman. I do not want your consort. Though it amuses me how fate has brought you together. The cause of the Great Fall, and the instruments of the End of Days. It is like the beginning met the end, and I love the irony of that." He looked past me to Sera. "Ah, you have always been a predicament, Child of the Fallen. Nurturing another Child who should not be. Causing another to fall. Fate is nothing if not cyclical. But I believe, as Hope Jones would say, you have been much sinned against already in your life. There will be no more interference from above. Be careful of the zealots of Uriel. Lucifer's Fallen are working at eliminating them, but they will want the child. He has worked them up into a frenzy that can only perpetuate evil, and you will have to bear the brunt of that."

He gazed disapprovingly at Livinius, who looked like he was about to shit his white pants. "The Father is here. I would start practicing your prostrating, Livinius," he said in a low, disapproving tone that made my knees turn to water. Livinius poofed out like the chicken shit he was. The fucking Archangel Michael turned his gaze back to me. "Until we meet again, Horseman."

Then they were both gone and I was alone in the room with the woman. She was sobbing on her knees, though I had no idea at what point she'd fallen from the chair. Wetness fell on my cheeks too, and I swiped through the single tear tracks on my cheeks, glad no one was here to see them. But standing in the presence of such immense power was painfully wonderful. Or wonderfully painful. I turned to the woman, putting my hands under her elbows, pulling her to her feet with gentle hands. She felt insubstantial, and I kept my grip on her tight.

"Are you okay?" My voice was rough, even mean. For once, I hadn't meant to be gruff.

She said nothing, continuing to tremble and cry beneath my hands. Fuck.

I followed my instincts and pulled her to my chest. She buried her face in my chest, and her cries turned from soft to full body-wracking sobs. Shit. Did I just make it worse? I went to move away, but she clung to my shoulders like I was the last port in the fucking shitstorm of her life.

"It's okay. We've dealt with fucking psycho angels now. Some shitty mobsters in cheap suits will be nothing. It's okay," I repeated but it didn't seem to help. I tilted her head back, until she was forced to look at me.

Then I kissed her.

Gently at first, but then with increasing pressure, until she was clinging to my lips with the same intensity that she was clinging to my back. I traced the crease of her lips with my tongue, bit her full bottom lip roughly until she whimpered. I consumed her, breathed her into the empty cavity in my chest. Then the doors opened and Solomon rushed in, Cain and Judas so close behind him that when he slammed to a stop they ran into his back.

I jumped away from her like she was poison.

I glared at my Brothers, the other Horsemen, until

they moved out of the way and I could step out into the war zone. I was more confident surrounded by dead bodies and bullets.

My chest felt weird. I thumped it with my fist, and realized it was because my heart was racing.

18

SERENDIPITY

The aftermath of the battle was a blur to me. Lucifer had cleaned up his own mess apparently, the dead bodies of Uriel's Army just poofing away like dust in the wind. I was in bed, squashed in between the warm bodies of Cain and Solomon. My body had trembled for hours, apparently my immortal body's way of coping with very human shock. The guys had eventually taken off their shirts, pressed me between them, and whispered barely audible promises.

Eventually, the trembling had stopped, and reality had begun to sink back in. Fucking Uriel. Even damned, he was making my life hell on earth. I'd wanted this to be the end. I just wanted the whole thing to be over.

But I realized now that it would never be over. I'd

been kidding myself. Delusional to think that it would all end with Uriel.

The whole day had been a lot to unpack. I'd been in the same room as the Devil and the Archangel Michael. The Fallen had been here. Hope had been here. My fa-. I cut the thought off. I didn't even want to think about how close that had been.

Then there was the warning about Tenebrae, whoever the fuck they were.

Kissing Goliath. That kiss...

So much had been said with that kiss. Long remembered pain, promises and threats. I tasted the desolation on his lips and I wanted to taste it again.

The baby moved restlessly, hopefully oblivious to the fact that it was the cause of so much of my turmoil. I didn't want to give the poor little thing a complex so early in life. I rolled on my back, searching for a position where we were both comfortable.

Cain put his big hand on my stomach, and the baby slowed its movements. I think it liked Cain. As if a baby could like anyone in there. It liked it when I put my electric toothbrush on the outside of my belly and that's about it.

Cain kissed the back of my neck, and I had my head on Solomon's chest. It was a damn good chest, muscled and inked, mostly smooth. His fingers were threaded through my hair, his nails scraping gently across my scalp.

I was perfectly content and totally lost all at once, the two sensations threatening to tear me in half. What did I do now?

Someone knocked on the door of Cain's room, and then Trigger let himself in. His dark eyes took in our positions, the guys' state of undress, and although I was still fully clothed, the intimacy was glaringly obvious.

"What?" Cain said softly, his tone gentle though his eyes were hostile. He was trying not to startle me so I didn't turn into a quivering fucking wuss again.

I was disgusted with myself. Once upon a time, I'd been a badass. A warrior queen. A survivor. Now I'm knocked up and crying on a man's shoulder.

I was suddenly uncontrollably mad at myself. At the situation. At every fucking shitstain who thought they could come in and take me, take my baby, like we were merely possessions to be had.

Trigger looked between the three of us once more, then shrugged. He walked over and slumped on the end of the bed, picking up my feet and placing them on his chest.

"That was some crazy shit, Hombre. Some fucking crazy ass, wild, LSD while on crack, shit. There were angels with huge ass wings. I saw..." he trailed off, and I understood. I petted his chest with my foot, and somehow, I felt a little better about being a wreck. We all saw shit we shouldn't have seen today. The war between Heaven and Hell wasn't ours to fight.

Then I remembered what Michael had called Goliath. Horseman.

What the hell did that mean?

"Yeah. Fucking nuts. But if you keep touching my girl, Trigger, I'm going to rip off an appendage you'd like to keep," Cain said pleasantly.

Trigger looked up at me and winked, but he gently shifted my feet back onto the bed and sat up. "The Pres wants to hold Church. Wants to know what everyone saw. Probably to ensure people keep their mouths shut about the angels and you guys being the Four Horsemen of the Apocalypse," he said nonchalantly, like they brought it up in conversation all the time, but I felt both Cain and Solomon's bodies go rigid.

"I don't know what you mean, kid," Cain growled.

Trigger waved a hand, rolling his eyes. "Come on, Cain. I'm not stupid. And neither was my dad. He knew what you were. He'd been here since the beginning of Damnation MC. He'd known, you know."

Uh no, I didn't know. But the look Cain gave to him quelled any thoughts of elaborating on his part. I made a mental note to corner Trigger about it though. "Anyway, Dad knew. And he told me before I patched in. No one else in the Club has made the connection, but the old timers suspect. It's been thirty years and you guys look like you are still twenty-five. I'm pretty sure no ladies face cream is that good. And I know for a fact you haven't been bathing in the blood of virgins," he laughed. "Your secret's safe with me. But it seems to me, sooner or later, you're gonna have to make some decisions and I've been ensuring that those decisions are easy for you."

Cain was standing now, pulling his shirt over his head, hiding those glorious inked abs. "What are you trying to say, Trig?"

"I've been getting you fake identities, setting up offshore accounts, making it so you can disappear for a little while."

Cain and Solomon seemed to be in shock. I tilted my head at Trigger, trying to find his angle. "You want to be President after they disappear?"

He grinned at me. "Fuck yeah I do. But that's not for another decade or two right? Unless the world ends and they have to go full Horseman before that, but then it won't matter if the MC has a Pres or not, because we'll all be in Hell." He laughed. "Not gonna complain because some of those angels were hot as fuck."

I had to laugh. It bubbled up in my chest until I couldn't breathe from the laughter spilling over my lips. "You are a horny bastard, Trigger."

He grinned, his teeth so white and straight they should have been in a toothpaste commercial. "I've started one for you too, Dippy. And the baby, though that'll have to wait until we know if it's a boy or a girl. I don't know what you are, but I can't imagine that a fucking big ass angel would want a normal human, no matter how hot you are."

Cain growled and Trigger just grinned at him some more. The guy obviously likes taking his life in his hands. I stood up and walked over to the cowboy hat wearing biker. What an enigma he was. "You'd be right. Thanks Trigger. I appreciate it."

"You're welcome, Dippy. And all it'll cost you is a kiss. Aren't I generous?" Solomon and Cain lunged for him but he ducked away, laughing. "I'm joking. Jesus. Fuck, can I still say Jesus? Anyway, Pres says Church now. Also, bring Dippy."

I raised an eyebrow. "You guys let women in Church?"

Trigger shook his head. "No, but we can make an exception when the woman that has the entire upper hierarchy of the MC wrapped around her little finger, and that little finger is in mortal peril."

"Not the whole upper hierarchy," I said, and Trigger waggled his eyebrows.

"I could be convinced," he mock whispered, and Solomon came up behind him and slapped the back of his head. "Even think it, and I'll let Goliath chop off your dick."

Trigger laughed, straightening his hat as he walked

toward the door. "Two dick threats in one conversation is a bit of an overkill, don't you think?"

He laughed as he walked down the hall.

"That little fucker talks too much," Cain grumbled, threading his fingers in mine and walking out the door of his apartment. He looked over his shoulder at Solomon. "Almost as much as you. Actually, I'm kind of regretting apprenticing him with you during his Prospect days. He's picked up way too many of your bad fucking habits."

Solomon just laughed, stepping closer so he could rest his hand on my spine.

We were in front of the huge double doors before I knew it. My steps slowed. I wasn't sure I was ready to be back in that room. I could still feel the power of the Archangel Michael like an ache in my skull.

But I'd had my quota of weakness for the week. I straightened my shoulders and let out a breath through my nose. *I've got this.*

I shook out Cain's hand from mine, giving him a soft smile to let him know it wasn't something he did. Solomon seemed to get it, and dropped his hand from my skin.

They stepped around me, walking in first, because they were VP and Road Captain. They commanded the respect of the other members. I slinked around the corner, not trying to interfere, but regardless of my stealth, every head turned to face me. Trigger and

Shots gave me warm looks, and some of the others gave me respectful nods. Some outright death glared at me. Including Goliath.

But that glare didn't erase the kiss.

Judas cleared his throat, drawing my gaze from Goliath. His stare was intense, and just like the first day I met him. I couldn't help but shrink back from the power he emanated. Now I knew that it was more than a charisma that powerful leaders had. It was preternatural. Otherworldly. Straight from fucking Hell.

"Take a seat, Serendipity." He indicated the chair behind him next to the wall. The naughty chair?

I kept my snarky comment to myself, and walked to the spot he indicated like a good little girl. I wasn't an idiot. I owed these guys. If it wasn't for them, I would be dead right now, my baby too. Or worse, they would have cut it from my body and raised it up as some kind of Second Coming.

Cain and Sol settled in their chairs, and Judas banged the gavel. Then he sighed heavily. "Yesterday, we fought a very different enemy. Saw things we never thought we'd see. Some of you may have had your very belief systems shattered. It is hard to be faced with the idea that those fairytales your mother told you to make you be good are actually true." He held himself with such confidence. Such assuredness. It was hard to imagine Judas scared of even the Devil himself.

He could sip tea with the Devil, but a kiss from me

sent him running for the hills. I wasn't going to take offense to that.

"So today, I wanted to do something different. For the first time in thirty years, I'm going to let you leave the Club, break your vows, without reprisal. Now is the time. Hand in your cut, your weapons and we will send you on your way with understanding and a handshake."

A small gasp crossed my lips when two men stood, shrugged off their cuts and left them on top of the table. Judas' face turned down as he stood, sadness weighing down his shoulders as he reached across the table to do exactly what he promised. He shook their hands, as did every other man around that table. It was a solemn shake, the kind of embrace you'd do at a funeral for a friend.

When the door closed behind them, Trigger stood and relocked it. That was it.

I knew that that decision had probably seemed too easy to me, but those men had cut their identity out of their life, and it probably felt like cutting off a limb. Because of me. Because of my drama. I couldn't help the guilt that snuck up and threw a shadow over me.

"Anyone else? Remember, this offer only lasts until the end of this Church. Afterwards, abandonment of the Club will be treated with the same rules as before." He paused, and there were a couple of sweaty faces but no one moved. "Okay. It's been decided that every man who remains should reswear to the Club. We've also added a code of silence in the Charter. What happened yesterday... you can't tell anyone about it. Not your wives. Not your priest. Not your side piece. It won't be me enforcing the rule if you break it. The people-"

"Fucking angels. They were fucking angels, Pres," someone interrupted.

Judas nodded once. "Yeah, they were. And they will break every bone in your body and drag you to Hell themselves if anyone runs their mouth about what happened yesterday."

There were a lot of pale faces around the room, and I didn't blame them. I felt shaky too. Trigger seemed to know what was needed. He went and got a bottle of tequila from the side board and passed it to the heavily bearded guy on his left. Then he went and got a huge fucking knife. The thing had a bone handle, inscribed with some kind of demonic runes up the side. Where the hell had they gotten that?

Trigger handed the mean looking weapon to Judas. Judas sliced his palm, letting blood drip-drip into the neck of the bottle of tequila, turning the golden liquid the color of the sunset. Judas handed the knife and bottle to Cain, who repeated the process. Then Goliath and Solomon. Trigger was next, then the bottle and knife moved around the room. Most of the men remained macho and stoic, a few winced as the knife ran over their flesh. Shots had the dude next to him cut him with the knife and dripped the blood into the bottle. When one of the Prospects ribbed him about it, he glared.

"So I don't like looking at my own blood! I like looking at yours just fine and I'm happy to make you bleed out that big fucking honker on your face, Paulie."

When the bottle and knife got to the Prospects, Judas held up his hand. "You guys deserve to become patched members. You held your own yesterday, protected what we hold sacred, and that is good enough for me. But, you can leave now free of retribution. You aren't tied to the Club yet. But if you do this, it's for life. It's a bond tighter than that of marriage. Of mother and child. We are bonded for life, and you only leave when you retire out, or when you die. Today aside, there is no out."

Both Stevie and Paulie looked nervous, but neither left. I kind of felt proud of the Prospects. We'd bonded the last time we were in this room together. Stevie slid his eyes to me. "Nah, I'm good. I wanna patch in. I want to be in Damnation for life." A small smile curled Judas' lips and he gave a nod. "You Paulie?"

The other Prospect didn't have Stevie's eloquence. "Yeah. Patch me in."

Solomon was grinning like a proud Mama, and even Goliath had a contented look on his face. Not a smile, but not his normal scowl either. May as well be a cheesy grin from the Enforcer.

"Give me your left hands." They both held out their hands, though Paulie stopped to think about which one was left for a beat, and Judas grabbed the knife from the table. He sliced both their hands, and Paulie bit his lip at the pain. Guess he hadn't had twenty years to dull himself to the sensation like the rest of the members.

"Paul Joseph Hutchins, do you swear to uphold the values of the Club?"

Paulie nodded. "I do."

Judas ran the knife along his palm again, the first cut having already healed but I hoped no one else had noticed that fact. He reached out and grabbed Paulie's bleeding hand with his own in a handshake. "May you ride into Damnation with your Brothers at your back. Welcome to the Club." He turned to Stevie. "Steven John Hutchins, do you swear to uphold the values of the Club?"

I had no idea that Stevie and Paulie were related. Brothers? Cousins? Stevie nodded. "I do."

Judas repeated the handshake and the oath. Then he handed them both the bottle of tequila and they dripped a drop or two of blood into the liquid that was now ruby red.

Judas took back the bottle and looked around the room. "Today is a day to celebrate. To strengthen the bonds of Brotherhood that are so important to us all. We have lost two members, but have gained two more.

Each and every one of you is important to me. I take your blood into my body, making us more than a Club. It makes us kin."

With that, he sucked back a swig of the tequila and I resisted the urge to dry heave. Gross. Paulie looked like he wanted to throw up, and given where most of these guys had been, god knows what diseases they had. Eesh.

The bottle went around the room once more, each of them drinking a swig of tainted tequila until it was back at the Prospects again.

They each took a swig, and Paulie looked like he wanted to puke, but he kept it down.

Judas finally smiled, his good eye crinkling at the corners. "I'm so proud to be your President," he said softly. "Now, let's get out there and clean up this place, so we can trash it again having the biggest fucking blow-out that Damnation MC has ever seen." He slammed the gavel back down on the table. "Church closed."

They all hooted and yelled, racing out of the door of the room. Judas came over, holding out his hand to help me up from the chair. I took it, smiling softly. "I haven't said thank you yet," I said in a low voice for his ears only. "I'm alive because of you."

Judas shook his head. "No. You are alive because of Hope. We just provided a convenient battleground."

"I saw Goliath. He definitely wasn't standing back letting Hope have all the fun."

Judas gave me a rare smile. Two in two minutes? Must have been a record. "Goliath enjoys a battle more than anything."

I looked around the room, realizing everyone but Judas, Cain, Solomon and Goliath had left. "Because he's one of the Horsemen of the Apocalypse. You all are." It wasn't a question.

Goliath glared at Solomon, who held up his hands. "Don't look at me. Trigger let it slip."

Judas' head whipped to the blond biker. "How the fuck does Trigger know?"

"Smoke told him. Apparently he figured it out before he retired out. Let Trig in on the secret."

Goliath growled. "He's known all this time?"

Cain shrugged. "Yeah. Apparently he's been creating us contingency plans for when we need to disappear for awhile."

Goliath swore, and Judas sighed. "I need a fucking drink."

19

"This was a terrible fucking idea."

I looked over at Judas as we watched Cain try and teach Dippy to ride a bike in the parking lot of the Club. She'd sputtered and bunny-hopped her way around in a circle, as Cain stood in the center and tried to coach her through changing gears with a panicked look on his face.

Judas was right, this was a terrible fucking idea, but I didn't have the heart to stop it. As she rode around in jerky circles, she was laughing and smiling and she looked so fucking happy. Miserable and scared Sera was gorgeous, but this creature? She fucking glowed.

It was almost painful to watch how beautiful she was. It was hard to work out how much was her half angel nature and how much was being pregnant. It had been nearly a week since they'd come for her, a week of walking on eggshells, waiting for the blowback. But there was nothing. Cain was even talking about reopening the tattoo parlor next week.

Goliath was beginning to pace the walls of his self-imposed cage, and I knew that one was about to explode in all our faces. We all knew that she didn't need to stay now. The threat of Uriel was nullified, and there were only the vague warnings of some zealot organization named Tenebrae. But as the time went on, and nothing happened, it seemed like even that wasn't much of a threat any longer. Judas had said that Hope and her, uh, consorts were mopping up Tenebrae.

The bottom line was that Dippy could leave whenever she liked. She didn't need us any more. Even the thought of her leaving us behind made my chest ache.

The bike wobbled, and Cain lurched toward Dippy, catching the handlebars. Luckily, he was faster and stronger than any human or she would have ended up on her ass. Finally, it was too much for Judas.

"That's enough for one day before she cracks her fucking skull!" he yelled, and Sera flipped him the bird but she was laughing as she did it. I watched his face soften and the fist around my heart eased a little. He wouldn't let her go either, even if he wouldn't admit it to himself. He wanted her. Cain and I wanted her. Goliath *needed* her.

That was it. She was staying.

"We should take her for a ride. Just the four of us," I said softly. "Go to that little seafood shack out past the lake."

"Why?" he rumbled, his voice low as Cain and Dippy walked toward us.

"So we can convince her to stay."

He didn't say anything else and when Dippy bounded up to us, I wrapped her in my arms. "You're a natural. You'll be a better rider than the Prospects before you even know it."

Cain punched me in the shoulder. "They aren't Prospects anymore."

I rolled my eyes. "Until they come up with names better than Bear and Goose, I'm going to keep calling them Prospects."

Judas turned away, muttering about fucking geese. We walked toward the back entrance of the Clubhouse, and Judas paused with his hand on the door. "We'll go for a ride tonight. Just the four of us. Be ready by six."

With that, he disappeared into the darkness of the hallway. I couldn't help the shit eating grin that lit my face. I'd been right! He did want her.

Cain leaned over and kissed her lazily. "I told Paulie, I mean uh Bear," he rolled his eyes, "that I'd help him with his bike. I'll see you tonight." It was a promise. I didn't know what they got up to at night, but I had a feeling they hadn't gone the whole way yet. I didn't know what was holding them back, but I wasn't sure I had the same scruples. My balls ached just being in the same vicinity as her.

I grabbed her hand, pulling her toward my room. "Sol, slow down," she said laughing, running while holding her belly. If I could run backwards and hold her belly for her I would, just so she'd go faster and I could enact my master plan. As it was, I turned and grinned at her over my shoulder. "What are you up to? I don't trust that grin one little bit."

I was kind of making it up on the fly, but she didn't know that so I pulled out the old faithful, "It's a surprise."

Yeah, a surprise to us both. I just needed to get her alone for a bit. Just Dippy and me. I needed to be able to woo her so she'd never want to leave me. Leave us.

We finally made it to the door of my room, and I wondered if stripping off her clothes and fucking her until we both forgot our names was enough of a surprise? It was certainly my favorite kind.

I shifted my eyes to the left, my eyes falling on the door to my bathroom. Hell yeah. "Wait here."

I ran into the bathroom and turned on the taps to the freestanding tub. It was my one luxury. The thing was huge, because I was not exactly compact in size. It took forever to fill but it was worth it.

I poured in some of this flowery bath shit, because I

liked fucking bubbles and they don't come in manly scents. Like men don't like fucking baths.

I walked back out, and Dippy was walking around my room, looking at my stuff. I didn't care. I wanted her to know everything about me, because I wanted to know everything about her. She'd paused in front of my dresser, picking up a photo frame that was face down on the polished wooden top. It probably looked like it had fallen over, but it hadn't. I just couldn't look at it, but it felt wrong to put it away in a drawer. Instead, I sat it up there and looked at it occasionally for penance.

I didn't need to see the photo inside the frame though; it was permanently etched into my mindseye. I walked over and stood close to her anyway, breathed her scent in, let it soothe the raw wounds that still weeped inside me.

It was a photo of a woman with a gummy baby in her arms. She was surrounded by four men, Judas and Goliath on either side of her, Cain and I behind her. Only that wasn't our names then. We were all smiling at the camera, and the woman between us was smiling widest of all. God we were so fucking happy.

"Who is she?" Dippy asked softly, and I swallowed hard. This wasn't what I had in mind when I said a surprise.

Ah, fuck. "Come on. I ran you a bath. This shit is better talked about surrounded by bubbles."

Dippy looked once more at the photo, and nodded. It wasn't just seeing Laura that was the hard part about staring at the photo. It was looking at my Brothers and knowing how they would never be that happy again. It hurt my heart so much.

I grabbed Dippy's hand, and gave her a sad smile. Well, never say never. Cain certainly seemed happy. The other two would get there too, if they just got out of their own damn way.

I led her into the bathroom, glad I'd cleaned it up the day before. The water was almost done, the water a couple of inches below the rim.

"Woah. I think I'm in love." She started stripping off her clothes at an alarming rate. Her shirt went over her shoulder, and she struggled out of her yoga pants.

I knelt on the ground, slipping her shoes off her feet, then her socks. She rested her hands on my shoulders as I peeled her pants over her ankles and off her feet until she stood in front of me in nothing but her underwear.

Fuck. She was so fucking beautiful. I ran my hands up her long, tanned legs. They weren't perfectly smooth, because shaving your legs pregnant is a tough ask. But I didn't care. They were the highway to exactly where I wanted to be. I slid my hands to the outsides of her thighs, missing the apex of her body as much as I wanted to bury my face there and never come up for air. I let my thumbs

brush over the round, firmness of her stomach, then I
stood.

"Dippy, I'm going to kiss you."

She let out a relieved sigh. "Thank God."

I wasn't sure we were allowed to say that anymore,
but I still kissed her. Tiny, sipping kisses at first,
sucking her lip between mine gently. But she wanted
more, increasing the pressure and deepening the kiss,
and I was more than happy to give it to her. I'd give her
whatever she wanted. I trailed my fingers down her
spine, and she shivered into me.

My dick was now rock hard and I swallowed down
my moan. I tore my lips away. "This isn't your surprise.
Get in the bath before I remember I'm a fucking biker
and not a gentleman."

She laughed at me, and I turned away as she
stripped off her remaining clothing. Again, not
because I was a gentleman, but because I had shit
fucking self-control. If I saw her naked, I'd have her
propped up on my vanity and fucking the hell out of
her in 3.5 seconds.

I heard her contented sigh, and knew I made the
right decision. She needed to be treated like a fucking
Queen. I needed her to stay. This was just step one.

I turned around and she was surrounded in
bubbles, the bath so deep the water touched her chin.

"Oh Sol, this feels so good." She bent her knees and
dipped her head beneath the water, her hair fanning

around her head like a mermaid. When she came back up, bubbles dripped from her chin. "I think I'm going to live in this bath," she said, leaning back and resting her head on the edge of the tub.

I smiled softly, sitting beside the tub near her head. "Hopefully there's room for two, because I love it too." I rested my head back against the tub, the tips of my hair getting wet.

She reached out damp, warm fingers and stroked them through my hair. "Always room for you," she said softly. "Want to tell me about her?"

No. I didn't really. I wanted the past to remain the past. But I would tell her, because I wanted Serendipity to be a part of my future. I sucked in a deep breath.

"Her name was Laura. She'd been my best friend since I was six when she moved next door to my mother's house. We lived in a shitty part of town, filled with drug deals and fucking drive-bys, but she was this little ray of sunshine. I even remember the first time I saw her in her front yard. She wore this bright orange dress, and had a doll that looked like it came out of a dumpster. But she had the biggest smile, and it was the first time I ever thought that a girl was anything but a cootie factory." I huffed out a laugh at the memory. Seeing her had been a revelation. "I'd decided then and there that we should be friends, so I went around to her house and told her parents we were going to be friends. I was this dirty, underfed kid, and I think they felt sorry for me, because they sent us out the back to play. That was it for me. I loved her."

Laura had been everything to me from that point on. "Eventually, we went through elementary and high school together. It was like the plot line of a cheesy teen movie. I pined for her from afar, but fucked anything that walked. She'd tease the shit out of me, and kiss all the jocks. The guys who were the opposite of me. I had a bad attitude and a fucking chip on my shoulder the size of the continental US. Laura got caught up in my bullshit all the damn time, but it didn't stop me. We'd sneak into bars, clubs, we'd party all night. But we always went home together. I always made sure she was safe." I clenched my jaw. Yeah. Safe. Except when it fucking counted.

"Anyway, one day I decided we would party at a local biker bar. No bouncers in a fucking biker bar. I thought it would be fine. I would protect her against any fights that broke out. I thought I was fucking king shit, but I was just a dumb kid. Fuck, I wish so bad we'd never gone to that damn bar. Because a fight didn't break out. What happened was even worse. She met Judas, and there was more chemistry between those two than a science lab explosion. Judas was the son of the MC's Vice President. He had this big fucking friend, Goliath, and before I knew it, Judas had whisked Laura off her feet. They started dating, and we started going to that bar more and more."

I shook my head. "We went so often I'd eventually become a Prospect, just so I could hang around. They dated for years. We graduated, but neither of us went off to college. Laura because she'd fallen in love with Judas, and me because I refused to leave the one woman I loved above all else buried in an old school MC where women were more property than people."

As I spoke, Dippy's fingers traced up and down my forehead, down over my cheeks, as if she was memorizing my face. "Eventually, I wanted to patch in so I could keep an eye on her. Besides, I'd gotten kind of fond of Judas and Goliath. The other Prospect that year was this fucking young ass punk tattooist who thought he was king shit too, and built like a fucking brick house. Cain. Same year we patched in, Judas proposed."

A small smile curled my lips when I remembered that moment. "Laura said no. I don't know who was more shocked at that moment. Me or Judas. Goliath was beginning to watch her like she was the fucking sun, and Cain doted on her like she was his. Anyway, Laura said she loved Judas, but a part of her heart belonged to me. I'm pretty sure my heart stopped beating when she said those words. But then she added that she had feelings for Goliath and Cain too. It was a fucking mess."

Those few months were fucking nuts. I'd already patched into the Club, my loyalty was supposed to be to them first and foremost. But everyone knew that my loyalty was to only one person. To Laura. "But Judas, he loved her more than himself. More than the Club. More than his Old Man, who threatened to disown him if he chased 'the whore'. His dad was a piece of shit."

Fuck, I'd hated that old bastard. When he'd died not long after Laura had turned Judas' marriage proposal down, it had seemed like fate. I rested my arm along the edge of the tub, and tilted my head back until I was almost hanging upside down. Almost all my hair was wet now.

"Anyway, Judas took the Presidency. He'd been groomed for it, and it only took a few beatdowns to get the job. Once he was Pres, he made Goliath his enforcer. Back then he was mean, but he wasn't a monster yet. Judas and Goliath beat the shit out of me and Cain, then Judas told us that he was going back to propose to Laura, and that if she wanted to love us too, then he'd allow it."

Fuck, that was funny as hell now, but it hurt like a bitch at the time. Goliath threatened to gut us if we so much as made her cry once. I'd believed him too.

"She'd said yes, and we'd all moved into one big house, and lived a moderately happily ever after for a few years. There were fights sure, more than a few slammed doors and black eyes, but eventually we were so fucking happy. Then she got pregnant, and had Max and I thought I was going to burst with how perfect my life was."

I swallowed hard. God, even though it was so long ago now, sometimes I missed Laura like an ache in my soul. I wasn't trying to replace Laura with Serendipity; how I felt about them was completely different but the end result was the same.

"Then it all went bad. Laura died. So did the baby. And we were no longer the men we were. We became the men you know now. Her death, their death, it broke us." My voice was shaky, and that huge dead lump in my chest ached at the memory of that pain.

I tensed, waiting for the inevitable question, and Dippy didn't leave me waiting for long. "How did they die?"

I shook my head then, shifting until I was kneeling so she could see my eyes. "That's not my story to tell. Needless to say it was tragic and violent and it was the death of everything good in the world for so, so long. But not anymore."

I leaned forward and kissed her because I needed to kiss her more than I needed to breathe. She kissed me back, her hands fisting the front of my shirt as she pulled me closer. I kissed her like her lips could chase away the painful memories. She pulled me closer, until I slid into the bath with her, the denim of my jeans instantly clinging tightly to my legs. I didn't care.

I moaned as I thrust my tongue into her mouth,

settling my body between her thighs and holding myself up on the edges of the bath. Her back arched so she could kiss me back with just as much heat. Fuck, so much heat it was a wonder the water wasn't boiling us both. Her hands gripped the back of my rapidly dampening shirt, her nails digging into my shoulders and one of her ankles hooking around my thigh to pull me harder into the sweet spot between her legs.

My cock was hard as a rock, and that was basically torture in wet denim, but there was no way I was going to stop. I slid my hand down her collarbone, down further until I was cupping her heavy breasts in my hand. We both moaned. Shit, her tits were glorious.

I pulled my lips from hers and moved my mouth down to where my fingers were currently gently tweaking her nipples. The way she writhed under me almost had me creaming my fucking boxers already, but I gritted my teeth and took that sensitive bud in my mouth and sucked hard.

She nearly rocketed out of the bath, but her hand came up to twist her fingers in my hair, holding me where she wanted me. Funny, it's where I wanted me too. Just to torture us both a little more, I ground my hips into her pussy and she moaned so loudly I was pretty sure someone was going to burst in here thinking I was trying to murder her.

So I did it again. It was the sweetest damn sound in the world and I could listen to it all day every day.

Switching to her other nipple, because I was an equal opportunity boob lover, I smoothed my hand down over her hip and then between our bodies. My fingers brushed gently over her clit, and she gasped like she'd been electrocuted.

"Sol," she moaned in that deep, whispy voice that made me so fucking rock hard. "Please," she whined, and I swirled my tongue around the hard bud of her nipple.

"Don't worry, Sweetheart. I'm going to take real good care of you." To make good on my promise, I stroked that sweet little nub in gentle circles and her whine echoed around the room. I wanted to bury my face between her thighs, but there was just no space. Soon. Soon I'd taste her on my tongue. Instead, I slid my fingers between her slick folds, and slid one finger inside her.

We both moaned this time. I wanted it to be my cock so bad, but I slid it in and out, making sure to hit her sweet spots before I added another finger, and her moans turned into pants as she gripped my head to her breast harder. "Yes!"

I stroked and sucked her body like I owned it, as if it was my instrument to play and I knew just how it liked to be played.

When her body tightened around my fingers, she cried out and her body clenched around my fingers.

Gripping my hair hard, she pulled my head back

towards her face and I happily obliged. Kissing those beautiful lips was never a hardship. "Sol, I want you to fuck me."

I'm pretty sure my thought processes flatlined at her words, and the only coherent thought in my mind tripped over my tongue.

"Yes!"

Paulie was either hungover as hell, or getting the flu, and either way I didn't want him in my garage, banging around on my tools and dropping shit.

"Kid, go to bed. Come back when you can see out of your bloodshot eyes, hey?"

Paulie grimaced, but didn't protest, which let me know that he was probably sick. He was a good kid. He didn't shirk his responsibilities to the Club, never cut corners so he could start the party early. He was methodical, honest and he'd be a great member.

I locked up the shop now that the strip club had opened its doors, because some people are stupid enough to steal from a criminal organization that enjoys beating people into mush. I strolled across the asphalt, watching the sun dip below the roofs of the surrounding buildings. I pushed through the front door of the Clubhouse, waving at a few of the guys who raised their chins in greeting. I couldn't see Sera, or my Brothers. Everyone was apparently getting ready for the ride tonight.

I took the stairs two at a time. I wanted to change out of my work clothes, but I'd check that Sera didn't need anything first. Honestly, I just wanted to see her. If that made me fucking whipped, then so be it.

I was a few steps from Sol's door when I heard a groan of pain. Shit. Something was wrong. I wrenched the door open, and then stopped.

Sera was naked on the bed, and Sol had his face buried between her thighs.

Oh. Not pain then. They both turned to look as the door slammed against the wall. "Oops?"

"Get in here and shut the door, dickhead," Sol growled and then went back to lapping his tongue against Sera's center. Holy fuck.

Sera held my gaze for a little longer, the heat in her expression making me hard as steel, before she threw her head back against the pillows and let out another guttural moan. Her hands fisted in the blankets, her face screwed up in a way that made me want to get naked and slip my cock between her lips. She let out a gasping scream as she came, and she was the most perfect thing I'd ever laid eyes on.

Sol was still in his jeans, though they were

completely soaked and sticking to his legs. They creaked as he sat up onto his knees.

"Either get naked or get out," Sol tossed over his shoulder as he attempted to remove his pants. "Fuck this shit, it's going to take me ten years to get out of these. Someone get me my knife," he grumped and Sera laughed, the light sound wrapping around my heart.

Luckily for us all, I wasn't even a little bit damp and I was naked in the time it took me to be across the room and pressed along the length of Sera's naked body. I looked down at her beautiful violet eyes. "Hey," I whispered against her lips, taking tiny, sipping kisses. "Is this okay?"

She bit her lip and frowned. "Two hot bikers in bed with me? Hmm. I'll have to think about it." She slapped my arm and grinned. "Yes, I'm okay with it."

I MIGHT HAVE THANKED Satan himself in that moment as I took her mouth with mine and pressed my body as close to hers as physically possible. Sol had her primed to perfection, but I couldn't help but trace my hand down her body and feel how wet she was for myself.

I shifted my eyes down, and they caught on the large round globe of her stomach. I paused unintentionally.

"Is it too weird for you? It's okay, I understand," she

whispered against my cheek, and I shook my head. No, she was beautiful. Besides, I'd been around long enough to know general human anatomy. We wouldn't hurt the baby having sex. I wasn't going to give it nightmares because it could see my dick aiming for its forehead or any of that rubbish.

Sera had needs that I could meet, and I sure as fuck was happy to meet every single one of them.

So I bit her lip and growled, "No fucking way." Then I plunged my fingers inside her, making her arch against my palm. Hell yeah. But as much as I didn't care that she was pregnant, it would mean a bit of different maneuvering. I rolled onto my back, pulling her with me until she was straddling my hips. She ground against my dick and we both let out a guttural sound. I slid my hand between us, holding my cock as she slid down onto me and I found fucking heaven.

She was so hot and wet, and when she ground against me, I almost came like a fucking teenage boy. I bit the inside of my cheek, placing my hands on her hips and I coaxed her back off my cock so I could bury myself again.

"Cain," she said in a gasping sigh as I buried myself in her again and again. Sol appeared beside us, naked as the fucking day he was born.

I had no interest in his dick beside my head, but the way Sera was looking at him like he was fucking candy stopped me from protesting as he stepped closer and kissed her. And when she clenched around my cock, squeezing me, I didn't give a shit if the asshole took up permanent real estate beside my face.

As she kissed Sol, my hands moved her up and down on my cock, her glorious tits bouncing. Her body felt like it was made for mine. Made for us.

Actually...

I lifted her hips and slid out of her, ignoring her sad mewling noise. "Spin around, Baby. I feel bad I'm taking advantage of all of Solomon's hard work." I helped her shift around so she was sitting on my abs, reverse cowgirl style. I guided my cock back to her entrance, and she pushed back into me like she couldn't wait to have me inside her again.

Her ass was as glorious as her tits. The long line of her back, the gentle curl of her golden hair.

Fucking sweet jesus. She leaned forward and took Sol's cock between her lips, and I started to pant as I kept thrusting up into her, moving her hips, finding that perfect rhythm that had her moaning around the cock in her mouth.

Everytime she moaned, Sol's eyes rolled back into his head. So I made it my mission to make her come as quickly as possible and see if I could get him to pass out. It'd keep me distracted enough that I didn't blow my load like some kind of two-pump-chump.

When Sol's hand slid down and flicked against her clit, she squeezed me so hard that it was a wonder I didn't come on the spot. Fuck, he was playing dirty. I ground harder, deeper, and he continued to thumb her clit until she was coming around my cock, and I was roaring down that beautiful damn rabbit hole with her. I unleashed deep inside, and it was so perfectly right, that I forgot how to breath.

Sol had his fingers curled in Sera's hair as he thrust his cock into her mouth, and she moaned even as her body shook from the aftershocks of her orgasm. When she reached up and rolled his balls in her hand, he crumbled like any red-blooded man would.

"Fuck, I'm going to come," he growled, and Sera kept running her mouth up and down his cock like she loved it. He stilled her head and roared, coming in her mouth. When she looked up at him and swallowed, I almost came again.

She was so damn perfect.

I gently slid her off my dick and laid her down beside me. Curling my body around her back, Sol slid beside her front. His hand on her hip, their legs entwined.

She wiggled against my dick, and I let out a groan, putting my hand on her hip to still her. "Stop that or I'll be back inside you again."

She looked over her shoulder at me. "You say that like it's a bad thing."

She was going to be the fucking death of me. "It's the best thing ever. But Pres said we have a night ride, and I want you on the back of my bike." She wiggled again and I moaned. "Nah, on second thoughts, fuck it. Let's stay home."

She laughed but stopped wiggling. "Don't want to piss off Judas. He's scary when he's grumpy."

Sol laughed. "You aren't fucking wrong."

She ran a hand down Solomon's bicep. "Sol?"

He kissed her forehead, his eyes a little droopy. "Mmm?"

"I gotta tell you something." He quirked a brow. "I'm seeing Cain behind your back."

She grinned at him, and the way he smiled softly back at her, I was pretty sure he was a goner. His heart was hers now. He met my eyes over her shoulder. "Ah, Dippy? Pretty sure I'm seeing Cain behind your back. Pretty sure I'm about to see him dry hump your ass."

I flipped him the bird, but I was smiling so widely my face hurt. Sharing Sera with him was right. It felt right in my soul. Like she had been hand delivered by the Ghost of Laura, or fate or the universe, just for the four of us.

But Judas and Goliath weren't going to be easily swayed. Didn't matter. I would love her enough for ten men.

The baby kicked beneath my hand, and Sera winced, looking down at her stomach. "Don't worry about it, kid. Not like I needed my liver anyway." She sighed deeply. "As much as I want to cuddle, I need to pee. And pancakes."

I laughed and kissed the back of her neck, then I shifted off the bed, watching her stand on shaky legs and head to the bathroom.

I looked at Sol and saw the same expression that was probably on my face. Awe. Fear. Dumbstruck.

"Cain..."

I nodded. "Yeah man, me too."

I pulled my clothes on, and waited until she came out of the bathroom. "I'll go have a shower in my room, maybe get changed out of these clothes before our ride. I'll see if I can get Sweetie to bring up some pancakes. Want them here or in your room?"

She looked over her shoulder at Sol, who was still lying naked on his bed, though he'd pulled a sheet up over his junk.

"I think I'll stay and have a nap here for a bit."

I leaned forward and kissed her. "A nap. Sure. Is that what we're calling it now?"

I heard the sweet sound of her laugh in my ears even after I'd shut the door to Sol's room behind me.

I stood out the front of the Clubhouse, wearing stretchy waist denim jeans, a skeleton face mask around my neck and one of Cain's oversized hoodies. There was no way leathers were going to go up over my stomach, and besides, this was big, warm and still smelled faintly of the man himself. I tilted my face to the setting sun, letting it warm my skin, a weird feeling in my chest. It might have been the baby kicking me in the lungs, but it felt an awful lot like happiness. Even thinking the word made me panic though. Happiness was just the precursor to misery in my experience

I pushed the thought away as the leader of Damnation MC rolled to a stop in front of me. Solomon was next, and I could see Cain getting on his bike where it sat in front of the workshop. Goliath was the last to

appear, staring daggers at me like this ride had been
my idea.

Uh no. I'd been quite happy pressed between two
big, sweaty, tattooed bikers. I'm pretty sure that was the
worst case scenario for a lot of women, but I enjoyed
the fuck out of it. All eyes turned to Solomon, and I
remembered he was Road Captain. Apparently, what
he said went when it came to a ride, even one this
small.

"You better ride with the Pres, Dippy. Cain has
already taken you for a ride today," he said, his half
smirk making me narrow my eyes and heat flood my
panties all at the same time. Sexy ass.

Judas narrowed his good eye at Solomon, but
shifted forward a little on his bike. Apparently, Sol's
word really was gospel on a ride. I walked gingerly
toward the Chopper that Judas rode, its body long and
sleek, its high handlebars showing off Judas' impressive biceps in his tight black tee.

He looked like a wet dream. I threw Sol another
annoyed look and lifted my leg over the leather seat,
settling myself a few inches away from his back. When
I grabbed his sides, I felt his muscles bunch under my
hands.

Judas confused the shit out of me. I couldn't work
out if he liked me or loathed me. At least I knew where
I stood with Goliath. Apart from that ill-timed kiss, he

had made his hatred of me thoroughly known. But Judas sat in the grey area.

Fuck it. Why was I worried about how Judas felt? I was one lucky bitch already. I had Cain and Solomon, and quite frankly that was enough. Things were better in twos. Two hands. Two feet. Two holes. See?

I did not need to collect the whole set.

"Let's head to that seafood place on the other side of the lake," he told Solomon, and I couldn't help it when my hands flattened out just so I could feel the rumble of his words in his chest. He tensed beneath my hands and I curled my fingers into fists, gripping his shirt. This was going to be so damn awkward. I made a mental note to punch Sol in the dick next time he was in arm's reach.

Sol grinned at me as if he knew my murderous thoughts, kicked his bike into gear and roared away. Goliath went next, then Cain. Judas and I brought up the rear. When we turned onto the freeway and the guys kicked it up a notch, I threw my arms out and laughed.

This, riding fast down the freeway, was beginning to be one of my favorite feelings. It felt like flying. Maybe my angel half enjoyed the sensation. I would never have wings, but I still yearned for them.

Judas let me fly for a moment or two more, before I heard his stern voice in the wind. "Hold on. Wouldn't want you to fall off and break your neck."

His tone said he wouldn't care either way, but I still placed my hands back on his waist. He grabbed my hand, pulling it further around him, before grabbing the other and doing the same. I had my hands wrapped around his waist, my torso pressed tight to his back, my fingertips pressed in the slight indents of his abs. I swallowed hard, glad that he couldn't see the blush on my cheeks or the lust in my eyes.

I mentally told my crazed lady-bits to get a grip, she'd just had two dicks literally hours ago. But I'm pretty sure my hormones had led a coup against my sense of reason, because all I could think about was dick.

Brushing my teeth in the morning, I wondered how much better it would be if Solomon was bending me over the sink. Putting on my yoga pants? I'd wonder if Cain would put them on for me after he ate me out like his last meal. Late at night, when the building creaked, I wondered if it was Goliath trying to sneak into my bed, to fuck me until I was nothing more than a mess of come and raw sexual need. Sitting on the back of this bike, I wondered if Judas could still ride if I took off my pants and sat on his dick.

Now I didn't have the guillotine of Uriel hanging over my head, my brain had decided to turn itself toward sluttier pursuits.

As if my body was in total agreeance with my wayward brain, I stroked my thumb over Judas' hard stomach, and felt the muscles tense in response. It could be in repulsion. It could be in lust. I might never know. Fuck it. I was riding with Cain on the way home. Solomon was on my shit list.

But when I went to move my hands back to his sides, he captured them both in his long fingers and held them on his stomach. He didn't move them the whole way, his hand covering both of mine.

I had to tell my heart to stop being a traitor.

We finally reached a weird little restaurant that looked more like someone's shack than an actual eatery. There were big, wooden bench seats out the front, just off the road, and there seemed to be more out the back which overlooked the woods. The sign on the front window said "Authentic Crawdad Boil".

An old man wandered out, in honest to goodness denim overalls, with about as many teeth as a jack-o-lantern, and grinned wide at the guys. Like they were his favorite nephews and not the leadership of the most scary MC in the State.

"Well, I'll be. What do I owe the honor of your stoppin' by?"

Solomon went over and pulled the old man into a weird man hug. "Uncle Thierry, couldn't stay away from your boil any longer."

The old man rolled his eyes, and then they landed on me. Then my stomach. "Which one of you no good *couillon* done knocked her up?" He gave each one of them the stink eye. "Remy, catch me my gun," he yelled behind him at an open window. "We'll have you married sooner than y'all boil be ready, cher."

I laughed and shook my head vigorously. "It's okay, the baby doesn't belong to any of these guys," I said, feeling a bit embarrassed for the first time ever, like I had something to be ashamed of.

Cain muttered something in Cajun then spat on the ground. The little old man nodded, almost yelling something that I could tell was cussing just from the tone, and spat on the ground too. Solomon just laughed, tucking me beneath his arm and leading me over to one of the long bench seats.

"Thierry is from Louisiana. How he ended up here, trying to dredge up a bit of the South for us Northerners, I'll never know. But I bet there was a woman involved," he whispered in my ear. The infamous Remy appeared in the doorway, holding Thierry's gun, looking confused. He must have been a grandchild, because he couldn't have been more than twenty or so. He looked around for the threat, the gun halfway to his shoulder, but when he didn't see anything, his eyes stopped on us and he grinned. He had a beautiful smile and looked nothing like his grandfather. He was all warm, tanned skin and big dark eyes.

"I don't like how you are eyeing that Cajun kid," Cain whispered in my ear and I scoffed.

"Are you kidding? I've had naps longer than he's

been walking the earth. Trust me, I have my hands full." I resisted the urge to look at Goliath and Judas. *Remember, two hands, two dicks, Sera!*

Remy turned and went back inside, Thierry following behind him, the flow and speed of his accent making it impossible for me to comprehend whatever he was saying to the boy. But when Remy reappeared, a big tub of beers and soda in his hands, I got the general gist. He gave the guys a respectful nod and grinned at me. He was cute. Way too young, but sweet all the same.

"I'm still gonna join when I turn twenty-one," he told Judas, his eyes bright with intelligence, and if I knew humans, mischief. "Only one year to go."

Judas stared at the kid, then grinned and shook his head. "Thierry really will take his gun to us then, Kid."

Remy laid down some newspaper on the table, placing four shiny stones on each corner of the paper. "Naw, he likes you guys. Even though, you know, you are all scary as fuck. I'm pretty sure he thinks he could still take you."

Goliath laughed this time, and I startled at the noise. I'd never heard him laugh. I hadn't heard him sound anything but cold or filled with rage. I must have been staring at him like he was an alien, because his eyes met mine and the mirth slid right from his face. Yeah. Maybe he laughed a lot when I wasn't around.

I dropped my eyes to the newsprint on the table in front of us, tuning everyone out as they talked to the kid. I chewed my lip, and wondered if I should move on. The thought made my heart ache, the idea of not seeing Cain and Sol anymore was like a punch to the chest. Maybe I could get an apartment close by. Still in Damnation Territory. I didn't want to make Goliath, and even Judas, uncomfortable in their own home.

I tensed my jaw and nodded to myself. I'd start looking when I got back to the Clubhouse. It's not like I could have raised a baby in a Clubhouse for outlaw bikers anyway. It didn't matter the thought of leaving the place made me feel almost sad. It had felt more like home than any place in a century. It had little to do with the four walls, and more to do with the people inside.

I looked up and noticed Judas watching me. Remy had scuttled off to bus the tables.

Judas saw too much, like he was mining my eyes for secrets. I was waiting for the day that he laid them all out for everyone else to see.

I cleared my throat. "How'd you guys find this place?"

"Remy's Dad used to ride with us. Died when a gang banger robbed him on the street. Thierry took the kid in, and we made a point to eat here as often as we could. We also pay a bit of every score into a trust for Remy for when he turns twenty-one, in case he wants to go to college or something," Cain says, nuzzling my hair. I smile softly up at him, and fall into the warm pools of his eyes. So damn hot.

He must have seen the look on my face, because he leaned in close and nipped my earlobe. A full-body shiver ran through my limbs and my horniness ratched up to one thousand. "You keep looking at me like that, babe, and I am going to lay you across this bench and eat you instead."

I could feel the flush on my cheeks burn over the rest of my face, and dropped my eyes to my hands and breathed through the huge wave of lust that seemed to flow through my body and pool in my lady-bits.

I refused to look up until the conversation had moved on to bike parts and gossip. Yeah, dudes gossiped like girls. Don't let them tell you otherwise. Even big fucking bikers. When I decided that enough time had passed, I looked up so I could rejoin the conversation, but I got caught straight in the tractor beam of Goliath's glare. His nostrils flared and his eyes were dead. But his tongue slipped past his lip, the pink tip darting out to wet his full lower lip. I wanted to chase that tongue with my teeth.

He startled a little at my gaze, and we were both saved by Thierry coming over to tip a huge pot of cray-fish, shrimp, corn, potatoes and sausage onto our newspaper covered table. My mouth watered at the smell of the spices wafting up with the steam. A big basket of crusty bread, as well as melted butter, Tabasco and lemon came over too.

"Eat Dippy. You look like you're about to orgasm over there and I'm kind of jealous of the dead crustaceans right now," Sol teased.

Heat lit up my cheeks, but I didn't argue. When Cain asked if pregnant women should even eat seafood, I may have actually growled like a damn animal.

They leaned back and laughed, drinking beer and picking at the huge feast in front of us. After I'd eaten nearly my body weight in shellfish, I sat back and watched their dynamic. They were Brothers, that much was obvious. Even Goliath looked at them with something that resembled fondness. It softened his face when he wasn't staring daggers. Judas chatted and joked, but he rarely ever smiled. Luckily, Sol laughed enough for all four of them combined. Cain peeled my shrimp for me, his eyes never leaving whoever was speaking, but he would peel himself one, then one for me, and so on. I don't know why that made me want to cry, but it did.

When all the food was gone, and the sun had left the sky and the shack was lit up by string lights and flood lights on poles, we got up to leave. Judas left two hundred bucks under one of the plates, and we waved at Thierry and his grandson on the way back to the bikes. As the night breeze picked up, I shivered and

Cain tucked me under his arm. I snuggled in further. "Can I ride back with you?"

The look he gave me was pure sex, and it heated my body right through. But he shook his head. "Sol is in charge of these things. If he says you ride with the Pres, that's where you gotta ride, Babe."

I huffed, narrowing my eyes at him. Solomon gave me another shit-eating grin, and I suddenly got why everyone was always smacking him about. I moved over to Judas' bike, and climbed on not at all gracefully. I was pregnant, had just eaten a shit ton of food, and there was no way I wasn't going to need to pee twice on the way home. Still, I strapped my helmet on, pulled up my facemask and placed my hands on Judas' sides.

But when he pulled them until they wrapped around his middle again, I was glad he couldn't see my smile.

22

JUDAS

I probably could have overruled Solomon when he told Serendipity she had to get on my bike. But I didn't. And I didn't want to fucking examine why I didn't. I probably didn't need a shrink to tell me that I'd enjoyed the feel of her arms around me. That her laughter when she spread her arms wide and pretended to fly had made my chest feel tight with wanting.

I also didn't examine why I made her wrap her arms around me again on the way back. I told myself that it was for her safety, but that was bullshit. I'd had other Club members ride bitch with me before, and I never insisted on hugging it the fuck out. I forced my body to chill beneath her hands, to relax like her holding me meant nothing. I focused on the feel of the road beneath my bike, the traffic around us, my three Brothers in front of us.

After a few miles, I'd relaxed into the ride for real. Until she slid her hand down my abs, closer to the button of my jeans. My body went rigid, and the wandering hands stopped, moving back up to a safer spot.

I didn't think, didn't reason, just pushed her hand back down so it could continue its exploration. I sucked in a gasp when her hands moved underneath my t-shirt, her soft fingers playing along my stomach. It simultaneously tickled and made my dick hard. Her nails followed the light dusting of hair that moved further down towards my cock. When her fingers paused again, foiled by the button of my jeans, I traced my own fingers over hers, shifting them out of the way while I popped the button on my jeans. I didn't think. Didn't reason. Pushed all the guilt down into a little box that I was sure would fucking explode later. Because when her hand slipped into my boxers and freed my cock, I almost ran off the fucking road.

Maybe this wasn't such a great idea. When her hand slid beneath my boxers and grabbed my dick, it didn't matter what kind of idea it was because I was helpless to stop it. She literally had me by the cock. Her cheek rested against the gap between my shoulder blades, warming my skin. When she stroked my cock in her tiny fist, I swerved a little and gritted my teeth, white knuckle gripping my handlebars as she began to stroke at a leisurely pace. Fuck!

She held it tightly, her thumb brushing the sensitive head, her pace increasing. Sweet jesus, I was going to cum all over myself in a minute. When her other hand moved into my pants to cup my balls, I groaned so loud that I heard her satisfied chuckle behind me. She knew what she was doing to me, and I gritted my teeth as her pulls got faster and rougher. I felt her stiffen, but I was too caught up in the sensation of her hands on me and the road in front of me. She continued to stroke me, rolling my balls in her hands.

"Fuck," I growled. "I'm going to come." I didn't know if she'd hear it over the bike, but she must have gotten the gist because she pulled up my shirt, not skipping a beat until I was coming all over my stomach in hard spurts.

I swallowed hard, waiting for the blood rushing in my ears to subside. She gently pulled down my shirt and tucked my dick back in my pants. Finally, I had my shit back under control enough to look around. I hadn't noticed Goliath drop back a bit, but by the way he was staring at Dippy like she was the antichrist and I was actually my namesake, I was going to gather that he'd seen the whole fucking thing. Damn. Fuck.

Dippy must have felt my body tense, and she went to move her hands away again, her own body stiffening. This shit was so damn hard. I gripped her wrist, and pulled her hand back around, placing it on my thigh and covering it with my own. I would put it back around my waist, but then we'd both be covered in jizz.

Goliath roared off, overtaking Cain and Solomon, breaking protocol, and I knew I'd pay for this later. But right now, I couldn't find it in myself to give a shit. Cain looked over his shoulder, confused, and I was glad I didn't still have my dick out. I'd have to explain later, and I wasn't looking forward to the smug, I-told-you-so look from Solomon, but he'd been right. I did have feelings for the woman.

I'd just have to work out if I wanted to do anything about it.

WE RODE the rest of the way home like that, and I let out a relieved sigh when I pulled into the Club parking lot and saw Goliath's bike. I was worried he'd go off the rails, go on a killing spree and Damnation would have to clean up his mess again. But he'd come home, and I was so fucking thankful.

I slid off the bike, the cum on my stomach crusted to my body hair, pulling painfully as I moved. Son of a bitch.

Dippy laughed, and I scowled at her. I held out my hand to help her off the bike, and she climbed off with shaky legs. Her cheeks were flushed and she couldn't look me in the eye, and it was awkward as fuck. I hated that. So I did the only thing I knew would solve the problem, other than laying her on the fucking asphalt and letting her ride me like a Fat Boy. I leaned forward and kissed her softly. I tried to express all the tender emotions I wasn't sure I was still capable of feeling in that kiss.

I moved back and looked down at her. "I need to find Goliath."

She looked so lost, yet so beautiful in the red neon lights from the strip club and I wanted nothing more than take her upstairs and fuck her until we both couldn't walk tomorrow.

But I had to find Goliath. I had an obligation to my Brother. I kissed her once more, this kiss far more of a promise than anything else. It was hotter, a vow that this wasn't the end.

I just hoped I had the follow-through.

I walked around the back of the Clubhouse, ignoring Cain's confused look and Solomon's knowing grin. I knew where Goliath would be, and I had to mentally prepare myself for the state he'd be in.

He wanted her. Dippy. We could both see it, no matter how much we denied it to ourselves. But it would be hitting Goliath harder. He had killed off that part of himself, the part that wanted to treat women as anything more than a glorified fuck-toy. The part of himself that *wanted* anything, other than the kill.

I walked past the back door to another single door at the side. It went down to the cellar, though we didn't keep beer kegs there. It was a wet room, and the things we did down here were very... wet. Easier to scrub down and bleach when we needed to have a conversation with a rat. A place to remove body parts, keep crying kidnap victims, stash drugs.

This was the nucleus of everything bad about the Club, and at the epicenter of that was Goliath.

He was naked, his body shadowed with hours and hours of ink. His back heaved as he punched the heavy brick wall repeatedly. His knuckles were already a mess. I noticed he had a make-shift cilice around his thigh, barbed-wire twisted around until it pressed tightly into his skin. It was something he hadn't done in a decade. I wasn't dumb enough to think he'd stopped using it because he'd gotten better; he'd abandoned it because we'd come to another agreement.

"G," I said in a low, rough voice, and his hand stilled.

He shook his head, still not turning to look at me. "I don't want to fucking talk. If that's what you're here for, then just get the fuck out." He punched the wall again, over and over again.

His shoulders were so taut, it was a wonder that his muscles didn't snap under his skin. "Stop. We won't talk."

I'd loved Goliath almost as much as I'd loved

Laura. We'd been childhood friends, who grew into more. Being bisexual in a fucking MC Club had been fucking torture, but we'd had each other and kept it a secret. When Laura had come along and accepted us, it had been a fucking revelation and we'd loved her the more for it. When she loved us both, it was like it was meant to be.

When she'd died, it had killed us all, but I'd buried my best friend in the ground that day too, left only with this angry demon who wanted blood and pain all the time. For a decade, we'd had nothing but self-loathing and pain. That had morphed into whatever the fuck we had now, but as much as I knew it was unhealthy, I couldn't live without it.

I shed my clothes until we were both standing there naked, Goliath's chest heaving, the dead pools of his eyes telling me the darkness was riding him hard.

The darkness in my own soul rose to meet it. I stepped closer, appreciating the hard as fuck bulk of his body like I did every time. He was a fucking beautiful weapon. Then I pushed against his chest with two hands, sending him flying into the wall with a thud. The rough bricks scraped at his back as I launched myself at him, forcing him to kiss me even though we usually didn't. I captured his face with my hand and slammed my lips down on his. Shit was different. He was going to have to get used to it.

I missed my best friend. I missed making love to this big, mean motherfucker.

We didn't make love anymore. Hadn't in decades. We fought with our bodies, the amount of abuse they could take now extreme. I needed to feel in control. He needed to feel punished. Once again, we'd become what the other needed without thought.

He ripped his mouth from mine and snarled, and I sneered back. Then I grabbed his arm and flipped him around roughly, slamming the front of his body into the roughness of the bricks. I could smell the faint stink of copper, telling me he was bleeding. Good. That would make him happy.

I pressed my hard dick against the cheeks of his ass. And it was hard, like a fucking steel bar. This brutality, compared to the sweetness of Dippy's hands, was the dichotomy of my life. I pressed G's cheek against the wall, holding him still as I kissed him again over his shoulder, then sucked and bit my way down his spine. My hand grabbed his hard, muscular hip and I ground myself against him. I reached around and tugged on his cock, nothing gentle and sweet about it. Luckily neither of us wanted sweet right now because he was hard as fuck in my palm.

I grabbed the chains that hung on the wall. The rest of the MC thought they were to keep those who screwed with Damnation stuck down here, and we sometimes did use them for that. But more often, they were used so I could chain the beast down here while I worked. Sol and Cain knew; of course they did. They'd known us when we were so fucking happy. When life was perfect. It was inevitable that it would devolve into this.

G sucked in deep ragged breaths as I chained him to the wall, already calmer for having the metal tight against his wrists like a security blanket. I unwound the cilice from his thigh and threw the barbed metal on the ground at our feet. He didn't need it. I was here to punish him just fine; to punish us both.

I kicked his feet apart, and I realized he still had on his boots. Well, so did I. This cellar wasn't a place to walk around barefoot, no matter how much of a masochist you were. I reached down, running my hands gently down his side, over the slope of his ass and the adorable fucking dimples that dipped there. Fuck, I'd loved those dimples once upon a time. Every time we made love, my tongue would trace the tiny indentations. I still loved them, but there was no place for that kind of gentleness here in this fucking sex dungeon.

I traced my hands down over his ass, squeezing the hard muscles and then down his inner thighs, making them tremble beneath my palms. I slipped my hand in his boot and pulled out his switchblade. It had its own pocket in his custom made boots, and he carried it around like a favorite teddy.

"Do it," he growled and I flicked out the knife. I knew what he wanted. He wanted me to carve Laura's name into his flesh before I could fuck him. Every time he would make me do this, and every time it turned my stomach. But I wasn't capable of saying no. I had lost my conscience when I'd lost Laura too. It would heal in a few hours, but when I was there, fucking him to make us both feel better, the ragged wounds of her name would lie between us.

Maybe my conscience was coming back. Maybe I was finally healing, because when I started carving letters into his back, it wasn't the L for Laura. It was an S.

G launched away from the wall, intimately knowing how the knife should glide through his skin after decades of this ritual. "What the fuck are you doing?" he gasped, but I pushed his head back against the wall and locked his lower half with mine.

"Laura is our past, G. She was everything good about this fucked up life. But Serendipity is our future, and I need you to pull your head out of your ass and see it. Feel it." I quickly finished Sera's name, then threw the knife across the room.

He stopped struggling, collapsing against the wall defeated. I spat on my hand, rubbing it on my dick, and then slipping my hand between us. I circled his tight ass with my finger, slipping my index finger into the knuckle and stroking, enjoying the shudder of pleasure that made his muscles twitch.

But that was all the softness he'd get from me. I pulled my finger out, lined up my cock, and slammed home in one hard thrust. He hit the wall hard, and the feral sound that came out of him made my balls tighten. I pulled out and slammed home again, setting a punishing rhythm, as my fingers drifted from where they were tightened in his hair, down over his shoulders, and then around the front of his body. I gripped his cock hard, tugging it in time with my thrusts. He placed both of his palms against the rough bricks, pushing back against me, taking everything I gave him eagerly. I leaned forward and bit the curve of his muscular neck, so close now I could basically feel the cum surging from my balls.

I leaned forward and licked the letters carved into his back, and he shuddered, shooting hot spurts of cum against the wall, the stickiness running down my palm as he yelled his release. I wasn't far behind, grabbing his chin and wrenching it toward me for a kiss, as I came hard inside him, only pulling away when the pleasure became too much and my head dropped back.

That's when I caught the flash of movement in the corner.

I turned my head and saw Sera staring at us from

the doorway, her eyes wide, her mouth dropped open in surprise.

"I heard... I mean, I'm sorry."

Goliath's head whipped around at the sound of her voice. "GET THE FUCK OUT!" he roared, and she skittered away, taking the stairs so fast it was a miracle she didn't trip and fall.

Fuck. What had we done?

23

SERENDIPITY

Oh shit. Oh fuck. Oh damn. My heart raced as I fled down the halls, Goliath's gut wrenching shout still echoing in my brain. I took the stairs two at a time, not stopping until I was safely back in my room, where I could process what I'd stumbled upon. I leaned back against the wall beside the door, calming my erratic heartbeat, the last fifteen minutes like an action movie chasing its way through my brain.

I'd been sneaking down stairs for potato chips, because it was eleven at night and I felt like damn potato chips, and Cain had collapsed onto my bed, asleep before his head hit the pillow. He'd been snoring so sweetly beside me that I didn't want to wake him up.

When I heard a pained roar, I hadn't stopped to

consider that going down into the creepy basement had been a bad idea. I hadn't stopped to consider anything.

I'd barrelled down the stairs to the celler, and stopped dead at the sight of Judas fucking the daylights out of Goliath.

At first, given how brutal it was, I thought maybe Judas was... punishing him. The thought had made me feel sick. But I'd watched the way Judas had kissed the other man's shoulders, had pleasured him even though Goliath had been chained to the wall, and it had silenced the shout in my throat.

It was consensual, and brutal, and when I'd seen my name carved across Goliath's shoulders, I'd wanted to throw up, but I couldn't look away.

It was beautiful. It was so damn tragic.

The door beside my head suddenly opened, a large tattooed hand snaking in and gripping me by the arm like he had x-ray vision.

I yelped softly, but his other hand covered my mouth. Goliath stared down at me with so much fire in his eyes I thought I was going to burn to a cinder. "What the hell is wrong with you? You'll forget what you saw and keep your mouth shut," he whisper-yelled close to my face. As I watched, the scrapes on his face were healing. It was like magic. "What you saw was private. You are not fucking welcome there."

"Mmmf mmm mmphmm," I replied, resisting the

urge to lick his palm considering I kind of knew where his hands had just been.

An annoyed look passed over his face and he removed his hand. "What?"

"There's nothing wrong with what was happening down there in the dung- err- cellar. As long as it was consensual. Was it?"

He growled. "Of course it fucking was."

I shrugged, hoping I looked a lot calmer than I felt. "Then whatever it was is between you and Judas, no one else." But of their own accord my fingers reached over his shoulders, tracing the wound in his back that spelled my name. Perhaps it was between Goliath and Judas and maybe me.

He stiffened, and shivered under my touch. "This means less than nothing," he growled, then his lips slammed against mine. I was imagining that I could taste Judas on his lips, as his tongue thrust its way into my mouth, his hand moving into my hair and holding me still with a tight grip. His kiss was angry, tasting of frustration and edged in sadness. But I kissed him back with all the hope in my soul.

My hands ran across his still bare chest, feeling old scars and bullet holes, and I wanted to taste every single one of them. When he bit my bottom lip, I whimpered, and when he lifted me and pressed me hard against the wall, I moaned. Fuck. Yes.

The sheer raw carnality of Goliath made me wet. I

feared and desired him in equal measures and it set my rampant libido on fire. I wrapped my legs around his waist, pulling him into my body.

Then the baby kicked. Hard. Goliath reared back, dropping me from his arms in surprise or horror or regret, or something, and only catching me mere inches before I hit the floor, like he suddenly remembered I was pregnant. He held me until I got my feet under my body, and then let me go like I was diseased.

"I hate you," he said with such venom I choked out a pained sound. He whirled away and strode down the hall, slamming into his room with such force that the windows rattled.

I sucked in a shaky breath. At the end of the hall, I could see Solomon's golden eyes, even in the darkness. He blew me a kiss and then went back into his room. At the other end was Judas, who stared for a moment, before nodding and turning back into his own room.

I jumped when two arms banded around my waist.

"Shh, it's just me. You okay?" Cain's smooth voice soothed my shaken nerves. I just nodded, because I wasn't prone to lying to anyone, least of all Cain.

"I'm fine. He's just..."

Cain squeezed me tighter and kissed my temple. "I know, Sweetheart. Come on, we'll go back to bed. You look exhausted."

I let him bundle me back into bed, and wrap his huge body around mine. It had been a hell of a day.

.   .   .

No one mentioned what happened in the cellar that night. I didn't tell a soul, but I had a feeling that the Horsemen all knew what went on down there. Solomon was extra attentive the next day, bringing me breakfast in bed, then taking me on a long ride down the highway in the sunshine. He'd found a beautiful grassy spot near the lake and made love to me until my eyes crossed. Cain took me to the diner for lunch, then pulled me behind the ugly beige building and kissed me until my lips were swollen and my hair mussed. I'd gotten some serious death glares from the waitresses after that.

Judas had pulled me into his office that afternoon, staring down at me like he was trying to judge how I felt without actually asking me. Then he'd spread me across his desk and devoured my pussy like I was his last damn meal.

Goliath avoided me like I was contagious.

It set the tone for the following month. I fought the instinct to nest, a part of me still worrying that this wouldn't be permanent. That eventually I would need to run again, or the guys would make me leave after the baby was born. Apparently, it was hard to shake the habit to move around. Never stay in one place. Always look over your shoulder. It was a mentality that had settled in my subconscious over centuries, and I knew it would take decades to rid myself of it, if I ever got that opportunity.

Sweetie had asked when my doctors appointments were, and I had to lie. I was worried if they did the ultrasound, they'd be able to tell that the baby wasn't entirely human. No, avoiding human medical facilities was paramount. Maybe nothing would come of it, but maybe it would be that one small mistake that led to everything turning to shit. Which pretty much summed up my mental state. I was here, waiting for all my happiness to collapse in a heap around me.

Because I wasn't allowed to be this happy, to feel like I'd found my home in the arms of the Four Horsemen.

I'd popped even more, and now I wondered how I didn't just topple over when I leaned forward more than ninety degrees. Getting up and down the stairs was becoming exhausting. Most of the time, if there was no one around, I just let Cain carry me up.

Luckily there weren't any feminists to judge me in an outlaw MC, but still, I was a strong independent woman and all that. But I'd be damned if Cain carrying me up the stairs didn't make me feel like a Queen.

I wandered down the hall, in Cain's massive Damnation shirt today. The baby was sitting low, and my yoga pants dipped low over my pubic bone. I stopped outside Judas' office door and knocked softly.

I found myself drifting toward one or another of

the guys all the time now, a little because my libido was in freaking overdrive, but mostly just because I liked to be with them all the time.

"Come in," he said softly. I stepped into his office and my heart did a weird little flipflop at the smile on his face. Judas didn't talk about his feelings or his past. Mostly we didn't talk much at all. But that soft look on his face was filled with emotion, and I could wait for words. He stood and came around from behind his desk.

He wrapped his arm around my back and kissed me gently, the rough scratch of his beard on my chin felt delicious. I kissed him back, running my tongue over his lower lip, making him let out a little grunt of pleasure. "Mmm, you taste good. Such a distraction," he chastised as he pulled away. "I'm up to my ass in paperwork, but right now I want to spread you on the couch and see if you taste this good everywhere," he rumbled against my lips, making my nipples hard. He sighed and stepped away, rubbing a hand over my stomach. "How are you feeling?"

There was always a touch of sadness coloring his voice when he asked me about the baby. I knew why. Solomon had explained. But I didn't know what to say, how to act, without making out that I was trying to replace his wife and son.

"Fine. The baby isn't moving around as much now it's so cramped in there, but it shifts every now and then to let me know it's okay. My back aches. My ankles look like hams and I've developed this weird blotchy rash on my neck, but other than that, I'm good," I laughed.

Judas kissed me. "You look fucking beautiful right now. Sit down. I'll rub your feet."

I looked at the low couch warily. I was pretty sure if I got down there, I was never getting back out again.

Judas must have seen me eyeing the couch like it was an alligator, and pushed me gently into it. "I will help you back up, I promise. Relax."

He slipped my flip flops off my feet, because I could no longer bend down to put on my Converses.

I moaned as his fingers pressed into the sore arches of my feet, and I wondered if you could orgasm from a foot massage.

The door of Judas' office slammed open, making me jump. Goliath walked in, his eyes sliding from Judas' empty desk to him kneeling at my feet. They flickered with something like panic between us both, before he stormed back out again, closing the door with violent gentleness.

I sighed and stared sadly at the door.

Judas squeezed my knee. "He'll come around. Some things cannot be healed in a day or week or even a decade. But he will heal. And he does like you."

I made a rude sound. Goliath might want to fuck me, but he hated my guts. I was all about angry sex, but it was hard to have hate sex when you looked like a beach whale and cried all the fucking time.

Judas continued to rub my feet with single minded focus. I reached down and ran my fingers down his face, and he turned his face into my palm. My fingers snagged on the thin elastic of his eyepatch, and I ran my finger underneath it. He stilled, but I felt him force himself to relax. I wanted to know what was under the eyepatch. Wanted to see all of the man who was so willing to make me feel good, but kept himself so guarded behind a nearly impenetrable wall. I'd seen him once without the eyepatch, the inky darkness making it look like it was just an empty socket of darkness.

"Can I look?" I asked softly. I didn't want to pressure him, and if he said no, that would be the end of it. He looked up at me with the remaining piercing blue eye that seemed to see everything, before nodding. I sat forward, not as easy as it sounded, and pulled him up onto the couch beside me. He came willingingly, no hesitance in him, and that did something funny to my chest.

I traced my fingers under the elastic of his eyepatch, not moving it, just pressing my fingers to the slight indents on his skin. I leaned forward, took his soft, full lips with mine, gently nibbling at his lips, assuring him that this meant something to me. That he meant something to me. I continued to kiss him, closing my eyes as I removed the eyepatch completely, slipping it over the dark strands of his hair, and pulling it back to my lap.

I moved away from his lips and opened my eyes.

I don't know what I was expecting, but it wasn't just a normal closed eye, essentially. There was a bit of scar tissue, sort of ragged edges that had healed roughly. When I pressed my finger to the closed lid, something hard was still beneath the surface and I frowned.

"What happened?" I asked softly, running my fingers across his cheekbones and up to the ragged corner of his outer eye.

"Lucifer took it when he made us the Horsemen as payment. Tore my eyeball right out of my head and then made us immortal. Which was fairly lucky, I guess. No risk of infection or the like. But it meant I couldn't get a prosthetic because my eye began to heal itself immediately." He pressed his own fingers to eyelid. "About a year later, after a lot of research and threatening a whole bunch of ocular surgeons until I knew everything I could, I got them to put a prosthetic about the size of a ping pong ball, then sewed it shut because the bastard just kept trying to heal over anyway. And here we are." He waved at his face.

"Well, quite frankly I appreciate the whole villain thing. I think it's sexy as hell."

He let out a low chuckle that went straight to my core. Damn, he was hot. "I think you are pretty fucking beautiful too, Serendipity." He leaned forward and kissed me again.

I leaned forward and bit the rough stubble of his chin. "You're a fucking liar. I look like a bloated cow. But I appreciate the compliment."

He grabbed my chin and held it tightly, tipping my face up so his lips were only an inch from mine. "Don't be coy, Dippy. You couldn't be more beautiful than you are right now. The only reason I'm not bending you over this couch is..." He snapped his jaw shut on his words.

Yeah. I wasn't letting that shit go. "Is what, Judas?"

"Is Goliath." He sighed and scrubbed his hand through his hair. "He needs me to be... impartial," he winced at the word, "just for a little while longer. He'll come around, Dippy. We just have to give him time. Me and Goliath, we have a long history and I've loved him longer than I've loved any other person and I just have to wait."

I nodded sadly, because I'd already known the answer. Judas and I would have this weird distance between us until then, like we were friends who got naked and gave each other orgasms. But I was going to win Goliath over eventually. If I didn't run out of time.

I made out with Judas on the couch like we were horny teenagers for a little while longer.

Someone else knocked at the door, and Judas pulled away, standing and trying to adjust his hard dick. He threw his hands up in the air and went to sit behind his desk, sending me mock-disgruntled looks as I grinned like a cheshire cat.

"What?" he barked at whoever was on the other side of that door.

Shots put his head around the door frame. "You better get out front, Pres. There's someone at the front door."

G oose, or Bear or whatever other stupid name he'd chosen, came over to where I sat at the bar chatting to Shots.

"Sol, there's someone here trying to get in. Won't tell me his name. Got two kids with him."

What the actual fuck? Who brought kids to an Outlaw MC Clubhouse? Even members usually didn't bring their kids unless it was a family event or an emergency.

I frowned toward Shots. "Go get the Pres."

Shots didn't waste time, and I slid from the barstool and followed Goose.

I looked through the windows beside the front door at the figures standing in the middle of the parking lot. A guy and two kids. Something about the guy's stance, his body seemingly relaxed, set me on edge. He was standing far enough away that he was out of accurate shooting distance, and it unsettled me that he knew that. I pulled my gun and rested it down at my side. I wasn't about to go aiming guns at kids, no matter my criminal status. Another one of Cain's strays, maybe?

"Get Cain too. We'll see if he knows anything about this."

I stepped out onto the covered front porch of the club house. I plastered on my most pleasant smile. "I think you've got the wrong house, Friend."

The dude remained motionless, that faux calmness nearly impenetrable. He didn't say a word. I stepped closer, my gun slightly behind me so I didn't frighten the children, my face still a mask of graciousness. "I suggest you leave. This is private property and we don't like trespassers all that much," I yelled across the distance, moving closer. When I was close enough, I could see the bulges in his silhouette that told me the guy was packing and my body tensed. I moved the gun around to my front to let him know he wasn't the only one with heat. When I was close enough to read the guy, all the hairs on my arms stood on end.

This guy was a killer. Killers could always spot other killers, and my hands were far from clean. "What do you want?" I repeated. And when he refused to answer, I raised my gun. "You better answer or leave, or I'm going to blow your brains out in front of your kids."

I didn't want to shoot this guy in front of his children but something about him set me on edge.

Suddenly, the little boy, who'd been standing slightly behind him, a little girl behind his back, stepped forward. The girl stepped with him like a shadow.

"He's mute. He can't talk."

The man shot the kid a furious look, but his eyes flashed back to me quickly. I looked at the kid and gave him a smile. "Well, fair enough. Do you know what he wants?"

The kid gave me a sly grin. "He wants Serendipity to be his girlfriend."

I blinked, and the guy looked down and signed furiously. The kid blushed and looked contrite, but the mischief still sparkled in his eyes. The guy looked exasperated.

Unfortunately for him, or fortunately, I knew sign language. My older cousin had been born with deformed vocal chords, and even though he could speak, it was a rough, tortured sound. So instead of scaring us as small children, he'd taken the time to teach all of us ASL.

Dippy has that effect on men. Unfortunately you are shit outta luck. I love her, and she's mine.

The dude actually growled at me, and the kids eyes ping-ponged between us. He signed furiously at me, and I laughed. "Slow the fuck down man. It's been a while."

But that look in his eye? I knew all too well. Relief. He'd been scared for her. He slowed down his movements, keeping his expressions simple. *I want to see her. I need to know she's okay.*

"And I need to know who the fuck you are, because otherwise there's no way you are getting within a hundred feet of her."

I felt the presence of my Brothers at my back, the overwhelming force of the four of us together enough to make grown men cry. But not this guy. He narrowed his eyes and pushed the both kids behind his back.

Cain grunted like the guy had personally insulted him, which he kind of had, but the other dude wasn't to know that. "We don't hurt kids here." He shot me a quick look. "Who is this guy?"

"He's here for Dippy," I said softly, and everyone around me tensed. Even Goliath.

The door opened again, and the man's eyes shot behind me.

"Marco?" Dippy whispered behind me. She went to race down the steps, but Goliath's hand shot out and grabbed her. She threw him a furious look, but he didn't let go. Marco took in Goliath, who was a big scary looking mother fucker by anyone's standards, even before you got to the cold, dead eyes. Then he looked at G's hand on Dippy's arms and he pulled his own gun, pointing it directly at my bad tempered Brother. Fuck, this was going south fast.

Judas stepped forward, in full Pres mode.

"What do you want?" He shot a look at Goliath and Dippy. "Stay where you are for a moment Sera. Goliath, let her go." Goliath huffed, but he uncurled his fingers from her arm. Judas wasn't stupid enough to tell everyone to put down their weapons.

Marco signed, and Dippy quickly signed back, her face looking happy if a little pissed at us. She'd get over it. Her safety was my first priority. I'd fuck her to forgiveness later.

Judas raised an eyebrow. "Now for those who can't speak with their hands?"

I looked between this Marco guy and Dippy. "He said he finally got Hope to tell him where she'd stashed Serendipity. She was chewing him out for bringing the kids to a biker bar." I grinned as she looked at me with surprise. "What? I'm not allowed to have hidden talents?"

Finally, whatever was happening between us adults got too much for the little girl, who dodged around both her brother and the guy, and ran full pelt at Dippy.

"Sera!" she squealed, the sound drenched in happiness. I pointed my gun at the ground.

The smile on Dippy's face when she saw the little girl made my chest want to burst wide open. "Cara."

She walked down the last few steps and Goliath let her go. She opened her arms wide and the little girl barrelled into them. The boy wasn't far behind her. "Careful Cara. She's got a baby in there," he said in a voice that was far too serious for a little kid. Sera opened her arms wider. "Hey, Sammie. You look bigger! Did you have a growth spurt?" She dragged them both close and kissed their heads. We all stood around and watched this woman with her gigantic heart shower love and affection. God. I didn't think I could love her more. I was wrong.

In the face of such affection, it seemed stupid to still have my gun out. I switched on the safety and tucked it in the back of my jeans. Judas looked at the scene in front of him, and then back at the dude still standing still in the middle of the parking lot, his gun still pointed in our direction, his eyes never wavering.

"Well, I guess you better come in so we can figure all this out. Dippy?" The woman who had stolen my heart looked up at Judas, her huge violet eyes sparkling. "Why don't you invite your friends inside? I'm pretty sure I can get Sweetie to make pancakes."

The little girl squeaked with excitement, and I couldn't hold back my grin.

Dippy looked back at Marco. *Do you want to come in?* She signed.

This Marco re-holstered his gun, but he was still looking at us like he was wondering how fast he could splatter our brains on the wall. *Are they going to shoot me as soon as I step behind closed doors?* He signed back.

I grinned. *Not today.*

Cain groaned. "That's going to get old fu-" Dippy gave him a stern look, "er, old fast."

Dippy slowly got back to her feet, groaning and holding her lower back. Goliath reached down and yanked her up with hands that weren't exactly gentle, but he wasn't rough. Baby steps with the big guy. Goliath was still giving the killer in the parking lot death glares, totally contradicting my assurances of safety, and I rolled my eyes.

Judas turned and led the way into the Clubhouse, Cain following him. Dippy gently pulled out of Goliath's grasp, then surprised the shit out of him by pressing a gentle hand to his chest. He looked at her hand on his chest like it was a tarantula. He might be in denial, but when he'd thought the guy had been a threat, he'd protected her whether she needed it or not.

Marco whistled, and the kids ran back to his side like well trained puppies. Dippy waited until Marco was close, and she gave him a small, secret smile that kind of made me want to blow the dude's brains out myself. She led him into the Clubhouse, her hand holding the little girls. I went next, and the guy was so tense I knew he didn't like having us at his back. Well, bad fucking luck. He was in our house now.

We made it into the bar, and the kids scrambled onto the bar stools, completely unconcerned that they were in a bar full of bikers. I guess when you had a killer for a father, your perception of bad was probably skewed at a young age. Sweetie was there fussing over the kids, asking what they wanted on their pancakes, and Shots was giving them lowballs of milk. At this rate, we were going to have to up our milk deliveries.

Judas looked at Marco. "Come, we'll talk in my office. Sweetie will watch the kids."

Marco shook his head, looking around at the bar full of bikers. *The kids stay with me.* He looked at Dippy longingly. *Or with Serendipity.*

I translated for Judas, who rolled his eyes. "Fine. We can air all our shit out here in the open." Judas might sound annoyed, but I knew him well enough to know that Marco just went up a little in his esteem. He probably had a way to go though considering he'd brought the kids here at all.

Dippy kissed the cheeks of both of the kids, who were happily chatting to Shots. He had a bajillion grandkids, and he looked a little bit like a viking Santa, so he was pretty good with children.

She grinned at Marco. "Well, considering you are here to see me, I guess we are doing this right here."

Do you think we could go somewhere else and talk without such a big audience? He indicated the four of us, who were doing our best impression of looming killers. Oh wait. It wasn't an impression.

"Fat fucking chance," I replied on behalf of all of us. The dude looked annoyed, and seemed to be summing up whether he could kill us all and steal her.

Then he heaved a sigh. *Fine. Hope told me about Uriel. I'm glad that the bastard got what he deserved.*

She shuddered and rubbed her stomach. *Me too. Hope and her consorts are...* Dippy's hands stilled. *Different.*

A strange hissing noise let me know that Marco was laughing. *No shit.* All the mirth left his face, and his eyes slid around the four of us. *I want you to come home with me. The kids miss you. There's no threat anymore.*

"Like fucking hell!" I growled, startling everyone but Dippy and this asshole Marco. I would slit his throat before I let him steal my girl. "This asshole wants to take Dippy."

Goliath growled low in his throat, and Cain reached out to pull Dippy back against his chest. Judas looked at him, his eye narrowed. "Serendipity is not safe. The angels of Uriel's cohort made vague threats about her and the baby. Until I am certain they are both one hundred percent safe, they stay, whether they like it or not."

Dippy raised an eyebrow at his high-handedness, but didn't argue.

Marco grimaced. *This would be easier if this fucker didn't know ASL. Why couldn't he just be dumb and pretty?* I gave him a smug grin and winked. He gave me a hand gesture that didn't need translation. *I've hated not knowing what happened to you. Hated that I couldn't protect you even though you'd been given into my care. I didn't want you to think that I just pushed you out when it got too fucking hard. I'm not that guy. When you called me that day...* His jaw pulsed, but he trailed off. I knew that pain. The pain of knowing you were too far away to save someone you loved. I wouldn't wish it on my worst enemy.

Dippy stepped out of Cain's arms, and I saw my Brother flex his hands as if he wanted to pull her back to where she belonged. I know I did. She stepped close to Marco, giving him the illusion of privacy.

"I understood, Marco. I would never have stayed and risked the kids. When Uriel arrived here..." she shuddered, and I pressed my fingers to her back to reassure her that we would always have her. We'd keep her safe. She threw me a grateful look. "You would have died. The kids would have died. I would never have forgiven myself for that." She touched his cheek, and he stared at her like I imagined we all did. With awe, lust and possession. He wanted her. Maybe he even loved her.

I hated him.

Do you want to come home with me? When she went

to look at us, he captured her chin, turning her face back toward him. Goliath growled and grabbed his wrist. I wondered if he'd crush it. I also wondered if Marco could shoot straight with both hands. Marco, to his credit, ignored the giant angry bastard glaring at him, his eyes only for Dippy.

She looked so damn sad. "I miss you and the kids too. But I'm happy and protected here. I need to stay." She smiled sadly, like she knew she was breaking his heart. "I want to stay."

Marco nodded once, releasing her chin. He straightened his spine and shuttered his expression, probably so Dippy didn't see his heart was breaking.

He whistled and the kids both turned to look at him, pancakes halfway to their mouths. He signed to the boy, and the kid looked between his parent and Dippy. "Isn't Sera coming home too?"

Marco shook his head, and the little girl began to cry softly. But they both obediently slid from the barstools and went to stand beside Marco. Dippy's eyes looked too huge in her head, watery with unshed tears. Ah fuck.

She grabbed the kid and pulled her into her arms. "Hey, it's okay. I'll come and visit."

The little one's lip trembled. "Don't you like us? Don't you like Marco?"

I raised an eyebrow at the kid calling Marco by name. Wasn't he their father? "No! That's not it at all,

Sweetheart. I love you guys. You're the best kids ever. And Marco is amazing," her voice broke a little. "But these guys are amazing too. And I love them as well. I wish I could keep you all, but it isn't safe for the baby."

Cara chewed her lip, and gave her a wobbly nod.

"What if they stayed too?" Judas said softly, and every set of eyes turned to his. Not just those in our group. Every single set of eyes in the room.

"What the fuck, Pres?" Goliath growled.

But Judas wasn't listening to him. He was watching Serendipity's face, his own expression soft. He fucking loved her, even if he didn't know it yet.

Are you nuts? I can't bring my kids to live in a fucking biker clubhouse, Marco signed, and I kind of agreed. But the look of absolute hope on Dippy's face kept my mouth closed. Judas' eyes slid to mine. "What did he say?"

I relayed Marco's misgivings, and Judas shrugged. "You brought them here today, didn't you?"

Marco's face twisted into a frustrated look.

The boy piped up. "It's because he doesn't trust anyone else to look after us. Our dad..." his little face screwed up, darkness that no kid should possess clouding them, "he wasn't a good dad. He had lots of bad friends. And people who didn't like him. Now we own all his money and people keep trying to use us. Use me."

My eyes flicked from the kid to Cain. There was a

slight tenseness to his shoulders, but I'd known the big bastard for a lot of years. I knew it meant he was chasing his own memories out of his head. His own abusive father.

Judas was looking at his VP too. "They stay. We'll protect them all," Cain said tonelessly, then turned and left the room. Kids and women. They were Cain's weakness.

Marco watched him go, his eyes flicking back to us, then back to Dippy. *I don't know. I don't trust these fuckers at all. That one looks like he wants to gut me already.* He nodded toward Goliath.

I laughed. *Probably. But he won't. His relationship with Serendipity is rocky, but he'll come around. He's fighting it. He wouldn't lift a hand toward a child or woman though. We'd kill him ourselves. That's not what Damnation is about.*

Marco gave a lopsided grin. *She has that effect. You start out swearing to yourself that she's the worst thing that ever happened to you, but when she's gone, it's like she's stolen all the light in the world.*

I nodded, grinning. Yeah. This fucker got it. "I was telling him about our code here at Damnation. That the kids couldn't be safer if they were in Fort Knox."

Judas narrowed his eye. "You couldn't have said that out loud for the whole class?" I shrugged and he shook his head. "So what will it be? Just know, if you do anything to hurt Serendipity or this Club, I will put a bullet in your head and dance in your brain matter."

Sera gave him a horrified look, covering the little girl's ears and kicking him in the shin, but he ignored her. "Last thing. Sera belongs to us. Get used to it, because if you make her cry again, I'll chop your fucking dick off. Are we clear?"

Marco tipped his head back and did his huffing laugh. That was probably the first sign that he was going to fit in just fine.

The woman had changed everything. I hated it. Judas letting that guy stay had been a shit fucking decision he never would have made before she came along. This Marco was as fucking dead inside as I was. You could see the killer hiding beneath the pleasant surface. All big smiles and dead eyes. I knew the type. Fuck I was the type. Though I never smiled pleasantly at anyone. Bet he would slit all our throats in our sleep if it suited his purposes.

You didn't invite a fucking snake into your nest.

But no matter what I said, Judas wouldn't listen. He was soft over the woman. He would have given her the President's patch if she asked for it. Pretty sure he'd hand her his heart on a platter if she asked.

I sat on the asphalt, replacing some parts in my

bike that had come in the mail. I could have taken it to the garage, but I just wanted to be alone.

This Marco had been here for a week. They stuck them on the top floor in the only two bedroom apartment we had. It'd been closed up for years, and it took the sweet butts hours to clean it. Even Sera helped which had made Cain and Sol fuss over her like fucking pussies. Honestly, while no one was particularly warming to the killer, the whole Club fussed over those kids like they were fucking mascots or pets or something.

I scraped my knuckles and dropped a nut, swearing as it bounced along the gutter, stopping at a pair of light-up glitter shoes. Fuck, thinking about it had summoned one. I looked at the little girl, Cara, as she picked up the nut and walked over to hand it to me.

She dropped it in my hand and I grunted a thank you.

"You're welcome," she said sunnily, skipping around to the other side of the bike, taking in all the shiny chrome parts. "Your bike is pretty. I used to have a bike, but my dad made Marco run over it with his car. Marco said he'll buy me another one, one day. But I don't want a pink one. I think I want one like yours."

I grunted, continuing to work. I thought that maybe kids were like wild beasts. If you didn't make eye contact, they'd just wander off by themselves.

"Though my dad wasn't really my dad. Marco is

actually my dad," the girl said, dropping that little bomb as she sat down beside me. "He used to be my dad's bodyguard. Mommy would make faces at him all the time. Then Daddy found out and he'd hurt her, so she stopped making faces at him again."

My fist tightened on my wrench. "Your dad sounds like an asshole," I muttered.

She gasped, then giggled. "You swore." She tapped her feet on the ground, making the lights along the soles flash. "He was bad. Mommy was bad too. She used to hurt Sammie. Sometimes she'd lock him up in a cupboard. I didn't know how to get him out 'til I was a big girl." She looked sad, feeling a guilt that shouldn't land on shoulders so tiny.

"Not your fault." I continued to untighten the nuts, resting them in a cut off coke can. "You should go back inside."

She sighed. "Can't I stay out here with you? I'm sick of being inside. I want the sun. Sammie says I'm like a sunflower."

Something tugged on my face, and I realized it might be a smile so I shut that shit down. Instead, I handed her the coke can. "Fine. Be useful and hold this."

She took the can happily. "I like your pretty skin drawings. One day, I want some skin drawings too. Marco said no." She tapped her index and middle fingers to her thumb as she said it, and it didn't take a fucking genius to work out that was the sign for no. "But I think I'll get them anyway when I'm a grown up because people can't tell you what to do when you're a grown up."

I didn't answer her, but that didn't seem to stop her. "I asked Marco if he was really my new Dad, if Sera would like to be my new Mom, but that made him go all red and he changed the subject. Sammie said that was because I'd made him 'barrassed, but adults don't get 'barrassed. Sammie said he was red because he really likes Sera and he'd probably like to marry her. Sammie also says that he can't because Cain and Sol and the scary guy with an eyepatch want to marry her too and she can't marry everyone because it's against the law."

She stopped and looked at me. "But it shouldn't be against the law if they love each other right? Do you love Sera too? Sammie thinks you're scary but I don't think you are. I think you are just sad. You look sad like Mr. Budson next door at our old apartment after his dog Tilly died. Did your dog die?"

Holy shit. I was beginning to sympathise with Marco right now. "No. My dog didn't die," I grumbled. "My girlfriend died."

The kid's eyes got real big and shiny then and I thought she was going to cry. "Oh. That is sad. I'd be sad too. Don't tell Marco or Sammie but I sometimes get sad because Mommy and Dad are gone but it's not because I want them back, and they aren't dead. I just sometimes remember and feel sad, you know? But I think it's okay to be sad. Just not forever."

Jesus. This kid was slaying me right now.

"Pass me a nut," I grunted, pointing to the piece I wanted, hoping to distract her from her Mini-Doctor Phil antics.

"I think you should love Sera too and then she would love you back and make your sad go away. Then she could have five husbands, and one could cook, and the other could mow the lawn, and one could make her pancakes, and the other one could look after the baby, and the last one could vacuum the floor because vacuuming is the worst. I hate the noise. I can't wait for Sera to have her baby. Do you think I'll be able to hold it? Sammie says babies are small and break easy but I think I'm big enough to hold a baby." She took a deep breath but didn't actually stop speaking. "I like it here. Sweetie makes the best pancakes and has a really cool name and she and Shots sometimes kiss. I think Shots is a funny name, like who has a name like Shots? Guess it's not as funny as Trigger though. I like Trigger. I think I might marry him one day." I looked over at her, frowning. She was bright pink. "Do you think Trigger would marry me one day?"

I huffed. "Not if he likes all his teeth."

Cara nods sagely. "I don't think I'd like him if he didn't have all his teeth. Kenny used to come to the same park as me and he was Sammie's age and he lost all his teeth at once and looked like an alien. They grew back but even then he looked like a weird rabbit."

The back door burst open and Sera came out. "Cara! There you are. I was worried," she said softly, walking toward us, taking in the scene. I shut my face down, locking down tight any thoughts I might have about the woman in front of me until my face was impassive. She looked down at the girl, her hands on her hips, her stomach protruding in front of her like a beach ball. "You can't just wander out here. It's not safe."

Cara set her tiny shoulders, an equally stern expression on her face. "I was helping Goliath with his bike," she said, except she pronounced Goliath like Go-wi-af. It was kinda cute, but I wouldn't admit it under pain of fucking death.

Instead I looked up from where I was working. "You can call me G," I said to the kid, and she beamed.

Sera, I mean the woman, smiled softly at us both. "Come on. We better go and tell Marco that you've been found before he sends out a search party." The girl huffed but stood up.

"I'll help you another time, okay?" she said seriously, and I just nodded. The woman opened the door for Cara, who waved and ran inside.

"I'm sorry about that. I'll tell her to give you more space."

I shrugged. "It was fine."

I didn't look at her. When I looked into her eyes, it made me feel raw, like I was picking at a scab. She let the door shut again. "Goliath?"

I dragged my eyes up to meet hers, keeping my face impassive. "What?"

"Thank you for looking after her." She paused. "And looking after me. I never really thanked you. You looked out for me even when you couldn't stand to look at me. I appreciate that. I'm going to try and make it easier for you, after the baby is born. Maybe find an apartment close by or something."

Her words tore at me when they should have made me happy. That should be warning enough. She had to go, before she caused me more pain. I'd already lost the last piece of Laura to her, lost Judas. I couldn't lose myself too. I couldn't come back from that.

"Good," is all I said, but refused to look at her big sad eyes.

I didn't watch her walk away, didn't look up until the back door clicked shut. I felt like shit.

"Fuck!" I shouted.

I stood, eating up the distance between my bike and the door in a few short strides. I wrenched the door open, and tried not to think about how relieved that she was only a few steps away.

She startled at the sound of the door, spinning on her heel too fast. She wobbled, and I reached her in a single stride, grabbing her arms and straightening her. "My reluctant savior," she said, smiling sadly. I shook my head, stepping closer. "I don't want you to go after the baby is born. Stay as long as you want." It came out roughly, but it was my default and I couldn't fucking help it.

She looked at me with violet eyes that seemed to see too much. "This is your home, Goliath. I don't want to make you uncomfortable in your own home."

I stepped toward her a little more, crowding her until she backed away towards the wall. I chased her body with mine. I couldn't help it. "My Brothers love you. You need to stay. I won't take that from them again."

She tilted her head. "Is that the only reason?"

I clenched my jaw. No. It wasn't. But I couldn't fucking give her that power over me, could I? "I want to fuck you."

She raised both her perfectly shaped eyebrows. "Oh? Like, right now?"

I reared back. "What? No."

"So like, in the future when I'm not fat?"

Fuck. Shit. Had I offended her? Was she going to cry? I was fucking this shit up. "No. What?" I repeated like a goddamn idiot. "You are fucking beautiful. You know that. I'm sure those other pricks are telling you how damn beautiful you are a million times a day."

She made a disgruntled noise and her eyes welled

with tears. What the hell was with the crying women today? This is why I joined a goddamn MC because men didn't fucking cry at the drop of a hat. "I'm pretty sure they are lying. I'm basically Free Willy right now. I haven't seen my toes in like a month and the baby just keeps growing and I'm so scared and-"

I kissed her. Not like I normally kiss her, with hatred and anger. I just kissed her because I wanted to kiss her. No guilt. No punishment. But when she pressed her body against me, something in me cracked.

I wrenched away. "Don't get an apartment," I threatened, scowling. Then I strode away as fast as I could without running.

I didn't look back.

26

L ying on the couch in Marco's room, I watched the former bodyguard like he was a documentary. He did everything with a clear efficiency of movement, whether it was cleaning up Cara's toys or cleaning his gun. Right now, he was assembling a huge ass gun that I assumed was a sniper rifle given the scope that sat beside it. If the guys could see this thing, they'd freak the hell out. You'd have to be an idiot not to recognize the danger that Marco represented. Sure, he was pretty fucking beautiful too, in a kind of broken way. Scarred body and soul, his dark chocolate eyes drew your gaze away from the pale stripes of skin that littered his golden skin. His body was tight and lithe, muscular in a way that said he was quick but strong. He wasn't as big as the Horsemen, but he still made my mouth water.

That being said, Tom Selleck as Magnum PI made me hot under the collar the other day while I was watching reruns, so my lady bits weren't all that picky right now.

But ever since Marco nursed my battered body back to health after Purgatory, after Hope had basically dropped me off at his door like an unwanted kitten, he'd had a little bit of my heart. Even when he disliked me, or at least pretended to. I had my theories about Marco, but you didn't move into the middle of an Outlaw MC for someone you merely liked, right? No matter how much the kids loved me.

But he'd been here over a week and hadn't made a move. Just what I needed, another guy who had the emotional range of a fucking rock. "Why are you assembling a rifle?" I asked. I shifted, trying to get comfortable. I'd been uncomfortable all day. Hell, I'd been uncomfortable all week, but it was worse today.

Got a job for the Mob taking care of a problem. No rush, but I'd like to get it out of the way. Get some cash.

While I'd be recuperating, I'd devoured ASL course after ASL course so I could communicate with Marco. There were just some things that didn't need to be translated by Sammie. Sign language had the best insults. Honestly. Even with all my study though, I wasn't very good. I know Marco signed slow for both me and Sammie. I couldn't imagine how frustrating it would be. So much of sign language was facial, and

Marco only had two expressions most of the time. Neutral and pissed.

"Do you need money?" I could try harder to liquidate some of my shit now that Uriel was no longer a threat, and every angel and his dog seemed to know where I was. I wasn't hiding any longer. I was pointing my finger to the sky and saying, 'Fuck you!"

No, not really. We have money, but Sammie and Cara's is in a trust fund until they are older, and my employer kind of got murdered by a pissed off Angel in jail and I got two dependents in the process, so it would just be better to have a little nest egg.

I nodded, but I could tell from his face he didn't want me to offer what I wanted to offer. He wouldn't take my money even if I had it. It would hurt his male pride. At least while they were here, they wouldn't need anything. Damnation MC provided for those in its care, and at the beginning I'd been a lot like Marco. I didn't want to take their charity, because then I'd owe them something. But I came to realize that many of the members felt like helping others somehow balanced out all the bad shit they did on the karmic scales. I think they were misguided to think that making me pancakes and blowing a dude's brains out were of similar karmic weight, but I wasn't about to burst their collective bubble.

"Marco, why are you here?"

He stopped assembling his gun and put it on the

table. I could see his jaw flex. He came closer until he was sitting on the coffee table in front of the couch.

I wanted to see you. See you were okay with my own eyes. Then when I was sure you were okay, I couldn't leave again. I couldn't make myself walk away. Sammie says it's because I want to marry you. He grinned fondly, and it transformed his face from scary to something that took my breath away.

"Is he right?"

Marco shrugged. *I know I want to kiss you.*

My breath caught in my throat as he knelt on the carpet beside the couch, leaning over me so he could kiss his way along my jaw. He reached the corner of my mouth and I turned my face so I could meet his full, soft lips. God, he had a mouth made for kissing. It was beautiful and perfect and I could have done it all day. But the front door slammed open and Sammie and Cara burst back in.

Sammie frowned. "Were you two kissing?"

I said, "yes" at the same time Marco signed *No!*

I raised an eyebrow at him and he blushed. It was fucking adorable on his killer face. "I must have been confused. Marco, help me off the couch?"

Marco stood up and carefully lifted me from the low settee. I rubbed my stomach where it was getting increasingly uncomfortable. "My mistake. I might just go have a lie down and think about it some more, hmm?"

Marco stood there, gaping like a dummy while I kissed the kids heads and walked toward the stairs. I was exhausted. I didn't know how many weeks along I was in comparison to human pregnancies, but I had to be getting close in angel human hybrid gestation terms. The baby was sapping every last ounce of strength I had.

I almost wept at the sight of my bed. I was seriously considering turfing over all five of my prospective love interests and having a committed monogamous relationship with my pillowtop innerspring mattress. I collapsed onto my side, and rubbed at the ache in my stomach. It was beginning to come more frequently, and my hindbrain knew what it was. I just wasn't ready. But it wasn't something that was going to go away if I ignored it though.

I pulled out my phone and called the one person who was my safe space.

"Hey Beautiful," he said, his voice instantly assuaging my fears. Cain was my protector. He'd make everything okay. "What are you doing?"

"Oh you know, lying down. Going into labor, I think."

"Nice... hang on, what?"

I took a deep breath so he didn't pick up on my panic. "Lying down. Going into labor. I think it might be you know, the time?"

Something clanged in the shop, as he whispered

the words "fuck, fuck, fuck." To me, he said, in a faux calm voice like I couldn't hear him freaking out, "Alright. I'll be there in a second. Don't worry, Beautiful. It's all going to be fine." He hung up but not before I heard him yelling for Solomon.

Cain appeared a minute later, puffing like he'd just run a one minute mile. He gave me a beautiful smile, nothing in his demeanor giving away the sheer panic I heard a moment ago. "Sol has just gone to get Judas. What do you want to do, Sera? Hospital? Why the hell haven't we thought about this before?"

Judas strolled into the room, looking so calm it was hard not to feel perfectly at ease along with him.

He slapped Cain on the back, "I've been thinking about it for all of us."

I sighed out a relieved breath as he came over and kissed my forehead. "No hospitals," I said softly, and he nodded.

"No hospitals. I've got someone lined up. I'll go make some calls."

He left the room with one more stroke of my hair. Cain was pacing back and forth, but Sol finally appeared in the doorway, looking golden and beautiful. He walked over and climbed on the bed beside me. He curled his body around mine and stroked my stomach. "Soon, little one," he murmured softly, then kissed the back of my neck. "How are you feeling, Dippy?"

I grinned at the pacing Cain. "Better than the big

guy, I think. He was meant to be the calm one."

Solomon huffed a laugh, the puff of air cooling against my neck. "Yeah, normally he's level headed. It's just you who turns him into a mess." He sat up a little. "Hey shithead, you don't have to run a marathon over there. Sit your ass down."

Cain gave him two fingers, but sat down in the rocking chair that had come from Sweetie. It groaned ominously, but held. I wondered if he'd rock my baby there? I was so fucking terrified.

Judas walked back in like he didn't have a care in the world. He looked at Cain. "I need you to go to this address. Tell them you are Damnation, they'll know what I want. Take the truck," he said softly, totally in control. But that was just Judas, wasn't it?

Cain looked at me, fidgeting. "Can't you send one of the guys? I need to be here."

Judas put on his Pres face. "You need to do something. You are freaking Dippy the fuck out. I need you to go do this pick up, then calm your ass down. She's going to need you; the normal you. The cool ass fucker who would lay down his life for hers. Now go."

Cain still looked torn, and I smiled. "Go. I read it will be hours yet."

He leaned forward and kissed my lips softly. "Don't you dare fucking have a baby without me. Cross your legs if you have to," he teased, then he grabbed the address from Judas and left.

I grinned at the remaining men in my room. The golden god and the one-eyed villain. A contraction hit me and I curled up, glad Cain wasn't here because there was no way he would have left if he'd seen this.

Solomon rubbed my lower back with his knuckles throughout the whole spasm, and I exhaled a sigh when it loosened. "Talk to me, Judas."

He sat on the side of the bed. "I've called in a favor from a friend of yours. Hope. I did a little research when she turned up to the Boss fight with three feathered boyfriends. Her father was a well respected neurosurgeon in his prime. Also, they aren't unfamiliar with the supernatural, if Hope is anything to go by. Seemed like the perfect option."

"A brain surgeon. Don't want to disappoint you there, Pres, but he's working on the wrong end," Sol teased.

Judas rolled his eyes. "Delivering babies isn't as complicated as slicing and dicing a brain, Dickhead. Maybe he can open your thick skull up and see if he can clean out the dust bunnies."

I laughed, and breathed out a relieved sigh. I trusted the guys. I felt like an idiot for not planning this sooner, but I somehow thought I'd have more time.

Judas leaned down and kissed me. "He's getting on a private jet. He'll be here in an hour. Cain will be back with all the equipment. This time tomorrow you'll be holding a beautiful healthy baby. Boy or girl? Have you thought of names?"

I'd be happy if it was safe and healthy. I hadn't thought of names. "I'm ruling out Uriel Junior," I joked, and Sol growled.

"Have you called Goliath? He will want to be here," Solomon said softly.

Judas looked worried for the first time since I told Cain that the baby was coming. "I sent him a text to get back here ASAP. He'll be here."

I bit my lip. "Do you think he would really want to be here? We aren't... I mean, he isn't as invested in all this as you guys are. Shit, someone should tell Marco."

Sol kissed between my shoulder blades so lovingly that I wanted to cry. "G is more invested than you could imagine. Don't worry about Marco, I'll get him for you. I'll get Sweetie and Shots to watch the kids too. I'm pretty sure they've adopted them as extra grandkids anyway."

Solomon gave me one last kiss and left the room. And then there was one. Although he held himself with absolute confidence, there was a tiny crease between Judas' brows that told me that there was more going on behind his eyes than he let on. I wondered if it had anything to do with his wife. "This must be hard for you," I said softly. "You don't have to be here, you know? I'd understand if it brings back painful memories."

He ran his fingers over my temple, down my cheek. "The day my son was born was the best day of my life. I remember every second of it. I want to remember every moment of the birth of this child too."

Shit, now I was crying. I sniffled and swallowed down the emotions that threatened to overwhelm me. "Help me up. I want to walk around a bit." Judas helped me to my feet, and kept an arm around me as I wandered around my bedroom, trying to ease the uncomfortable ache. "What happened to them? Laura and your son. Sol wouldn't tell me, said it was a story you should share."

Judas' face closed down. "That's not a story for now, Sweetheart. It is a sad, miserable story that can bring nothing but pain. This is a time to be happy."

I shook my head. I don't know why I wanted to press this. It was like I had to learn about the ghosts I was going to share my men with. They will look at my baby and see another one. They will look at me and see another woman. I just wanted to know the end so I could start my new beginning without standing in the shadow of their tragedy.

I didn't realize I was speaking out loud until Judas took a shaky breath and held me tighter. "Alright. But it isn't pretty. But know, when we look at you, we see only you Serendipity." I smiled and snuggled into his side.

"Soon after I married Laura and my father died, I stood for President of my old Club. There were a couple of guys who believed that she'd made me soft, who fought me becoming Pres, but we'd fought it out per the rules of the Club, and won. My opponent, Ricky, had taken the whole thing badly, because he was a fucking weasel, and the worst sort of psycho. Sneaky. Underhanded but compelling. He left the Club, took some of his friends with him, and I forgot about that shit, you know? It was done. I'd won fair and square." He shuddered, and I didn't need a narrator to tell me that it wasn't over.

"Laura got pregnant, had the baby, and for a few months we were the absolutely happiest fuckers in the universe. We'd bought her a home with a white picket fence and a wrap-around porch. There was a fucking tire swing in the front yard. It was everything a family home should be. A few months after my son was born, we went on a run. Small time shit, running some guns up the coast. No big deal. But Ricky knew. He'd joined a rival club, the fucking traitor. Told them Laura was my weakness. That she could bring us all down. That she was the Club's Achille's heel. While we were away running guns, they came and took her from us. Took them from us." Judas' voice cracked, and he turned away from me. "We found the baby first. A single bullet in the chest. Small mercy, I guess. But Laura, they'd shredded her. She was unrecognizable. The coroner had to use dental records to ensure it was really her. She died in so much pain because I'd dragged her into this life. But Ricky had been right, Laura was our Achilles' heel. When she'd died, we all shut down. Goliath turned into an emotional vacuum. I didn't see Solomon for three days. Cain organized their funeral. His breakdown came later. He kept his shit together long enough to make sure they were put in the ground properly. Then Lucifer came and made us an offer we couldn't refuse."

I wrapped my arms around his waist, pressing my head between his shoulder blades, my huge stomach between us. "Did you gut those fuckers? Did you make their deaths as slow and painful as possible?"

Judas gave a short, humorless laugh. "The things we did to them still haunts me, but they deserved every moment of screaming pain." I agreed. I hope Lucifer was down there, making sure their eternal damnation was as painful as possible with no relief. "We moved out here, started a new Club. Fed the darkness that now resided in us all. Avoiding getting attached to anyone." He turned in my arms. "Until you. You have the power to destroy us all over again. I handed you that power myself. Maybe Goliath, that big, mean motherfucker, is the smartest one of us all."

I brushed my fingers through his hair, kissing his lips softly. "I'm not going anywhere. I'm not so easy to kill."

Another contraction had me leaning over and panting. Ouch. Judas rubbed my back, making soft, soothing, nonsensical noises. I straightened slowly. "Thanks for telling me."

He nodded, leading me back toward the bed. Solomon and Marco walked in, the latter coming toward me at a breakneck pace. He looked at my face, looking for something. God knows what.

If I'd known kissing you was going to send you into labor, I would have kept my lips to myself for a few more weeks.

Solomon translated for Judas. "I'd prefer it if you kept your fucking lips to yourself permanently, asshole," Sol added with a growl, but there was no heat in it. Sol and Marco had bonded. Not because they were both good-natured either. Marco was a prickly asshole, and there was a darkness inside Sol that he hid under that shiny exterior. Might have been having someone else to communicate, which made Marco friendlier than normal. Plus the kids were basically adorable icebreakers.

Marco ignored him. *Are you okay?*

I leaned forward, resting my forehead on his chest. "It hurts. And I'm scared. So fucking scared."

He ran his hands up and down my back, the circle of his arms reassuring. Now that I was in fucking labor, all the shit that I'd pushed down started to rear its fugly head. How did I think I was going to balance five guys? Not like they were the sharing type. They were alpha and angry and honestly there wasn't one clean hand between them. They were all bathed in blood. And I wanted every single one of them.

Maybe I would have to leave, because there was no damn way I could pick one of them. Marco had been my savior when I had needed it most. He'd protected me when I was too weak to walk. Fed me when I was too beaten down to sit up. He'd seen me at my absolute worst after I'd been freed from Purgatory, and he'd still chased me all the way to an Outlaw MC Clubhouse. What I felt for Marco was all mixed up in those emotions, but I knew that I wanted to explore where they went, and if the guys made me choose... I don't think I could.

Marco caught my eye, leaning away a little, and I could sense his frustration that he had to give up the closeness between us in order to communicate. *You are the toughest bitch I've ever seen. You faced down psycho angels. Survived purgatory. What is a little childbirth after all that. Stop being such a cry baby.*

I laughed, and nodded, letting him hold me for a little while longer. I laid back down, and Solomon laid back down behind me, his presence comforting. I managed to doze for a bit, don't ask me how. When I woke up, a handsome man in his fifties was standing beside my bed, talking in a low voice with Judas.

"How long has she been having contractions for?"

Marco signed that I'd been rubbing my stomach in his apartment six hours ago, so probably since then.

Sol translated. I had to thank him for willingly taking on the role of interpreter so Marco could feel included. Heard.

I blinked awake, as another contraction made me huff out a pained breath. All eyes turned to me. "Ah, you're awake. Serendipity, yes? My daughter Hope speaks very highly of you."

I smiled softly, his slight British accent making him sound very proper. "Hope is a wonderful person. You should be proud."

A warm smile lit up his eyes. "I couldn't be more proud. My name is Eli. I'm here to help you deliver your baby. Don't worry, I have delivered dozens of babies, not that many in this century, but it's a process as old as time itself."

I blinked, my pain-addled brain obviously mishearing him. Did he say this century?

"Let's have a look, shall we? May I suggest your beaus shift to the non-business end of the bed? Take my word for it, fellas." I noticed Cain was back, and shot him a relieved smile. I held out a hand and he came, squatting beside the bed. I squeezed his hand as another contraction hit me. Fuck, they were so close now.

The doctor pushed up the sheet, talking to himself. "You are fully dilated, but there's no crowning. Let's just see what's going on here." He covered back up my lower half and exposed my belly. He pressed around, his brow creased in concentration. At least I was hoping it was in concentration. "When was you last ultrasound?"

I shook my head. "There aren't many ultrasounds in Purgatory, Doc. You know the story of this?" I indicated my belly, panting between contractions that barely let up.

He nodded sadly. "Yes."

"Argh, I was worried about what human medicine might see. I just couldn't."

Eli didn't say anything more, didn't chastize me for being a shit parent already. "Luckily, your friends have access to some good equipment," he said, his tone only mildly sarcastic. He pulled over an ultrasound machine. "No harm done. We can have a quick look now." Someone must have set up the equipment, because he was squirting some gel on my stomach, and that's when I saw my baby for the first time.

It was perfect. Except, were they...?

"Holy shit, are they wings?" someone whispered. The grainy image didn't lie. There, on my perfect baby's back, were two tiny wings.

Holy fuck. I burst into tears. I looked past the doctor to Goliath standing in the hall, his eyes on the monitor as well. Then his eyes shifted to mine. He gave me the softest look I'd ever seen on him. *Fucking beautiful,* he mouthed and I cried harder.

Then I clutched my stomach and screamed.

27

CAIN

The sound of Sera's scream chilled me to my very bones. She made a god-awful groaning noise, and I wanted to rip the doctor away, even though my brain logically knew he wasn't causing her pain.

Even Goliath had moved into the room, the look on his face murderous.

"I need you to stop pushing, Serendipity. The wings can't get down the birthing canal. We are going to have to do a c-section. I don't want you to worry, though. Emergency c-sections happen every day." He turned to Solomon. "I'll need vodka. Water, towels."

He looked back at Sera, who's face had gone from a flushed red to a ghostly pale. "Normally, I would suggest this is the part where we go to a hospital, but I understand that isn't an option. It just means that I'm going to have to do this without the benefit of an operating room or decent anesthesia. I can probably give you some morphine but that can cause some issues in newborns."

She gritted her teeth. "I'll be fine. Just get the baby out," she ground out. Solomon reappeared with hot water and towels, and a bottle of Grey Goose. At least he was using the good stuff.

I wrapped my hand in Sera's. She gripped my hand like I was her last anchor to her sanity and I held her steady. "I got you, Baby. I'm here with you, we all are. I love you so much. You'll be fine. I refuse to let you be anything else," I said, kissing the side of her head as she breathed through another crushing contraction. The doctor was gloved and ready in seconds, standing over her with a scalpel.

I prayed to God, something I hadn't done since before Laura died and I sold my soul to the Devil. *Let them be okay.*

"Are you ready, Serendipity? I'm just making the incision now."

His scalpel pressed down against her skin, but nothing happened. "What the ever lovin' fuck?" Eli whispered to himself, as he tried again. Still, the scalpel refused to pierce her skin.

She screamed again, the sound reverberating around the room like she was being murdered. Fuck, fuck, fuck.

Goliath leapt forward, handing the doctor the switchblade from his boot. "Try this."

Eli didn't argue, which was a point in his favor, but when he pressed the knife against her stomach, nothing happened. It seemed to pierce the top layers of her skin, but didn't even dent her womb. The whole thing healed up in seconds.

Jesus.

"It's like her stomach is made of titanium. Barely scratches the surface," Eli said, panic edging his voice. He seemed so self assured, that his panic made me fucking go nuts.

Marco pushed at Solomon, furiously signing. Solomon looked at the doctor. "Marco says she definitely isn't impenetrable. She was covered in cuts and injuries when she came out of Purgatory."

Judas' jaw tensed. "It must be the baby, protecting itself. Who fucking knows?" He sounded wild and uncontrolled, like he saw his happiness slipping away from him again. No, it can't happen again.

"The wings are too wide to get down the birthing canal." The doctor's eyes flicked around, like he was trying to find answers in the corners of the room. "I can try and remove them in the womb. There is a chance the baby would not make it. There is a chance that Serendipity wouldn't make it. If the baby tries to force its way out, it may get stuck, or tear her in half. I don't know what I'm dealing with here. There's a chance the baby is properly immortal and I couldn't slice his wings at all, which means I would be permanently injuring the patient for no good reason."

Judas stood, grabbing Eli's arms. "Save her, or so fucking help me, I'll make you wish you were dead," he growled.

The doctor didn't even blink at the threat. "Son, I've met beings that would make you shit your pants. Your threats don't compel me to save her any more than I want to right now. I want them both to live."

Goliath came to her other side while they stood around arguing what was the best thing to do. He squatted beside the bed. "I knew you were going to be the fucking end of us as soon as I saw you," he growled at her, but I could see the fear in his eyes. He looked like a cornered animal staring down the barrel of a gun. Sera was moaning like she was being torn apart, and he flinched as if every ounce of her pain was inflicted on him. "You better fucking fight and prove me wrong, woman, or so help me God, I will chase you into the bowels of Hell myself and make sure you never get any rest. Fight, Serendipity. Don't pussy out on me now."

Her wild, pain-addled violet eyes met his, and she gritted her teeth and nodded. Goliath reached out and stroked her face. "Good girl. You're so fucking tough. You can do this."

She squeezed my hand so hard I could feel the

bones in them crack. I didn't care. I would smash every bone in my body to take away her pain. "Tell them to save the baby. Fucking get a ....argh, a chainsaw and cut me in half if you have to. Look after it for me," she gritted out, aiming her words at Goliath, because there was no fucking way I was making that promise and she knew it. If she died, I was following behind her, even if we weren't going to the same place. I couldn't do that pain again, and Sera, she had all my heart.

Goliath nodded and I wanted to rip his head off. But she was screaming again and it was all I could do not to kill every fucker in this room until someone came up with an answer. I couldn't fight this one, couldn't threaten the problem away. I just had to pray, and that didn't come fucking naturally to any of us.

"We need help," Eli said. "We only have one choice. You need to make a bargain with the Devil."

I jumped to my feet. Fucking done. I'd sell my soul over and over to him if it saved her. "Lucifer, I wish to make a bargain," I yelled at the ceiling. "Lucifer, I fucking need you right now. Please." I'd beg if I had to. I'd get down on my knees and let him flay me alive if it would save her.

Lucifer appeared in the corner, no smoke or fire or fanfare. "I should have known I would see you sooner rather than later. I ignored you bastards for decades, and suddenly you've become clingy." Serendipity let out another one of those blood-chilling screams, and his eyes shot to her. "Ah. This isn't good. God knows Uriel's seed would continue to punish her even after the fucker was deep in Purgatory. He's like a damn plague. She's dying?"

Eli nodded. "The baby, it has wings, Luc. Fucking wings. It's stuck in her mortal womb, but has created some kind of impenetrability barrier around her stomach so I can't give her a C-section." He looked into the Devil's eyes like he did it every day. "I need Raphael."

Luc shook his head. "He won't come. You know him, he won't go against the Father. And this? This abomination is about as far out of his plan as you can get, no matter what the old man says."

"This child *is* outside the pattern, Luc. It has been sinned against enough in the name of the Father. Make Raphael come. Take Ace. Take Gus. He likes Gus. Just get him here already. She doesn't have long."

Luc looked around the room. "There will be payment for this."

I bared my teeth at him. "I'll give it a thousand times over if you save her."

Luc nodded, running a soothing hand over Sera's head. "I'll be back as soon as I can. Keep her alive, and I'll do my part."

Eli was beginning to look pale, which wasn't a good sign. "I'm going to give her morphine, try and ease her pain. I will deal with the problems as they arrive. But if she continues like this, I worry that she will stroke." He was dumbing it down for us, and I appreciated it. A needle slid easily through her arm. Apparently she was only impenetrable over her womb. I leaned over Sera, her hair sticking to her face, her tears streaming down her cheeks.

"I'm sorry," she whimpered, and I hushed her.

"You should be sorry for making me prematurely grey, but I promise you, we will have eternity for me to give you hell about it. You aren't going anywhere."

The morphine must have worked slightly, because her screams became moans of pain. I leaned toward her stomach. I rubbed a hand over the undulating mound. *Just stay a little longer, kid. You're killing her and I need her to live. I need you both to live.* I willed with my mind. *Please, please let them live.*

Several things happened in that moment. Luc reappeared with a being that could only be a fucking Archangel. Raphael was the goddamn Archangel Raphael. I didn't care if Luc brought Jesus himself, as long as he saved her. Behind them was one of the Angel's from the battle with Uriel, the big golden one. He looked at Sera and went pale, the gold seeping from his skin like it was being drained from the soles of his feet. "It can't be."

Sera was oblivious to the other people in the room, pain giving her tunnel vision. "Cain, I can't," she whispered. Her eyes rolled back in her head and her hand released mine. Her chest rattled, then stilled.

"NO!"

They were too fucking late.

To Be Continued....

ABOUT THE AUTHOR

Grace McGinty is eclectic. She has worked as a choco-latier, a librarian, a forensic accountant and finally a writer. Like her professional career, the genres she writes are also eclectic. She writes romance, reverse harem romance, fantasy, contemporary young adult and new adult books.

She lives in rural Australia with her crazy family, an entire menagerie of pets, and will one day be crushed by the giant piles of books that litter every room.

Keep reading for a sneak peek at the first book in my Dark River Days Series: Newly Undead in Dark River.

facebook.com/GraceMcgintyAuthor
twitter.com/McgintyGrace
instagram.com/gracemcgintyauthor

NEWLY UNDEAD IN DARK RIVER

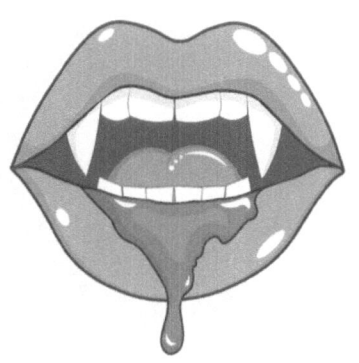

DARK RIVER DAYS
BOOK 1

GRACE MCGINTY

NEWLY UNDEAD IN DARK RIVER (DARK RIVER DAYS BOOK 1)

CHAPTER ONE

I woke to a rat scuttling across my chest, its tiny nose twitching as it paused to stare at me before scurrying off. Damn, I was hungry.

The fact that my initial reaction to a rat was hunger and not disgust was the first sign that something was very, very wrong. The second clue was that I was lying in a drain pipe in the middle of the night. Although it was hard to concentrate on anything but the hunger clawing at my stomach, I could hear the nocturnal animals shuffling around in the silence, smell the stale water that now soaked my clothes.

I tried to sit up and banged my head on the slimy concrete. Groaning, I rolled over and crawled my way out into the open. My body felt like I'd climbed Everest. Twice. I couldn't see my backpack anywhere. Panic began to fill my chest. Everything was in that pack. But it was pitch black, the moon not even visible behind the clouds. I became acutely aware that I was standing in the middle of the wilderness, at night, alone. I was a serial killer's wet dream right now.

I stared down the road, looking for the oncoming lights of a car or truck or something. Maybe I could hitch a ride into the nearest town. It was probably hitchhiking that put me in this predicament to start with. My mom was going to be pissed that I'd been so irresponsible.

I felt dazed like I'd been tranquilized, but I patted down my clothing with sluggish movements. Nothing was torn, and all my clothes were still on. I didn't feel violated in any way. My brain was cloudy, and I tried to sift through the fog to remember why I was lying in a ditch, outside of...

I looked up at the road sign. *Welcome to Dark River.* Where the hell was Dark River?

Hunger tore at my belly again, a burning ache so painful I moaned into the darkness like a wounded animal. First, I needed to eat something. Maybe then I'd be able to work out what the hell was going on.

I stumbled down the side of the road, and I could see the muted glow of the town lights once I was over the small rise.

Electricity surged up through my chest, and the edges of my vision dimmed. The last thing I felt when my body buckled was the rough gravel scraping my cheek.

I snapped back to consciousness all at once, like when you dream you're falling. My head felt too full, and panic was beginning to mingle with the overwhelming hunger.

I was now in town, beneath the striped awning of Bert and Beatrice's Old Fashioned Diner. How the fuck did I get here? Everything was completely blank as if someone had plucked the memory from my brain like a bad apple. A clock tower sat in the middle of town, proclaiming it to be almost midnight.

I pushed through the glass door, and a little bell tinkled above my head. The place was filled to the brim, which was unusual seeing how it was basically the middle of the night.

Every set of eyes turned to look at me, and the old guy behind the counter dropped the soda glass he was drying, the smashing sound shooting pain into my skull. I must have really looked like hell. An elderly woman bustled out of the swinging doors, which probably led to the kitchen.

"What's goin' on out..." she trailed off when she saw me standing in the doorway. She nudged the old man out of the way.

"Lass, are you feelin' alright? Bertie, get the girl a drink. The house special," she said slowly, her accent a thick Scottish brogue. "Tilda, call the Sheriff, please. Get him down here, quick smart." She was rounding the counter now. "Here, Lass, take a seat."

I took the stool she indicated obediently. She had a no-nonsense, matronly tone that soothed my panicked nerves.

"I lost my money and my passport." My voice sounded so weak that I hardly recognized it as my own.

The elderly lady just patted my shoulder.

"Not to worry, Sweet. It's on the house."

I could hear the sound of Tilda murmuring quietly into the phone down the other end of the diner.

"Yes Sheriff, just stumbled in the door. Looking like death, if you know what I mean."

The old man, Bertie I guess, slid a cardboard milk-shake cup in front of me, complete with red and white straw. It smelled so good that I fell on it like a half-starved animal. When I'd sucked down the last drop, I looked up, embarrassed.

"Sorry. I was really hungry." Bertie just took away my empty cup and put a fresh one in front of me.

"Don't worry about it, Darlin'. Have another one." I was struggling to concentrate on her words. I found it hard to concentrate on anything but the milkshake in front of me.

The bell over the door tinkled, and everyone's eyes shifted in that direction again, even mine. A tall man in a chocolate brown uniform walked into the place, and everyone started talking at once. The cacophony after the complete absence of noise was hell on my eardrums. I pushed my palms over my ears to try and muffle some of the sounds.

"Quiet!" The guy was obviously the Sheriff, judging by the way that everyone's flapping jaws snapped shut with almost perfect synchronization. Silence again. The man strode over, his every movement elegant, to where I was sitting and gaping in his direction.

The man was hot. Like, spontaneous combustion, three-alarm, call in the National Guard, hot. He had sandy brown hair and deep green eyes. The uniform hugged his muscular body. He was so attractive it made my teeth hurt. Literally.

"Ma'am, my name is Sheriff Walker Walton, do you need some help?" His deep voice was gentle, almost as if he didn't want to startle me.

"I don't know how I got here," I whispered. It was all a blank.

I'd been backpacking my way through Canada with my friends, but they had gone home last week, while I continued to travel up through Alberta by myself. I'd missed my bus to Yukon, so I'd decided to hitchhike my way through the last stretch to the border of British Columbia. After all, what's life without a little adventure? I'd been picked up by a family with teenage sons, but they'd let me off near Grande Prairie. I walked down the highway a bit more, and then poof, every-thing else is blank.

"Do you remember your name?" the Sheriff asked in the same soft voice.

"Mika McKellan. From Boston."

"That's good, Mika. I'd like you to come down to the station with me, so we can get this all sorted out. The town doctor will meet us there, just to check you over."

I nodded absently, and followed Sheriff Walton out of the diner, clutching my take away cup to my chest like a lifebuoy. He walked me over to the squad car, and let me sit in the passenger seat, instead of the back.

We drove in silence around the block, and I took the town in. It was actually quite beautiful. Not the cemetery stillness of most small towns after dark. Fairy lights were strung around the town square, and people milled about. The lights were on in all the shops, and small clumps of people were talking to each other on well-lit sidewalks.

"Is there a festival going on or something?" I asked Sheriff Walton.

"Or something," he replied, letting silence fill the cab.

Within a minute, we had pulled up in front of a skinny brick building. There were shiny bars on the windows, and a police sign hanging over the front lawn.

Sheriff Walton moved around the front of the car and opened the passenger door. I heaved myself out of the seat. Moving wasn't as painful as it was when I first woke up, but I still felt sluggish.

A plain woman with sparkling eyes met us at the front door. She looked me over and then sent a pointed expression to Sheriff Walton.

"Mika, this is Doctor Alice Sommer. I'm gonna get the Doc to check you for any signs of, uh, injury."

He held open the door of the station for me, and I gave him a polite smile.

"Let's go into the conference room. We need to have a chat after the Doc has looked you over. I'll be out here doing some paperwork."

He opened the door to an interrogation room. No windows, just a metal table with two chairs. Conference room, my ass.

"Thanks, Walker. I'll give you a shout when we're done," the doctor said softly.

The door closed with a click. The doctor sat a leather doctor's bag on the metal table. "Have a seat, Miss McKellan."

"Mika."

"Okay, Mika it is. But you have to call me Alice. Now, let me have a look at you." She shone one of those penlights in my eyes, and I let out a little squeal.

"Ouch."

"Hmm, light sensitivity. You have a little bruising

on your throat too." She got out a measuring instrument and measured the width of the bruise. "Anything else feel off to you?"

"Except for the starving feeling, my muscles aching, the weird blank spots and the passing out?" My sarcasm was obnoxious, but I couldn't seem to help it. "Other than all that, I'm as healthy as a horse."

The doctor clicked her tongue and wrote down the measurements. "Walker, can you get the cooler from the backseat of my car and come in here please?" She barely raised her voice, but the Sheriff must have heard because the front door of the station slammed.

"Don't worry, Mika. Your symptoms should lessen in a few days."

"Lessen?"

But the Sheriff was striding in the room, cooler in hand. Damn, he was fast.

"It's confirmed, Walker, though let's face it, it was obvious to everyone as soon as she walked through the door of the diner. You can smell it just as well as I can."

The Sheriff ran a hand down his face and sighed. "I know, but I didn't want to believe it. I didn't want to think someone we know could have done this."

What the hell were they talking about? I sniffed my armpit stealthily. I didn't think I smelled that bad, considering I'd been sleeping in a ditch. My nose twitched. A tangy metallic smell was coming from the cooler. A smell that was so familiar, but I couldn't quite put my finger on what it was.

"You know, I'm still in the room. Do you think someone could take me out to the ditch and see if I can find my wallet and my backpack? Everything I have is in that pack."

"Ditch?"

"The one I woke up in. Under the welcome sign."

The Sheriff's eyebrows knitted together, and I could basically see the cogs turning. "Sure. We'll go take a look out there first thing tomorrow night."

"Why can't we go in the morning?"

Alice laid a hand on my arm and rested her butt on the table. She was looking down at me sympathetically. In my experience, that was never a good sign.

"Mika, we have something to tell you. This is going to sound outrageous and frightening, but I want you to know that we are here for you."

My heart started to race, something in the back of my mind screamed that nothing was going to be the same again.

"Did my pet goldfish die? Are you two getting a divorce?" I deflected awkward situations with sarcasm. My therapist and I were working through it back home.

It was the Sheriff that answered. "No. Well, maybe, I don't know. I've never seen your pet goldfish, but I understand they die quite frequently." Walker ran his hand through his hair, and my hands itched to follow suit. "Look, Mika, I know this is going to sound strange, but it's our opinion that last night, you well, uh, you died."

I laughed. Maybe I'd stumbled into one of those reality TV shows. The producer was going to jump out any minute and make me sign a media release and a Non-Disclosure Agreement.

But the door never opened, and the two people opposite me never cracked a smile. "In case you guys didn't notice, I'm sitting right here, conversing with you. I haven't seen many dead people in my life, but I went to Great Aunt Milly's funeral when I was twelve, and she didn't talk back to me from the coffin."

Alice gripped my hand. There was something off-putting about a doctor holding your hand like you were about to get really bad news.

"What Walker is trying to say, Mika," they kept saying my name over and over like I'd suddenly forgotten it, "is that you are the undead. We believe you have been turned into a vampire. I should say, we *know* you've been turned into a vampire. It's the *how* that we don't understand yet."

I blinked. And then blinked again. They were actually serious. They thought I was a vampire. I'd definitely stumbled onto a TV set. It sounded like something the SyFy channel would come up with. But my heart was thudding, and I felt like I was going to throw up. It was like my body knew they weren't kidding, and it was just waiting for my mind to catch up.

"A vampire?"

Walker nodded sympathetically. "The hunger, the light sensitivity, even the blank spots, are all symptoms of the Turning."

"And you guys know this because..." No, that can't be right. My mind rebelled.

"Because we are vampires. The whole town is populated by vampires."

I stared at them dumbly, expecting something, I'm not sure what. For them to turn into bats, or broodingly sparkle in the overhead fluorescent lights. But nothing happened. They just looked like ordinary people. Not overly pale, their eyes weren't glowing red, they didn't have crooked, needle-like teeth. Nothing.

Alice had mocha-colored skin and smooth blond hair that went all the way down her back. She wasn't unearthly attractive by any means. She was pleasant and professional; exactly what you'd want in a physician. Okay, so Walker was hot, but from what I remembered of the diner, it wasn't like I'd stepped onto the stage at Milan Fashion Week or anything out of the ordinary.

"Do you have any questions?" Walker asked. Uh, yeah, I had a few. Like could he pinch me so I would wake the hell up from this bad acid trip?

"So, I'm a vampire, and you're a vampire. And she's a vampire." He nodded. "Do you, I mean I, have fangs?"

Walker bared his teeth, and there, gleaming white against his pink lips, were two pointed fangs. They were actually quite sharp, and I wondered how he didn't cut his mouth up with them. I looked at Alice, and she too was baring her fangs, which weren't quite as long as Walker's, and sat in her mouth with more ease. I eased my tongue over my own canines and found they'd elongated. I cut my tongue on them, and the blood dripped into my mouth.

Blood.

Hunger clawed at my stomach like a ravenous beast. Suddenly, I understood what the smell coming from the cooler was.

"Please." It was a half yell, half sob, as I dived for the cooler. Walker was around the table in a flash, his arms like iron bands around my body.

"Calm down. Alice is going to get you something to eat right now." As he said it, the Doc was getting a blood bag out of the cooler, like the ones you see in hospitals. She unscrewed the cap on the tube and handed it to me.

Walker released me from his hold, and I closed off the part of my mind that was grossed out at the thought of drinking blood, and let my body take over. I sucked that baby like it was my first cocktail on Spring

Break in Cabo. All that was missing was the little umbrella and the frat boys trying to convince me to come to a snow party.

All too soon, the bag was empty. "I want some more." My voice wasn't weak anymore, but it sounded slurred like I was drunk. Alice shook her head.

"With the two you had at the diner, and now this one, you've had enough. If you gorge yourself, you'll be vomiting for the rest of the night. I'll come see you tomorrow, and we'll discuss how everything works. For the remainder of the night, you need to rest." She picked up the cooler and her doctor's bag. "Are you taking her to your place?" she asked Walker.

He nodded. "I'll find somewhere more permanent for her to live tomorrow." He walked the doctor out, leaving me alone in the windowless room.

The shock settled over me like a numbing cloak. My mind spun as I tried to process, well, everything. I placed my hand on my chest, and my heart was slowly beating in there. Somehow, that made me feel better. I may have been dead, but my heart was still beating. The illogicality of that statement was something I'd deal with another day.

Walker was suddenly back, and his warm hand was on my shoulder. "There are a lot of things we have to discuss, and we can do it here, or back at my place. I know that sounds almost creepy, but I promise you'll be safe." He shifted from foot to foot, almost uncomfortably. "You are new to this world, and I wouldn't feel right about leaving you on your own. There are rules, life or death rules that you need to know. But, if you'd like, we could do it somewhere a bit more comfortable."

I nodded absently, every warning my mother uttered about going home with strange men now defunct. What was the worst that could happen? I was already dead. Plus the guy was the sheriff of a vampire town. If I couldn't trust him, who could a girl, err vampire, trust?

We hopped back into the squad car. I looked at the town through the window in a new light. I really studied the people, their inhuman grace, the fact that there were no children around. A guy stood on the pavement waiting to cross the road, and then magically was on the other side. I didn't even see him move in front of the car.

"Did that guy just teleport? Can we do that?" The thought was exciting. To just close my eyes and picture anywhere I wanted to be in the world, it would be amazing. Such freedom!

"I'm afraid not. He just moved really fast. As your vampirism settles into your body, you'll see him move as slow as a human. We can all move that quickly."

I was disappointed, though moving at super-speed was still pretty cool. "If we can move that fast, why the hell are we driving? Wouldn't we be wherever we are going almost instantly? Unless your house is in Alaska."

"Two reasons. Firstly, I didn't want to freak you out, plus you'll need a bit of time to get used to moving at that speed. Secondly, I enjoy the slower pace that a vehicle has to offer. Just because you can go at break-neck speed, doesn't mean you should." He sounded like my Dad teaching me to drive. Thoughts of my parents made me feel homesick.

"I need to call my parents and tell them I'm okay. Sort of."

Walker looked uncomfortable. "If you want, but just wait until tomorrow. Give everything you'll learn tonight time to process first."

He pulled up in front of a cute little whitewashed cottage, with a wrap-around porch and a perfectly manicured hedge. I looked at the man in the driver's seat and then back at the house. I saw him as the log cabin type of guy, not the gingerbread vibe that this place had going on.

I followed Walker up to the front door. I don't know when I started to think of him as Walker instead of Sheriff Walton, but it was probably around my third dirty fantasy.

When we walked in the space had a bit more of a masculine feel. Leather couches, a big-screen TV, and a scarred wooden coffee table occupied the living room. A large breakfast bar separated the living area from the kitchen, with three old diner stools tucked under the overhang.

Walker went over to the kitchen counter and poured two glasses of scotch into crystal tumblers.

"I can still drink?"

"Sure, you won't get drunk, but sometimes it's nice just to indulge in the nostalgia. You can also eat and go out in the sun. Though I wouldn't suggest going out in the daytime just yet. The increased sensitivity to light makes daylight extremely painful. It's something to work up to over time. Please, have a seat."

I walked over to the big scarred leather armchair. There was a burgundy throw rug over the arm, and I pulled it over my lap, even though I wasn't cold. The softness of the mohair was amazing. I could see the intricate pattern of the weave, the tiny flyaway fibers on each of the strands of wool. It was like my sight had become microscopic.

Walker handed me my drink and sat across from me, his elbows on his knees.

"I know this has been a lot to take in, but you have some serious decisions to make, Mika. This is a whole new world, with all new rules. Especially Dark River. We aren't your average community, as you know."

"Because everyone is the undead."

"Right, because we are all vampires. But it's not just that. Even within our own race, Dark River is rather unique. I'll explain the rules, and then it is up to you if you stay or you go. We can't keep you here against your will."

Well, that sounded ominous.

"Rule number one, there is absolutely no drinking from humans. Blood is delivered and distributed around the town by the Town Council, and no one goes hungry. The penalty is banishment from Dark River, forever."

That didn't sound so bad. It's not like I wanted to go around munching on people, giving them the hickeys from hell. I nodded for him to continue.

"Rule number two, you can never, ever, turn a human. The Town Council has decreed that the penalty for disobeying this rule is death. Because, in our eyes, turning a human is essentially murder." He looked at me imploringly. "This is what has happened to you, Mika. Someone has murdered you, and it is my job to find out who and bring them to justice. You are young, beautiful, and full of life. You should have had the opportunity to do everything you wanted to do. The opportunity to have children, get married, grow old with a loved one, live out in the light. You deserve retribution." His eyes lit up, and I don't mean sparkled with fervor, I mean literally started to glow.

"Uh, Walker, what's going on with your eyes?"

"Sorry. I didn't mean to freak you out. That some-times happens when we get worked up. Plus I need to feed."

He walked over to the fridge and pulled out a bag of O positive. I knew it was O positive because there was a huge sticker on the side. He poured it into his tumbler on top of his Scotch. Ew.

He sat back down in front of me.

"Okay, the third rule and usually the most problematic for new vampires who want to join our community is that you must cut all ties with your old life, both for our safety and the safety of the people from before. You wouldn't know this yet, but being around humans is..." he let out a shaky sigh, "an overwhelming temptation. Especially when you are only just learning to control your new body."

I collapsed back on the couch. I'd have to cut ties with my family? Never see my mom smile again, or hear my dad tell a lame joke? Never watch my youngest brother graduate high school? Tears welled in my eyes as my death sunk in. My mind was in the denial stage of grief, apparently. I mean, I felt fine now that I'd drank that blood bag. Maybe I could go home and become a goth or something. I lived alone in my apartment, so I could keep the blood hidden.

"I know what you're thinking. Really, I do. But think about it. You will never look older than you do today. You will live hundreds, if not thousands of years. If you go home, you'll watch your parents die, and your siblings, and their children, and then their children's children. Trust me when I say that it is a soul-shattering experience to watch everyone you have ever loved whither and die." The level of pain in his eyes told me that he knew from experience.

I couldn't decide this now, I needed time to think it over.

"What if I choose to leave?"

Walker bit his lip, his fangs pressing into his full lower lip. "If you choose to leave, then you are subject to the rules of the Vampire Nation. No telling humans what you are, or revealing your nature in a way that could bring Vampires as a whole in the limelight. If you feed on humans, you must do it in a way so that they do not suspect your true nature. Which basically means that unless you have the ability to wipe memories, which some vampires do, you have to kill them and dispose of their bodies discreetly. If you break these rules, Enforcers will come, and you will die. Trust me when I say that Vampire Nation always finds out if you break the rules."

Well, okay, then.

Walker's shaggy hair slipped over his eyes, and he combed it back with his fingers. The move made his shirt pull taut against his chest, and a completely different kind of hunger overtook me. The need to lean over and rip open his shirt was almost impossible to resist.

Walker's eyes met mine, and whatever he saw in

them made him look nervous all of a sudden. He stood quickly and took a step away.

"Okay, I'll let you think it over. The guest room is the second door on the left, and the bathroom is right next door. Make yourself at home, if you need anything, just give me a yell." With that, Sheriff Walker Walton hot-footed it out of the room, faster than my eyes could follow.

www.books2read.com/NUDR